SCHERZ PHOENIX BOOKS

VOLUME 4

ERIC KNIGHT

THIS ABOVE ALL

I

Second Edition
Copyright 1942 by Alfred Scherz Publishers Berne
Printed in Switzerland (Effingerhof AG. Brugg)

ERIC KNIGHT

THIS ABOVE ALL

I

THE SCHERZ PHOENIX BOOKS
ALFRED SCHERZ PUBLISHERS
BERNE SWITZERLAND

To My Lass with the Bright Blue Eyes

This above all: to thine own self be true,
And it must follow, as the night the day,
Thou canst not then be false to any man.
Farewell: my blessing season this in thee!
                                            Hamlet

CHAPTER I

WHEN spring was almost done the war began in earnest. In that town, people walking along the Esplanade could hear the guns.

The people were somehow relieved. They said: "The sitz-krieg's over at last."

They walked in the hard sunshine, and waited for news of victory and listened to the guns. The guns were not loud for they were far away, far up the Channel, over on the Continent. But when the fine breeze came in gladly from the sea the sound of the guns came muttering with it, and people said: "Hear that? Now he's catching it!"

Sometimes the sound was a single one, a trembling of air as if someone had stroked a big drum with one finger. Sometimes the sound overlapped into a long mumbling like a dog's first growling.

But still the holiday people and the seashore trippers walked gladly in the unusually good weather. They promenaded on the stone-faced Esplanade, breathing deeply of the rotting-kelp and brine smell of the sea. Only occasionally they would stop and say:

"Listen! Hear that? The guns!"

"Yes. Now he's catching it at last."

They listened half anxiously because it was, after all, a war, and half gladly because now all the nervous strain of waiting was over. But they were confident about the boys over there and the Allied armies, and the sounds were too crooning and remote to have evil meaning.

In a curious way they were personally proud when they heard the far-off cannonading. It was as if hearing the guns allowed them to take some small but important part in the war; as if, by the mere act of listening, they also were serving.

The weather was beautiful for walking. Sometimes the people strolled out beyond the town, going up to the cliff top. There, high up over the Channel, the sea breeze came over more steadily, like greater music. That steady wind always blew. The grass tops were riffled in sweeping planes so that they reflected the blue of the sky. Far below in the bays and coves the waves moved in like a slow-motion picture.

The guns sounded much plainer up there. Just sitting or lying there and listening made one feel in some indefinable way like a pioneer.

The guns sounded louder in the town, too. Some of the holiday people started leaving.

After that, to the regular townspeople, the unusual spell of beautiful sunshine began to seem like a wasteful gesture of nature, like an oversupply of fruit in a peculiar glut season, or an inexplicable run of herring when every fishing smack had such a remarkable catch that no one could sell any in the overcrowded market. For fine weather in that town was a business.

If there hadn't been a war the place would have been jammed: all the boarding houses, all the hotels—even the Channel Hotel which was the most exclusive. That was the only way to make money—to be packed to capacity in the fine weather.

They said:

"After all, it's only a short season at best, and you have to make what you can to carry you through the winter."

Now, at last, they had good weather, and yet the place

was, as they said, getting practically empty. They did not blame the war much. Rather, they blamed the weather. It wouldn't have been half so bad, they said, if it had only been rainy. They wished it would rain, so that all the fine sunshine wouldn't go to waste.

But they tried not to complain. After all, they said, there is a war on. One should be ready to do his bit without complaining—now that the war had really started at last and you could hear the guns.

You could hear them very plainly now, especially at night when the blackout made the town unusually still and hushed. Then the place went dead. People went for a short stroll after dinner, and when they came back for a nightcap in the bar they said it was curious how clearly you could hear the guns at night.

They listened to the B.B.C., and discussed tactics. Just let him wait a while. It wasn't Poland or Norway this time. He was up against a real army and he was getting a nasty shock. The French generals were the best in the world. Hitler had made his big mistake at last. The way the guns were going meant that we were giving him hell.

No one thought of it the other way round, not even when the gunfire came nearer—not even when it got so that you could hear gunfire at night when you were indoors.

You didn't have to go out on the Esplanade or on the cliff top any more. Lying in bed, you could hear the sound of the steady wind, and the sound of the waves thumping—but you could hear the thump of the guns, too. The window-panes would chatter. Sometimes you could even hear the shells going through the air.

There would be a boom and then a long, sighing sound. It was like a train in the Underground, only heard at a great distance. The sighing would go on for thirty seconds, forty seconds, fifty—and then a crrrump. That was the way it sounded. Boom—then a sigh for as long as you could hold your breath—then crrrump! It had landed. The sound blanketed in the air. More often than not the crrrump was louder than the boom.

Before May became June you could see the gunfire. The sky to the southeast blinked and flashed and sometimes broke into a sustained glow. Each night the glowing crept farther west.

The situation seemed confused. In the Channel Hotel bar everyone listened stolidly to the B.B.C., but that didn't make it any clearer. When the news was over they said, well, you couldn't expect the B.B.C. to broadcast information that would give away our plans to the enemy, could you?

It was all very confusing until Churchill declared it was the Battle of the Bulge. That made it easier to understand. The Germans had pushed into a great salient. If you drew a picture you could see how simple it was. All we had to do was press at the neck from the north, the French do the same from the south. Anyone could understand it. One wondered why the Germans had been so utterly foolish as to get into such a situation.

But soon no one spoke of the Battle of the Bulge any more; just as no one spoke about Hitler missing the bus any more.

Now the guns were drumming away and rattling windows all the time. They blazed away to the southeast, the south, and finally to the southwest, too.

The war was going farther and farther along the Channel, and everyone seemed so impotent. Something seemed to be wrong. It was as if the Esplanade were a grandstand and the war was parading past right under your eyes—and you couldn't do anything to help.

The guns drummed away all day and all night; but no longer they said: "Now he's catching it!" For at last they began to think that it could be the other way round. The shells might be dropping on their own men.

For the first time, people began to think about high explosives and screaming steel and human flesh.

All but a handful of the few remaining visitors packed up and left. It was too terrible to sit in the glorious sunshine all day while the guns told you of this horrible thing happening almost under your eyes. The British army was being slaughtered, practically as you looked on. For it was clear now that it wasn't the German right wing that was surrounded—it was the British army.

It came out over the B.B.C. that the Belgian king had surrendered, and left the flank open. The Belgians had let them down. The French had let them down. There was nothing now but the British army, surrounded by greatly superior forces. The Germans had Calais. They were within a few miles of Dunkirk. The British army was fighting for its life.

And then, at last, war became terrible. When people heard the guns they shuddered. It was horrible to think of that endless cascade of shells being poured in on the tightly compressed body of the British army.

The nights became a torture of sound. There were crashes that almost shattered the windows. It meant the warships were in action. The Fleet was trying to help hold back the German army.

Now, at night, the skies erupted bursts of light and glowed with flame. In the day V-shaped squadrons of planes went roaring out over the cliffs. They snarled away at top speed, and people knew they were racing to help plug up the leaking left flank. The planes tore away and came back. They shuttled over the Channel with their loads of bombs so endlessly that it seemed as if both men and machines should drop from the sky, in defiance of aerodynamic laws, from sheer weariness.

It was then that, at last, the fine weather ended. It turned foggy.

The very last of the visitors left. They felt it had been a terrible experience, but they had stuck it out. And one thing, the weather *had* been fine. It was no use staying now that the one good thing about it had come to an end.

The fog kept up for two days. In those two days they got the British army out. Naval craft, private craft, it didn't matter. Tugs, destroyers, yachts, trawlers, barges, pleasure boats, rowboats, canoes—anything that could float. They got in and got them out while the rear guard fought the enemy off. The beggars' flotilla went back and forth—all day and all night and all the next day and all the next night—as long as boats stayed afloat, men sailed them.

That way they got most of the British Expeditionary Force home again. But not all. For the fog lifted and it was fine again.

The guns still went on pounding, and people knew that some of the rear guard was still alive in Dunkirk. Those men fighting knew there wasn't much chance of getting boats to them now—now that the fog had lifted, but they fought on.

As long as the guns went on it meant there was a rear guard left. Standing on the Esplanade, the people of the seashore town knew that. They thought that and listened to the guns, pounding away at human flesh. They stood in the sunshine and thought of it, over and over. They were hearing the British rear guard being smashed to bits.

Suddenly everything became very quiet. The sun shone uselessly and splendidly on the holiday town. It shone on the empty splendor of seaside resort magnificence—the Esplanade, the unbroken regiments of ornamental lampposts, the steadfast battalions of benches.

The guns had stopped. It was all over. The Germans had Dunkirk.

CHAPTER II

BY THE time summer came the town began to look disused. It was strange to the people—such endless sunshine—and no seaside crowds. The hotels were, as they said, "starving to death."

The place became more and more desolate. By August, in the bandstand opposite the Channel Hotel, the sand had drifted up and lay, undisturbed by feet. Even the Channel Hotel was starving to death now. The assistant manager, sitting on his high stool behind the grille, thought of that. He thought of it as he stared from the window. He stared, studying the windblown patterns of sand on the bandstand floor jutting out from the Esplanade. He thought it was hard luck. The manager had just been called up with the Class of 1907. He himself was younger, but had the bad luck to be quite physically unfit. And the bad luck might have been good luck—in a business sense—if it weren't for such rotten business. After Mrs. Tirrell, he was next for the job of manager. He lifted his head as the silence was broken. The lift was coming. He tried to look happy. The modernistic lobby was empty. But beyond in the lounge, one man sat, slumped in one of the chairs. The sunlight struck the brown tweed of the man's suit, making a warm, lively splash. It harmonized with the color scheme of the lounge, and made the assistant manager a little happier in a vague way.

The indicator on the lift moved round. The door opened. A woman, a nurse, and two children came out. The children and the nurse went out into the sunlight. The woman sat in one of the lobby chairs and read a magazine. In a few moments she put her finger in the place and went to one of the windows looking over the Esplanade. She stood there a long time, watching the nurse and the children.

A bell tinkled with terrible too-loudness in the lounge. The waiter hurried in, came back, went to the bar, and returned with a cherry brandy on the tray. As he passed he caught the assistant manager's eye. He rolled his own eyes a little in a suggestive way and held up his open hand with the fingers extended. He meant to say this was the fifth brandy he had taken in. The assistant manager did not smile; he merely nodded. He dropped his head and tried to appear busy.

He heard the woman coming from the window, her heels first sounding on the tile of the floor, then quiet on the carpet, then again clicking and firm on the tile. He looked up and smiled.

"Did you put my call through?"

"Yes, Mrs. Cathaway. We'll let you know the very moment we get it."

The woman tapped her foot impatiently and then clicked back to the window. She went on tapping her foot as she stared out. The clicking sounded clearly in the emptiness of the lobby. It went on and on.

The splash of warm color in the sitting room eddied and moved. The young man in the brown tweeds came into the lobby, going a little unsteadily. The assistant manager gave him a smile of recognition—one given in passing. The young man did not pass. He came straight to the grille.

"I'm moving out," he said. "Will you have my bill?"

"Oh," the assistant manager said. "I'm sorry, Mr. Briggs. I understood you'd be staying—at least a week."

He looked so crestfallen that the young man frowned. He thought: Why should the bastard make me suffer for it? Why should I have to carry his woes? I can't help it.

"No, I'm leaving", he said.

The assistant manager cocked his head on one side and smiled belatedly.

"Pardon me a moment," he said. "I'll have the bill made out."

He went away and the young man leaned his elbow on the desk and half turned. He could see the woman looking out of the window. Her back was to him. Her legs were slim and very well shaped. The seams of her stockings were perfectly straight. Her heels were perfectly set.

He watched the tapping foot. His eyes came upwards. Her flanks were slim. She was the type that did not need to wear a girdle.

Without reasoning it, his mind shied away from undressing her, and his vision went beyond through the window. He could see six of the ornamental lampposts along the Esplanade. They were exactly like the ones he had seen through the window of the lounge—except there he saw only five. Exactly the same. It was the sameness that he couldn't stand. Five then six. But the same.

He moved slightly so that the six should be perfectly balanced in the frame of the window. He leaned his body far over. At last they were spaced properly. He felt a sort of comfort.

The woman turned, and he saw she was staring at him with something like disdain.

He thought: I'm not looking at you. I'm looking at the six lampposts. I have a right to look at the lampposts.

So he stared on, stonily; but he turned quickly when he heard the sound of the assistant manager. He was following a woman in a black dress. She had a slight mustache, but her gray hair was finely coifed.

"This is Mrs. Tirrell, the manager," the assistant manager said.

The young man thought: What the hell do you bring her into it for?

The woman smiled.

"You're leaving already, Mr. Briggs?"

"Yes."

"We understood you would be here for a longer stay."

"No, I'm leaving."

"Is there anything wrong—with the service?"

"No. I just—I'm moving on."

"I see."

He thought: Oh, Christ, why do they load their burdens on me. Their damned hotel is empty and they're worrying about even one bloody guest. It isn't my fault their hotel's empty and they're losing money, and they'll lose their jobs. It isn't my fault. They've no right to pass it on to me.

The woman looked up, slyly, and spoke quietly, confidentially.

"If it's a matter of rates, Mr. Briggs . . . ordinarily we couldn't do it, but because we're having such a low season, I could make some adjustment."

He thought: Oh, God! Oh, God!

"No, I've got to move," he said. "I'll go and pack my bag. If you'll have the bill ready when I come down..."

He went up the stairs, ignoring the lift. In his room he picked up his already-packed Gladstone bag. He came down again and went to the desk and asked for his bill. He wrinkled his forehead as he saw the name which was written across the top in a neat, clear hand: "Clive Briggs, Esq." He shook his head slightly as if throwing off his own thoughts. He paid the bill and the assistant manager counted the change primly. As he did so the buzzer sounded on the telephone exchange.

"Pardon me", the assistant manager said.

The woman by the window tapped her way over quickly. The assistant came back and smiled.

"It's your call, Mrs. Cathaway. I'm sorry it took so long..."

"I'll take it in my suite," she said.

She turned and faced the young man in tweeds.

"Pardon me," she said.

He stood aside quickly so that she could pass toward the lift. She could have walked round him as easily as not. He paid her back by watching her legs as she went into the lift. When she turned about, in the second before the door slid to, she was aware of his intentional insolence. He smiled, almost happily.

"Oh, could you take care of this for me?" he said.

He lifted the new Gladstone bag onto the counter.

"We'll be glad to, Mr. Briggs."

"I'll pick it up again some time—or let you know where to forward it."

"Yes, Mr. Briggs."

The young man lifted his chest as if in relief. He went quickly to the door and out onto the Esplanade.

Iris Cathaway took off her hat primly, smoothed her fine brown hair carefully as she looked in the mirror, and then went to the sitting room of the suite. She sat at the desk, prepared her mouth, lifted the telephone and said:

"Yes?"

She heard the man's voice at the other end, lifting gladly as one does when surprised:

"Iris! What in the name of goodness are you doing down there?"

"I've been trying to get you for hours."

"I just came in. When they said Leaford was calling I didn't think..."

"I'm in the Channel Hotel here. I've got the boys with me. We've got to move them."

"Well, where do you want to go?"

"That's why I called you. Hamish, I want you to decide."

"Me. But you know how I feel. I..."

"This is no time to go into that again. We've got to move them. I've taken Arthur out of the school."

"But, Iris, if you break up his schooling any more..."

"I don't want to break it up—but neither do I want the child dead. Why, there's a military airport practically next door to the school. It was supposed to be a safe area. That's why the school moved there. You said it would be safer."

"Hold on, Iris. I didn't say it would be. I admitted it, but under protest against moving them at all."

She heard his voice grow dryly pedantic as it did when he was angry. She kept her own voice cool.

"Now, Hamish. This is no time to play the barrister. The fact is that the school was about the worst place in the world for Arthur to be. I should think you'd want the children to be safe..."

"Nonsense, Iris. Of course I want them to be safe. Now bring them back here..."

"I will not go back to London, Hamish. That's the worst place in the world."

"I can't agree, Iris. There's too much protection here. The defenses are so well organized that I don't think they'll ever be able to bomb London."

„Well, I do. London's the last place I want to be."

"But, my God, Iris. I don't see what you expect me to do at this distance. If you'd done as I said in the first place, and gone to Oddale..."

"I will not go to Yorkshire! Now we won't discuss all that again."

"Well, where do you want to go?"

"It isn't where I want to go. It's your responsibility. You're the children's father."

She heard him expelling his breath in exasperation.

"See here, Iris. I have a case in a few minutes. I'll think it over..."

"If that is more important than the safety of your own children..."

"Oh, for God's sake, Iris. What do you want me to do? You won't do anything I say, and when I ask you what you want to go, you say it's my responsibility. You won't come to London because you think it won't be safe. You won't go to Yorkshire—where God knows there's nothing to bomb for miles around—because you have a silly feud on with my father; you won't go to *your* father's because there's a steel mill a mile away; you won't leave Arthur in school because there's an airodrome near by. And where are you now? Of all places you take the children..."

"I came here because this is safe. This is a seaside resort. There isn't a single military objective in the town."

„Oh, military objectives! They've dropped bombs on the South Coast already. And do you think they've been coming down first and inspecting the places to ascertain whether or not they're military targets? Those Nazi gentlemen..."

"Please don't make a speech, Hamish. You know my feeling about this whole silly war. The Nazis are quite as capable of being gentlemen as our own army. There's no reason on earth for bombing this town."

"Then why not stay there?"

"You advise me to keep the children here when you've just admitted yourself that it's probably unsafe."

She heard him blow out his breath. Then his voice came hard and balanced.

"If you wish to stay there, it is your choice. Now what do you wish?"

"We can't stay here. It's ghastly—this awful hotel. Now I'll put up with it until you can make some decision. I want a place that's perfectly safe—where the children can grow up normally and sensibly. That's all. I want you to help me find such a place."

There was a silence. Then he said:

"All right. I'll look into it. Are the boys there—I'll say hello to them."

"No, they're out on the sands with Mills."

"I see. How are they?"

"Very well."

"And you?"

"Quite well, thank you. How are you?"

"Oh, quite fit."

"Then you'll look into it? You could see Willfred. See someone about it."

"I'll look into it."

"All right, Hamish. I have your promise."

"Yes, you have my promise."

"Good-by, then."

"Good-by."

She heard the click of the telephone. She sat for a while, then rose and looked from the window. Farther down on the sands she could see Mills, a lonesome splash of white, on the brown rectangle of the blanket. Arthur was bending over, bending straight-legged as a child will, examining something on the sand by the water edge. Prentiss ran unsteadily round the blanket, wavered, and fell.

Iris put all her muscles in a lifting impulse—as if over the distance she would lift him. Mills went on reading without looking up. The child lay there.

Iris strained. The exertion left her feeling weak and frustrated. She watched, her teeth set until the child pushed himself up on all fours, rose, and staggered again round the blanket, going over the pale gold of the sands in a drunken circle.

Iris shut her eyes, and pressed the tips of her fingers on her temples, and stood thus, unmoving.

CHAPTER III

AFTER Clive left the hotel he went west, going through the town, then steadily along the cliff-top road. He marched, going in stolid, set gait, until the sentry challenged him.

"Halt, who goes there?"

"Friend", he said.

"Advance, friend, and be recognized."

The formula was over, and now he thought it had a humorous quality. The sentry was quite young. He stood with his left foot forward and the rifle correctly at the on-guard of bayonet fighting. But the gun had no bayonet. The boy shifted his feet.

"Come on," he said, uneasily. "What yer want?"

He walked over, looking at the boy's arm band.

"Hello, L.V.D.," he said. "What up?"

The boy grounded his rifle. He motioned with his head.

"It's a closed port, they call it. I ain't supposed to let no one down here less they got a pass. D'you have one?"

"No."

"Oh. Well, if you got business, like, you can go see 'em down there. You go down by the main road here. That's where the guardhouse is."

"It doesn't matter," he said. "I was just walking. So long."

"So long," the boy said, uneasily.

Clive turned about and went along the road. A half mile further back he struck a footpath branching north. He followed it for half an hour with the sun beginning to slant low on his left shoulder. At twilight he was on a metaled road going north. Just before dark, at a crossroads bus stop he saw two men standing. One had at his feet an old-fashioned straw satchel such as carpenters carry their tools in.

He stood beside them and caught the bus that stopped for them. He sat there, nodding with the sway of the bus, hearing the rear end grind, and going over in his mind all the things one would do to take the rear axle down, put the differential into shape, and put the job together again.

When the conductor came around for the fares, the carpenter and his helper said: "Gosley."

He said the same. It was a sixpenny fare. The bus went on, making many stops. It was long after dark when the carpenter bent down for his satchel. Clive followed the men out.

The place was dark from the blackout, but Clive felt he was in a small town—a village. He went along in the darkness, seeing dimly the narrow pavement. More from the heavy smell of ale than through sight he found the village pub. The bar was crowded. As he went in, the place was loud with the hubbub of thick county accents. Then the room quieted as people turned to look at him. He went to the bar.

"Can I get anything to eat?"

"Sorry", the bar man said.

"Well—where could I get something?"

"I dunno. You could try up the inn. Does he have any meals at the inn, Will?"

A man at the bar bent and spat.

"His daughter's poorly in bed. They'll not have anything."

"I could give you a cup of Bovril", the barman said.

"No, it doesn't matter. You might give me a double brandy."

"A double brandy, sir. Yes, sir."

Clive took his drink and went to a table. When he sat it was as if a signal had been given, and the men took up their clamor of talk again.

He sat with his head bowed. He could hear the plunk of the darts in the board. The voices chipped in singsong comments on the game. His ear became tuned to the accents, and he began to pick out the thread of sense in the voices. There was an argument at the bar. He heard a voice lifted.

"Didn't they kill three not twenty miles away?"

"Aye—and sunk a French ship taking surrendered Frenchies back to France?"

"Ah, to hell with Frogs—and Belgies too. Aye, they could walk through bloody Belgians, but when they hit a right army, they knew it. I bet we give 'em hell."

"I'll bet if the flank hadn't been opened we'd ha' stuck there yet."

It was a young militiaman. He looked about, hopefully.

"Them bloody Belgians," the man beside him said. "It was the same in the last war. You never knew where you were with a Belgian. Half of 'em were no better than Germans, the bastards."

Clive got up and went to the bar.

"Another double," he said.

His voice rang too clearly. The man beside him stared and the conversation died. The man turned his back and went on to the militiaman.

"Well, I say, this time we ought to do the bloody job right. Last war, we let 'em off light. They don't know what war is, in Germany. Well, what I say is, this time we shouldn't stop until we've shown 'em. Right to Berlin, and let 'em see what it is."

The man turned, pugnaciously.

"Isn't that so, mate?"

He picked up his glass. He knew the men were waiting. Terriers with a strange dog among them. They didn't really want to be unfriendly.

"If you say so," he said, quietly.

"What do you mean, if I say so?"

Clive put his drink down carefully before answering.

"What do you want me to say? Yes, with jam on it?"

The man glared at him, uncertainly, and the place was quiet.

Afterwards, when he had gone back to his seat, he could hear the men talking, now in lower tones. He felt as if among enemies.

But as he drank the thought of them went from his mind. He felt the deep, warm glow spreading through his body, and he lost himself in the peace of it. He felt his head nodding and rocking. The noise about him blurred, and the words tangled into meaninglessness. Sometimes he felt that he slept, and sometimes it seemed that only his mind was sleeping. It kept waking up to find his body going independently through normal motions—moving to the bar—picking up a glass—sitting opposite a young man and lifting his glass in salute—stepping carefully around a man with a dart poised in his hand.

Then he came from the curious sleep to hear a loud voice. He saw the heavy face, and realized that he was in the argument again.

"I say, land on the Continent and take him by surprise. And, by Christ, fight it out this time if it takes every bloody last man. No surrender for good old Britain."

"That's what you say."

"Bet your bloody life that's what I say."

"With your mouth."

"Yes, with my mouth."

"When does the rest of you go? When do you march?"

"I was in the last bloody war, and I'd go in this one if I wasn't over age."

"Too bad you're over age."

"Too bad about you, too. What about you?"

"I'm over age, too. I'm a grandfather."

"A grandfather! You'll be a bloody clout in the jaw in a minute."

Clive saw the man swinging, so he stepped back and then

struck out, gladly, viciously. He felt he had hit cleanly on the side of the jawbone. The man went down, and came up strongly, weaving his head in boxing manner.

He almost laughed, even though he felt that he had been hit over the heart. There was a curious peace at last—to be doing something. He danced back and chopped at the man going past him. He could hear the cry of the barman:

"Gentlemen! Gentlemen!"

No one was paying any attention.

There was a curious jump in time, and then he was in a press of bodies by the door. He had his head down and was slugging monotonously right and left. His arms were weary, but there was peace even in that weariness.

Then, like a broken film, the scene shut off, and there was only blackness and not knowing.

CHAPTER IV

OLD General Cathaway watched his son bend over, slowly, and strike the match on the holder as he spoke.

"And how's mother?"

"Oh, well. Never changes."

He was thinking: Roger's the soundest of the three. But he's the hardest one to get at. Never get behind his mind. Wonder how he stands Diane. She must weary him to death—she does me. But probably she can't get at him really any more than I can.

Roger Cathaway lit the cigar carefully, holding the match well away from his beard.

"You shouldn't smoke another before dinner," Diane said, plaintively.

"I shouldn't, should I?" Roger said pleasantly. He held the cigar in his hands, clasped behind his back.

That was it, Old Hamish thought. You couldn't tell wether he had let Diane bully him into not smoking now, or whether he was going to ignore her politely. You couldn't get at him.

Roger rocked on his toes.

"I suppose you know Prentiss Saintby's gone to America?"

"Why, no."

"Yes," Roger said. "Think it's buying airplanes or something."

Old Hamish nodded. It would be like Saintby to get a bombproof job. The thought of the Saintbys took his mind to Young Hamish.

"I wonder where Hamish is," he said. "Didn't he say..."

"Oh, he'll get here," Roger said. "Blackout—it's hard getting around London now, you know."

They were silent in the awkward way of people whose minds cannot be free until the awaited person has come.

"You saw General Bullyer?" Diane said.

Old Hamish coughed.

"No, not exactly. I'm seeing him later—in a week."

"Oh."

There was silence. Then Roger put down his cigar, carefully.

"That sounds like Hamish now," he said. "I'll go."

Old Hamish cleared his throat.

"It's been a beautiful summer, hasn't it?"

"Hasn't it?" Diane said.

She was listening with almost pained concentration to the sounds below. Old Hamish heard the voice of his youngest son. He went forward gladly.

"Father! Well, well. How's mother?"

"Oh, fit. Perfectly fit. Never changes, you know. None of us change in Yorkshire. It's the good air."

"I think dinner..." Diane said.

They edged to the dining room.

Old Hamish felt suddenly depressed. Why was it so depressing to eat at the home of one's own children? Children! Roger looked nearly as old as he did. At any rate, he looked every bit of fifty, Roger did. By God, he *was* getting to the fifty side.

"Did you hear Iris' brother's in America?" Young Hamish said.

"Yes—Roger just told me."

"Purchasing steel."

"Steel? I thought it was planes."

"Oh? No, steel, I understand."

Old Hamish thought: Soup incredibly hot—Roger seems to have removed himself in spirit.

"You came in to see Bullyer?" Young Hamish said.

"Yes. I'm coming in again next week. He—he sent me

25

out a note begging my pardon, asking me to make it next week."

"Oh."

Roger was carving the roast, carving with incredible skill. But then a surgeon—he ought to be able to carve with all the practice he got.

Old Hamish felt cheerful for the first time at his own thought. Then his face fell.

Mutton—it shouldn't be rare. Beef—rare as you could get it. Mutton—well done. Pork—done to a crisp. But Diane ——

"Bad about Somaliland, isn't it?" Young Hamish said. "What's going on down there?"

Old Hamish warmed up.

"Some damnable mixup. By God, by my very God, if I had two divisions there—just two divisions! I don't know what the idiots are doing."

"Well, the French Near East army was part of the tactical scheme, wasn't it? And when they dropped out.."

"That's it. We shouldn't rely on any other nation," Old Hamish boomed. "Rely on ourselves—we always did before."

Young Hamish bent over his food.

"Anyhow, it looks as if we're going to have to get out." They were silent.

"Don't you like the mutton?" Diane asked.

"Oh, yes—yes," Old Hamish said.

There was no chance to avoid eating it now.

"It's very good," he said.

If you had to eat it, might as well throw in a few words to boot.

"I'm glad someone appreciates it," Diane said, sorrowfully. "It's so hard trying to get good food now—and you go to all that trouble and..."

Old Hamish thought: I wonder how Roger stands it.

He's built up calluses, that's it. He just lives in some other part of him where she can't go.

He let his own mind drift away, until he saw Diane holding the coffee pot and speaking to him.

"Don't you think this is a beautiful design? I just got it..."

"Yes, yes. It's a coffee pot that looks like a coffee pot."

He knew his words should have been kinder. The affair was a beautiful piece of simply conceived silverware. Diane had that, at least, taste.

"Functional," Young Hamish said.

Old Hamish seized it gladly.

"Yes. Functionalism in architecture and everything else these days."

"At least we've got through the terrors of Victorian overdecoration," Diane said.

Old Hamish considered it, tempted to disagree with Diane for the sake of disagreeing.

"Decoration, functionalism," he said. "That's got nothing to do with it. Art and everything else goes bad the moment it becomes consciously something—consciously anything."

Diane stirred.

"Should we have coffee in . ."

The chairs were moving back. They were going to Roger's library.

Gloomy place, Old Hamish thought. Doctors seemed to gather gloom around them in their homes.

"What time did Will say he was coming, Roger?"

Young Hamish was saying that.

"Oh, after dinner."

"It's after dinner now," Old Hamish said, petulantly.

Waiting for someone always kept everyone else at such a sort of tentative stage.

"Oh, he really is busy," Young Hamish said.

"Willfred's quite on the uprise, isn't he?" Roger said, gently.

"Yes. He's going up with his party."

"The party!" Old Hamish said. "His party. Luck—that's all."

Young Hamish smiled.

"Well, he backed an outside shot, and it's in the running. It's a Conservative Government now, but God knows what it'll be before this war's over."

"Willfred," Old Hamish said, slowly, "is as cold as a piece of beef liver—and always was."

There was a silence, and then Diane rose.

"I must—I should see..."

She drifted away.

What nicety, Old Hamish thought. What outrageous nicety! And she's the kind who'd listen at the door as soon as not. By God, by my very God, why don't I like my sons' wives? Who's wrong—me, or them?

Well, Willfred *was* as cold as beef liver—and he had a right to say so. Always had been—even when he was a little chap.

"Willfred was always hard to understand—even when he was little," he said. "Hard for me to understand."

Willfred always had that sort of hard possessiveness—a sureness in knowing what he wanted. The other two didn't have it. Roger, the oldest—he was too gentle. Hamish, the youngest, was too generous. Both the kind that get stepped on by the world. But Roger built defenses against the stepping-on, and shut himself away in a deep world of his own. Young Hamish hadn't learned that. He would go on giving himself generously.

The givers. And Iris was a taker. She was like something—a female spider or whatever it was—battening on Hamish's generosity of self, consuming his kindness. Some day she'd exhaust the supply, and then...

"You look well, father," Young Hamish said.

Old Hamish brushed his gray mustache.

"I feel well. I feel well."

At that moment he did—and then he remembered the shortness of breath. Shortness of breath when he hurried too much. Perhaps heart! Heart failure. Pop off—like that.

He wanted to ask Roger about it, but he couldn't now. If he could get Roger alone...

"That sounds like Will now," Roger said.

He went from the room, and the other two stood, watching the door. At last they heard Willfred's voice. He came in, speaking sedately.

"Father—good to see you. How's the mater?"

"Oh, very fit. She always is."

"Well, the family gathering," Willfred said. "Let's see —it's two years—three, since we all ... how's Iris?"

Young Hamish nodded.

"She's—well."

"Where is she?"

"Leaford—South Coast."

"Indeed!"

Willfred looked around.

"Oh, that reminds me, I suppose you know her brother's in America?" Old Hamish smiled, grimly.

"Oh, yes," he said. "Buying steel."

"No, not steel," Willfred said. "Something else."

Well, why doesn't he say what it is, Old Hamish thought. Damned fool, going on as if he were carrying deep Government secrets. Superior ass. They were talking now of Somaliland, Roger listening, smiling; Hamish eagerly, Willfred superiorly. Willfred, at last, finished his speech. He had beaten Hamish down. He looked at his father.

"Did you see Bullyer?" Willfred asked.

"Why—er—I'm seeing him next week."

Willfred came closer to him, and shut the other two out from the conversation.

"Bullyer," he said.

He took off his pince-nez and regarded them. His long, sharp nose now seemed to jump out in bolder acuteness. Old Hamish saw that his hair was sanding over thinly.

"What's wrong with Bullyer?"

"Oh, nothing," he said, airily. "Only..." He dropped his voice. ".... You know, I don't think Bullyer's quite the man—not after Dunkirk, you know. I rather think Condout's the coming man. Now, would you like me to —put out a feeler to Condout?"

Old Hamish drew himself up. A father could do favors for his son—but not the son for the father. Not without saying: Here is an end to a phase of life.

Not from Willfred.

"Bullyer's my friend," he said. "We were lieutenants together."

"I don't doubt that," Willfred said, complacently. "But now, it's a case of what you want and who has it. Just what—do you want?"

"By God, what do I want?" Old Hamish roared. He saw the other two look up. "It isn't what you want at a time like this. It's how can you help. God knows they haven't done so well thus far—their new command ideas, and new tactics—the invulnerability of defense over attack! Pah! The young ones haven't done so well. We're in a hole. We're facing invasion. There's lots of us with a lifetime of experience. We're waiting to do what we can. Work to do—and experienced men ready to do it. A division—a brigade—anything. But do you think we can even get a chance to serve?"

Young Hamish saw Willfred opening his mouth, and spoke quickly to drown any chance of the words, "too old."

"But undoubtedly they're in a fearful jam of work, father. It'll take some time to get around organizing men in retirement."

Old Hamish's anger at Willfred still burned.

"Then they'd better hurry—for if they don't use us chaps—there doesn't seem to be any mad rush on the part of young ones to serve."

The moment he said it he realized that in his lashing out at Willfred he had struck Hamish.

He thought: Now eternally damn—you can't strike the thick-skinned ones.

Young Hamish was passing a hand over his reddening face.

"Yes," he said. "I suppose it wouldn't do to have a war without a Cathaway in it."

"Now, Hamish," his father said. "You know what I mean."

"No," Hamish said, almost angrily. "We've all secretly given a snort over Prentiss Saintby. And here's a war, and father the only Cathaway ready to get into it."

"Now, Hamish, I didn't mean..."

"But there is a Cathaway in it," Willfred said.

They stared at him.

"Roger's girl's in the Waffs, isn't she? That's one in uniform."

Willfred said it so smugly, that Old Hamish couldn't stop himself.

"That's what I mean," he boomed. "Women—girls going to war—and men standing around waiting. I don't see how you allowed it, Roger. That's one thing I wanted to talk to you about. I don't like it. Prudence is my granddaughter and..."

"And she's my daughter," Roger said, quietly.

"But—but good God, man. You don't know what sort of things come off in those women's camps. I don't trust them—women in uniforms and—and—what does she do?"

"She's a sergeant," Roger said. "And I don't think..."

"In the ranks," Willfred said. "Oh, why didn't you get in touch with me and..."

"But she did it herself, not I, Willfred."

"Then, goodness me, let me look into it. I can get in touch with someone and see that Prudence gets a rank compatible with..."

"No," Old Hamish said. "She's a right to stand on her own feet."

"But, father, I don't know which side you're on. First you say..."

"I'm against women in uniform—and I'm against politicians pulling strings in military matters," Old Hamish said.

He felt he had said it well.

"Just a moment, both of you," Roger said. "It's my girl—and let me explain it. When you have a child—an only child—you bring her up first with a basic feeling of security in her home. Then, next, you teach her to find security in a very complex world. You do that, not by protecting her and forbidding her to go into the world, but by letting her go out boldly, learning to stand on her feet, held up with the knowledge that there's home security to fall back on if she needs it.

"It's no use trying to protect girls from the world, because—some day you won't be here to protect them—and then they'd be out in the world without even an anchor to windward.

"I've—thought a lot about being a parent. I'm—I've thought a lot about it."

He stood, cracking his finger joints, as if embarrassed at his own speech.

They were silent. Then Young Hamish moved.

"I ought to be—be running," he said. "I have some stuff to clean up—this dinner was short notice and I'd planned to do it to-night."

"Righto," Old Hamish said. "I'll toddle with you. You'll drop me off."

"You won't stay here?" Roger said, mildly.

"Why—no. Put up at the club, and get away bright and early in the morning if I feel like it."

"You're not staying in town?"

"Can't say. Perhaps I'll run up home and come in again next week."

"I still think Condout..." Willfred began.

"No, no," Old Hamish said. He made his voice more amiable as befitting a farewell. "Nice of you—but I'll play along with Bullyer."

They began moving from the room.

When they were in the cab, Old Hamish began framing the words in his mind. He was startled when his son spoke first.

"It's the devil, being too young for the last one, and feeling foolishly a little too old for this. You know..."

"Pooh!" Old Hamish said. "Old at thirty-four?"

He felt this was too near to openly persuading Hamish. So he let his words race on.

"But then, I dare say we need barristers in war as in peace—law suits never stop, worse luck. You know, it's funny!"

His laugh boomed in the dark space of the cab, trundling along.

"I shall never forget when I came back from Egypt with the one over my kidneys. No—the one over the kidneys was at Ladysmith. It was the Boer War, that was it. Well, when I got home your mother was—well, very distant. And finally I twigged it. It was being wounded in the back. You know, the funny old romantic idea that a soldier always kept his face to the foe, and if he got wounded in the back it was a mark of cowardice—he'd been running away. I had quite a time explaining to her how shrap bursts. In fact, I don't think she's got past the old idea yet. Has no conception of what an H.E. does.

Still has the idea, privately, I think, that it's all like Omdurman—and I'm on a horse, charging into every battle."

He laughed appreciatively.

"Now what on earth made me think of that? I've never told anybody."

Young Hamish thought:

He did that for me—to make me stop thinking about not going. Once he was abler with his tongue and mind. It's sad to see a parent pass the peak of capabilities.

"It's a good way to be," he said. "Mother lives at peace with her ideas. I wish more of us could."

Old Hamish's mind jumped several moves in the gambit.

"What the devil is Iris doing at the seaside—what is it—Leaford? I thought Arthur was at—where's the damned place they went?"

"Oh, they moved the school right next to an airdrome —or someone put an airdrome next to the school. So Iris took him away. Planes all day. She thinks its bad for children to get impressions of so much—so much militarism."

"Ah, foolishness! It's better than all this chuckle-headed, panicky running around. Where is she now? Leaford? For the love of heaven. Right smack across the Channel from him..."

"It's temporary," Hamish said. "I've got to—I'll dig up some other place—it'll all iron out."

Old Hamish made a grimace in the darkness.

"Well, you know my feelings," he said, in a slightly aggrieved tone. "But I'm not going to put my foot in it. I'll be damned!"

"Oh, don't look at it that way."

Old Hamish licked his lips. Then the words got past him.

"Damn it all to hell, I don't see why she won't bring them to Oddale. Of all the places on this island that're isolated and safe..."

34

He felt his son's stony silence, and puffed out his breath. In for a penny, in for a pound, he thought.

"Damn my eyes, Iris is a good woman," he said. "Of all things on this earth, God save me from a *good* woman. You know, some day, someone will tell her what kennel she was whelped in."

"Now, father."

"Her father, Old Saintby! What a saint! By God, at least I never left any by-blows to get by on bastardy rates. And he did! I have proof. He was in court for it! And then she raves about me. Me, if you please!"

Hamish thought he had never before heard his father sound so gladly and maliciously gossipy. Probably another mark of age.

"She never says a word about it," he reproved.

"Oh, stick up for her," Old Hamish said. "Of course she doesn't. But she won't bring my grandchildren to Oddale—not if it were the only single place left in Britain where they'd be safe. She'll risk their lives..."

"Nonsense. I want to get them all back to London. They'll be safe..."

"The very devil they will."

"Oh, I don't think he'll bomb London. Why, the very effect on the civilized world would..."

"Poppycock. He bombed it last war, didn't he? What makes you think he won't again?"

"Well—this is different. We've anti-aircraft defenses and..."

"Before he's through he'll blast the daylights out of this place. Mark my words!"

Young Hamish moved the conversation away.

"Willfred looked well, didn't you think? Flourishing—like the green bay tree these days."

"You know—it would be fun to get Iris and Willfred together," the old general said.

He was thinking: Willfred and Iris over a clothesline with their tails tied together like a pair of Kilkenny cats. Two of a kind. Greek meeting Greek. Hard, capable people.

But his son's mind had moved simply.

"Oh, they get along quite well together," he said, mildly.

"Ah, yes. But now. Willfred going up in the Government—and everyone knows Iris is an out-and-out Nazi."

"Oh, come. That's not so. She's a peace supporter, that's all."

"I've heard her argue..."

"Not since the war."

"Ah, now they're keeping quieter. But it'd be dreadfully embarrassing for Willfred right now with an out-and-out Nazi sister-in-law."

"Anyone has a right to march to the music of the drum he hears," Hamish said.

"Yes. And talking of drums..."

The cab was slowing down.

"Here's the club," Young Hamish said. "Don't ring off, cabby."

Old Hamish was standing on the curb in the blackness, leaning forward into the cab. A good thought had come, and now it was eluding him.

"Er—I'm sorry I popped off about Old Saintby," he said. "I shouldn't have told you..."

"I knew it," Young Hamish said. "Will told me once."

"Ah," Old Hamish said. He felt his sails fall, flopping, windless. Then his mind warmed. Drums—that was the good thought.

"You know, Hamish. I don't want to poke in—but between you and Iris—you've got to stand up and fight. I'll give you some advice. I'm older than you, and... well, a woman and a drum..."

"Should be beaten regularly," Young Hamish said. "I

know, but just at this particular year of grace, the accent's on the drum. Good night."

Old Hamish shook his head, watching the cab creep away from the blackout lines on the curb. He shook his head and went into the club.

CHAPTER V

CLIVE woke feeling a hot pulsating in his head. Somewhere a band seemed to be playing. He saw small starched curtains. Then he remembered someone had wakened him by speaking.

He looked up. From his angle the young man in the room looked heroic in size, his head far up under the plastered gables of the room. There was a slight cut and discoloration beside his right eye. His wavy chestnut hair was still wet from the combing. He was smiling and holding out a mug of tea. Clive sat up and drank. Then he grimaced, handed the cup back, and laid his head on his drawn-up knees.

"Got a bad one, hey?"

He felt too ill to speak. He opened and shut his hand as a signal that he'd heard. The young man laughed happily and sat on the bed. The movement sent violet lights dancing.

"You shouldn't begrudge yourself a fat head after the binge you had last night."

"Perhaps so. Where am I?"

"My home. Told the old lady you were a sick friend. You were sick all right."

"Sick?"

"Don't you remember? Oh, my, what a do. One of the best the old Ram's Head's had in a long time."

"I'm sorry. I only remember being in an argument. I don't remember you."

"You don't! Why, we discussed everything last night—women, the world, and the war. Then Mouthy got into it and you smacked him. He got up and smacked you. Then you would ha' died laughing. Somebody gets between you to make peace and you hits him by mistake. He hits you, and then school was out for fair. It wasn't a private fight any more. Rare time we had, you, me, them, and a militiaman with his belt off smacking anyone impartial he could reach. Then the bobbies come, and we come out the alley door and over the back fences into High Street."

"It was good of you to help me. I should have had more sense."

"That's all right. It was anybody's fight."

"It was good of you to side with me."

"That's nothing. I'd do anything to upset Old Carlishaw—you know, the publican. The bastard—he opened his mouth about my mother."

"Your mother!"

"Yes. Oh, it was several years back. My mother used to make eel pies. You know, threepence each. I used to hawk 'em in a basket. Eel pies—get 'em while they're hot—who wants eel pies! You know, shouting 'em round at night. Well, I hear someone's giving it out that my mother's putting gelatin in 'em. And I trace it down, and it's Old Carlishaw. So I went down, and walked right in and took out this knife..."

Clive saw the young man whipping out a huge sailor's knife which flicked open, showing a half-foot blade.

"Oh, God, put it away," he said.

He passed his hand over his eyes. The young man clicked it shut.

"I waved it right under his nose and says: 'Mr. Carlishaw, you bugger you, I hear you've been sounding off about me and mine. If you open that dirty mouth of yours again about us, I'll take this knife and enlarge your mouth from ear to ear and give you a permanent smile that you'll wear the rest of your life.'

"So help me, I did. And me just a kid. Then the bugger

has me summonsed for threatening his life—and I bloody near went to reform school over it. Only I had good characters, so we got fined five pounds and costs."

"Why on earth do you go to his pub, then?"

The young man arched his chest. The grin spread over his cheerful face.

"Oh, just to help out. Anything starts—like last night—I do my best to keep it lively. Break a few of his windows and smash the place up a bit. It'll help get the Ram a bad name, and soon the good custom will go down the Chime instead."

Clive laughed despite the aches that the spasm produced.

"So you didn't help me, especially?"

"Oh, no," the young man said, with vehement eagerness. "Now don't look at it that way. Old Mouthy needed a smacking. He's a mouthy bastard. Going to fight this war to the last bloody soldier and the last bloody sailor. Warlike bleeder, he was. He wouldn't talk that way if he'd seen it like I did. Poor bastards wading out to us and bloody Stukas bombing the guts out of 'em. It'd ha' made your heart bleed, chum."

Clive studied the quilt, and then looked up.

"Are you in the navy?"

"Oh, no. I've been working around on packets—summers, like, we'd take out the *Island Queen*. Down Little Bourneton. You know, winkles and round the buoy for a bob a head, nippers under twelve, sixpence. We lay her up winters. Well, there was no summer business this year, so I was helping out down the garage, and the skipper sends up in a hurry that we're going over to help get 'em out of Dunkirk.

"You should have seen that bloody old *Island Queen*, chum, eight knots and she's racing—ten and she'd bust a gut. But she was good—you know, shallow draft. So we could get in close.

"And it was go in and load 'em up, and get out and land 'em, and go in again. What a time—everything afloat—a bloody pawnshop regatta it was. Tugs, trawlers, destroyers, motorboats—any bloody thing. And us with a shallow draft getting right in. They was on the shore—they come wading and swimming out to us.

"Ah, chum, it would ha' made you cry bloody salt tears, it would. The poor bastards. Poor bleeding bastards. Hadn't slept for ten days—and lying there on the shore on their backs firing rifles at the Stukas—and the bloody planes playing clay pigeon with 'em. Make your heart bleed.

"And pick 'em up and get out, loaded to the gunnels. And land 'em, and go back in again. Then, third day, the fog clears, and plonk! He drops one right down into the engine room, and good-by *Island Queen*. We swim around and a destroyer comes up and picks us up—and that's all for us. Now I'm back—and I dunno—you don't feel like going back to a garage, do you?"

"No," Clive said. "I don't think you could."

He swung his feet from the bed.

"I suppose I ought to get dressed," he said.

„Yes, you'll feel better if you get up. What do you do, chum? Don't mind me being personal."

"Oh, that's all right. I'm—just on a holiday."

"I see. What's your name?"

He hesitated only an instant.

"Briggs," he said. "Clive Briggs."

"Glad to know you. I'm Joe Telson. I'll take the cup down. You'll have to wash in the sink downstairs. Nobody's home—it's almost mid-afternoon."

Clive watched him go through the door. He held his head a moment. Then he began dressing.

In the dusk they leaned over the old stone bridge, looking down at the stream.

41

"Funny, you know," Joe said. "Looking down on the river. Always makes you feel you're going somewhere. Moving, like. Used to look down for hours when I was a kid and feel I was going the other way from the water. Of course, the water's moving and you ain't, but it feels the other way round."

"It's quite feasible that you are moving and the water's still," Clive said.

"Ah, science. Yes, that way. Well, how about a pint?"

"No, thanks."

"It'll do you good. Cheer you up—make you clap your hands and sing."

"I couldn't go it. And—anyhow I ought to be getting along."

Joe looked up.

"Where to? Where you going, chum?"

"Oh—just moving along."

"I know, but it's late to start today. Stay over another night. We could put you up."

Clive studied the water. He remembered the small room with the sloping gabled ceiling, the kitchen, the tiny quiet woman with bright bronze hair, the smell of the warm coal fire and baking bread and soapsuds. It was a familiar smell.

"Well, if I could make it all right—you know, with your mother. I'd be paying anywhere else."

"Oh, that's all right."

"I couldn't do it otherwise."

"Well, then. What you think. Since you can pay—the old lady could use it all right. Every bit helps out, you know."

"Of course."

"Well, what about a pint?"

"No, I've reformed."

"Oh—well, I tell you what. How about running up the Waffs Camp for the concert?"

"The what?"

"W.A.A.F. The Waffs. Didn't you hear 'em go past with their band this afternoon—when I woke you?"

"I don't think so."

"Well, they have a concert every Saturday night."

"I've heard concerts."

"I know—but I know a nice little number up there. And she could get a friend. Come on—do your duty to the girls in uniform."

Clive shook his head.

"Ah, come on. You're not a bad-looking chap, you know. You shouldn't begrudge spreading a little joy around. Don't be selfish. Share the blessing of nature with others."

Clive looked at the water, flowing darkly, steel-smooth.

"It's just what you need," Joe encouraged. "A nice girl to cheer you up."

Clive looked up at the cheerful countenance, and smiled.

"I doubt it. But one thing or another—what does it matter?"

"That's the way to take it," Joe said. "Come easy, go easy. Live, love, and leave when your welcome's up."

In the dark they met, not seeing each other. In the faint light of the clouded three-quarter moon they saw only a blur that was the whitened stones set beside the road at the camp gate. They heard voices around them and knew the untouching movement of people, yet they felt isolated, chained together against their own wills in the close prison of blackness.

But the thought of appearing together in the light seemed to each an offense now against himself.

He said: "Should we go to the concert, or—would you rather walk?"

Without answering, she started away, and they walked, untouching, down the dark road.

He thought: Let's get it over with.

They went far along the lane until walking had no sense.

He stopped by a low roadside wall where an overhanging beech made total blackness.

"Let's sit here," he said.

They each sat on the wall, waiting.

They felt the nearness of each other, and were ill at ease. Each had a feeling that there was a routine to go through, and the fact that it was a routine repelled them.

But Clive only knew that the girl beside him was silent, and that meant that she was waiting. He wondered what she looked like.

He drew his breath.

"How do you like it in the camp?" he said.

One could always talk and fight away routines.

"It isn't normal," the girl said slowly. "You can't have a purely feminine world. It builds slowly, day after day, into a sort of hysteria. Men—you've got to have them round, don't you think?"

Clive was thinking: The intellectual type. My God, this is worse. Why did I have to get stuck with one of the intellectual type?

He said:

"Did it take a war to make you find that out?"

"No, seriously. It's like a clock winding up, hour after hour, the spring getting tighter and tighter. You feel that if you are going to see any more women, or talk about women's things, or hear any more women, you'll break out screaming. That's why I came out with you."

"But usually, of course, you don't do this sort of thing?"

"You needn't be sarcastic."

"*Touché.* You're a bright girl. But I'm interested in the way you're trying to explain to me—or to yourself—why you're here."

"I've told you. You just want to talk to a man for ten minutes and get sane. Any man. Anything with a pair of pants on."

"I'm anything with a pair of pants on?"

"You mustn't," she said. "I'm trying to cover up my awkwardness at being here. Or don't you understand?"

Clive felt the genuine sound in her voice.

"All right, then," he said. "Just go on talking."

"Don't be angry. I was talking abstractly, and you are thinking personally. It's been a shock. I thought women were self-sufficient. I wanted to think so. I thought they could get along—but we don't. It gets like a bunch of hysterical schoolgirls. Of course, we bottle it up, but I suppose that's worse, isn't it?"

"Oh, yes. Very bad for the system."

"No, I don't mean that. But I never thought of it before. I never thought how it would be for men in the army—living in a purely male life. Do they get sick of men—of seeing men, of hearing men, of talking male talk?"

"No, a male world's a good world."

"How do you know? Have you been in the army?"

"It's true, all right. It's so in schools. And then soldiers in the army have another outlet."

"What? Oh—I see what you mean. I suppose there *is* that to it."

"Don't be superior. It's just that men are more honest in their relations with themselves, that's all."

"I don't know. That's a generalization. It's pretty rotten on women. This is a man's world—even in wartime when we put on uniforms and try to pretend that it isn't. I wonder why women don't fit in on organized life—because they don't."

"Most of them do, I suppose."

"Which means that I don't. That's it—I wonder, then, why I don't."

He thought: Oh, God. Now she wants us to talk about her.

"I don't know," he said. "From the sound of your voice I'd say that you're from a better background than most. Most of them are tough little devils.

"They're fine girls."

"*Esprit de corps* stuff, girl. They're just ordinary human beings with the same percentage of grubby, scatterbrained, insensate females as in ordinary life. And putting them in uniform doesn't suddenly make 'em all Maids of Orleans any more than soldiers are plaster saints."

"Kipling," she said. "Just the same they're fine girls."

"Of course they are," he said.

He slipped from the wall and found her with his hands. He wanted to have it done—to go through the motions and send her into acquiescence or revolt.

He pulled her toward him, half distastefully. Her forehead rested by his cheek. He smelled the odor of her hair. She smelled clean. Half instinctively he had prepared himself for the dry sweaty smell and slight, sickly powder overlay of none-too-clean females. Thinking this, he stood with her head touching his. She did not respond, nor did she move to repulse him in the coy routine of boy and girl situations.

He let her go. She leaned back and he could feel and hear her brushing her uniform with her hands.

"Well," she said.

"Well, what?"

"It was fairly disgusting, wasn't it?"

"What was so particularly disgusting?"

"I don't mean us—I mean, going through the motions—because we felt we had to. I came out here..."

"Under the impression that you thought I was different. If you tell me the one about being different I'll—I'll..."

They were silent. Then she said:

"You might have been nice about it."

"Shall we go back?"

He heard her starting. They went along the lane, under the arching trees that made the blacked-out night even blacker.

It was not until they halted that she spoke.

"This is far enough—and thank you."

"You don't want me to take you back to the entrance because someone might see you and..."

"That's true," she said. "Then I would be like the others. You have to get used to things little by little. You don't think so until the time comes."

"Like the others?" he said. "I thought you said they were nice girls."

"They are nice girls—in many ways."

"I see... well..."

"I'm sorry," she said. "About saying it was disgusting. I didn't mean you. I meant—both of us—starting something that neither of us had our hearts in—not really wanting to do it but only making the motions."

He stood silently a moment.

"That's true," he said. "I'm sorry I was ratty. What's your name?"

"Prudence. Prudence Cathaway."

"Prudence?"

He stood back and laughed. For the first time the tension of observing themselves left them.

"They should have called you Imprudence."

"That's what my father says. I'm always getting into so many scrapes."

They stood in indecision.

"Look, may I see you again tomorrow night?" he asked.

"I don't know. Probably I'll be busy."

"And possibly not."

"I couldn't be sure."

"I'll come anyhow. I'll restore all your feminine ego. I'll wait for you—up on the wall."

"I can't promise. What if I can't come?"

"If you can't come..."

He considered a moment.

"If you can't... it won't make any difference."

"At least you tell the truth," she said. "That's a kind of torture to oneself—telling the truth when it's so easy not to. Good night."

"Good night," he said.

He felt disjointedly ill at ease—as if he'd been hearing a tune that was interesting, and someone had turned off the wireless in the middle of it.

He listened for her going down the black road, but there was no sound.

CHAPTER VI

Joe came in as Clive straightened his necktie.

"Sure you won't change your mind, Briggs?"

Clive bent his head under the gabled ceiling. The late evening sunlight came in a shaft through the tiny window. He bent nearer the looking-glass to inspect his chin. The sunlight made it hard to see.

"Can't do it, Joe."

"All spit, shave, and shine, eh? Appointment?"

"That's it."

"The one last night?"

"None other."

"Ah—women! Once in a while's enough."

"Sour grapes, mate. You weren't a success."

"I was that. I am when I want to be."

"But you weren't last night."

"Ah, she give me a bellyache, that Violet. I haven't time to waste."

Joe sat on the bed and hugged a knee.

"You know, chum. There was a time when I'd go for it. You know—I didn't mind how long I had to work for it. Patient—that was me. But now I'm getting to a point where—well, hell, if it comes, all right; if it don't, to hell with it."

"You're losing your manhood, Joe."

"Me? Like bloody hell!"

"You are. Either losing your manhood or approaching mental maturity."

"I'm getting more sense."

"That's what I mean."

"Then whyn't you get sense, too? Come on—just drop in with me for a couple."

Clive picked up his hat and grinned. Joe had such a serio-comic pleading look on his face.

"All right. Just one quick one—then I'm away."

Joe grinned and jumped up.

"That's more like it," he said.

They went from the cottage to the warmth of the evening. The early August air was clear and soft.

They went along unspeaking to the pub. They ducked under the low lintel and their feet moved noisily on the sanded floor. The publican saw them and came over, wiping his hands on his apron. He drew up his bulk and sniffed.

"Now, you two. I don't want no trouble to-night, so..."

"Oh, go fry a fish," Joe said. "Bring us two mild and bitters."

"No, let's get out of here," Clive said. "I don't want to stay..."

"To hell with him. You'll have a drink first to warm you up. This is a public house. Come on, Chubby."

"No. Let's get a pint of whisky and get out."

"Not me. You hear, Carlishaw? Two mild and bitters and a pint of White Horse—and hop to it."

Joe laughed as he leaned back in the leathered wall seat.

"Fair gives him the gripes—the swine."

Joe looked around happily.

"You know, that's the right idea you've got."

"What is?"

"The pint. Always take a little along, I say. Give 'em a couple of healthy swigs. Then if that don't warm 'em up to you—save your time and energy. Cut your losses and run. It's no use wasting your time on a girl if she won't warm up after two drinks."

"You're cold-blooded about your women, Joe."

"No, I'm not. Just common sense, that's all. It's no use

wasting your time in sitting there and talking this and talking that, when both of you bloody well knows what you're working up to."

"Good bluff fellow, Joe."

"No. I mean, what the hell is there to talk about, anyhow? You sit and say the weather's nice, and then you sit and say nothing, and then first thing you know you're fighting the bloody war with your mouth."

"It limits conversation."

"Well, what's there to talk about any time—barring women, when you're young and single? I'll talk women and be open about it."

"Even if it's only talk, eh?"

"That's all right, chum," Joe said. He wrinkled his forehead. "If you talk women, that's only talk. And if you talk war—that's only talk, too. So you might as well keep your bloody mouth shut."

"About the war, anyhow. Let's not get going on that."

"Right! It was an effing mess, chum. I didn't like seeing the bloody British army standing up to its belly in the sea. It made you mad and—and it made you ashamed."

"Ashamed? About what?"

"I don't know. About something—against somebody. It made you ashamed. Well—here we go saying we won't talk about it, and you get me started on it."

"I'm sorry. Here we are."

"Seven-and-nine," the publican said.

"Too bloody much," Joe cut in.

"New taxes went in two weeks ago. There's a war on, me lad—in case you haven't heard."

"Here it is again," Joe said to Clive. He looked up. "Then why don't you go fight it?"

"You want to start another argument?"

"Oh, go fry a fish. You're getting yours all right."

Joe grinned as Clive put down a ten-shilling note. The

51

publican counted the change on the table and stalked away. They drank, and then Clive rose.

"Sure you won't stay, Briggs? Beer's better nor women."

"You can get a hangover from drink. I get too many headaches these days."

"That's nothing to what you can get from women. You can catch wrong honey. And that don't get cured in one day."

"I'll chance it. Don't get drunk."

"Not on this beer."

"And don't start an argument."

"It's never me starts 'em. It's always the other chap."

"That sounds logical. So long."

"So long, chum. And remember. If she don't go good after two drinks—don't waste any more."

Clive waved his hand and left the pub. It was dusk now, and he went slowly along the narrow flagged pavement, his eyes still used to the lighted pub. The voices around him seemed eerily disembodied.

Time had crawled like a beetle, and the night noises of insects had become pandemonium. But they faded into forgetfulness as he heard her coming into the darker-than-darkness under the tree.

He slipped from the wall.

"Hello," he said.

"Hello."

They stood quietly, not knowing what to say.

"I'm glad you came," he said, finally.

"I'm not," she said.

"Why not?"

"I still feel a little like a kitchen maid on her night out."

"You make it sound very attractive," he said, harshly. "If you feel like that—what did you come for?"

"Because," she said. "Because I kept thinking you'd look like such a fool, sitting on this wall—if I didn't."

His senses assayed the modulation of her voice—tense beneath its poised tone. In the darkness there was no distance between them. He moved nearer, until he thought he could feel the warmth of her face affecting the skin of his cheek. But they did not touch. He rocked backward slightly.

"Nice of you to think of me," he said. "And now—since you look at it that way—we might as well go back."

"Perhaps it would be better," she said, coolly.

They walked down the road in the blackness, going slowly and without speaking. Then, in a curious manner, their common malaise gave them kinship.

"You don't mind my walking with you, at least?" he said.

"No. It's good of you to see me back," she said. "This way."

She was moving through the grass at the edge of the road.

"It's a stile," she said. "Can you see?"

"Not a thing."

"Here, take my hand. I know it well enough."

He felt the warmth of her palm as he climbed the wooden steps.

"It's much shorter over the meadow," she said.

He followed her in the narrow path. At first he marveled at her sureness in following it. Then he found it easy to follow, too. In the years of coming and going the path had been tamped into a smooth runnel and one's feet bumped the turfed edge when they went astray. The blackout was giving new dimensions to some of the senses.

"Man used to live without lights—once," he said.

"Yes."

He realized that he had assumed in a curious way that her mind had followed his. Yet she was distant. He looked at the starlit sky and stumbled, bumping into her.

"Sorry."

"Not at all."

Her voice sounded small, feminine. He was sorry for her.

"How are things up in the purely feminine world?"

"Fine. They're a fine bunch of girls."

"I know."

"You know?"

"Yes. You told me. Remember?"

"Oh, that."

He felt his attempt to comfort her was missing fire.

"Oh, now," he said. "I'm really sorry—about to-night. You understand that, don't you."

Her voice came back in the darkness.

"I'm sorry, too. You'll pardon me, won't you?"

"It's all right. You can do as you like. It's a free country—they say."

"It's just—I suppose I'm not going to be any good at this sort of thing. And if I say anything—I suppose it sounds like all the coy things a girl's supposed to say and doesn't mean."

"No, it's nice of you to try to explain. Don't be upset."

She laughed.

"The silly thing is, I'm rather upset about you. You are really—well, you're decent about it."

"I'm a Galahad. My word—what's that there?"

"It's only the haystack."

"Heavens, I thought it was a diplodocus. Looming up like that."

She halted.

"Is this far enough?" he said.

"Yes, thank you."

They stood in silence.

"Shall we sit down?" he said, finally. "We've signed the armistice."

"Step number one," she said, in a small voice.

He heard her sitting in the hay. He sat beside her and

the rustle ended. Not seeing her, he was even more aware of her presence. They were silent long enough to hear their own breathing. He felt that she was waiting. He felt her shiver.

"Are you cold?"

"Just a little—I think."

He fumbled in his pocket.

"Will you have a drink?"

He heard her breath come and go twice.

"Step number two, isn't it?" she said.

But her hand followed along his arm until it reached his hand.

"The cork's out," he said. "That's proper upbringing. My mother told me always to take the cork from the bottle before you offered it to a lady."

He heard her laugh.

"Especially if it's a lady in a haystack," she said.

He sat with his elbows on his knees, not wishing to answer. He heard the soft gurgle. Then she said:

"Here."

He took the bottle and drank. The whisky crept hotly to the edges of his brain. The earth seemed to tilt slightly, and stayed atilt. He put the cork back, carefully.

"Did you ever get stinko?" he said. "Blind, unconscious stinko?"

"No. Have you?"

"Yes. Two nights ago. Blind! Blotto! Out!"

"Sounds restful. What does it feel like?"

"Fine. You wake up the next morning feeling like hell, but rather magnificent in a way. Empty, tired, chastened. In a way, rather purified and shriven—as if all your psychic sins had been bleached away—or washed down the sink, or something."

"It sounds as if it's exactly the thing I need. I might try it."

"I'll be honest, my lass. There's something I didn't mention. The headache the next morning."

"I'll risk it. May I have the bottle?"

He passed it to her, and then held it as their hands touched.

"There's remorse, perhaps, too," he said.

"You sound like my own conscience. I don't believe in remorse. Let go."

He let go of the bottle.

"And a feeling in your stomach," he said. "As if bile-green boats were pitching on a warm, greasy, dishwater sea."

"Now you sound like Mephisto, having successfully tempted someone, gloating as he provides himself with an alibi to prove that he warned them."

"Yes, I'm a stinker, aren't I? But be warned..."

"It's too late now," she said. "Will you tell me when I'm getting stinko—blind stinko?"

"You'll know."

"I don't feel anything."

"A delayed action effect. Wait a few minutes."

"No. I don't get drunk. I've drunk ever so much. Last Christmas at home I tried—I drank and drank. It didn't do any good."

"Don't get discouraged."

"I'll try again."

"No. Wait a while. You'll be sick."

"It's my sick if I want to be."

"If you say."

He gave her the bottle, and waited until he heard her breath expelled. He reached out and took it away.

"Should I see you back to camp?"

"No. You asked me to meet you, and now you want to hurry me back to camp. Is that being a Galahad?"

"I think perhaps it is—just that."

"No it insn't. It's more I-told-you-so to your own conscience. So that no matter what happens, you can say to yourself: 'Well, I offered to take her back.' You don't really want to go back."

"Nonsense."

"It's true."

"Yes, I suppose so."

"All right. Then we'll sit here and talk. We'll talk about you," she said.

"What about me?"

"What did you want to see me again for?"

"Oh, nothing much."

He wished she would stop talking. Her voice sounded strained.

"It's just that I'm woman."

"Nonsense."

"It is. You don't know me. We've never even seen each other in the light. You don't know what I look like. I'm just woman—something in skirts."

"Well, I'm something in pants. Pants and Skirts, that's all," he said, harshly.

"Yes. It does sound revolting," she said.

Her voice sounded thin and far away.

"Pants meets Skirts," she went on. "Object, seduction. Shortest distance between two points."

"You're gabbling."

"I have a right to if I want."

"You're getting tipsy."

"My head is perfectly clear. That was the idea, wasn't it—casual seduction of one of the Waffs. Walk arm in arm. Then clinch. Then—that's the part where it always fades out in the cinema. I wonder why?"

"Because the cinema has more sense than to try to talk about it."

"But it was your idea, wasn't it? Tell me the truth?"

She was clutching his arm. He took his hand and lifted hers away. He spoke coldly.

"Well, I can't say I wanted to see you because you're beautiful—I haven't seen you enough to know whether or not you are."

"I'm not—not very."

"And I can't say I asked you out for conversational exercise or a little chitchat. Or perhaps you can sing—or do parlor tricks."

"And that leaves—only the other thing."

She sat quietly. In a childish rebelliousness he determined not to speak before she did.

"It's no good," she said. Her voice had changed. It was soft and small. "I wouldn't be any good at it."

"At what?"

"You know. I think I'd be very disappointing. You'd better go after someone else. It would..."

Her voice trailed away. Then she spoke brightly.

"I'm sorry," she said. "Well, we've talked about me. Now let's talk about you."

"Yes," he said. "What do I think about you, eh?"

She laughed quickly, and for a second his ear was held by a sort of round beauty in the tone.

"Give me another drink," she said.

"Are you getting drunk?"

"Not in my head. But it's certainly helping me to talk."

"Ah, a garrulous drunk."

She took no notice of what he said. After a pause she spoke.

"Now. What do you do?"

"I'm on a holiday."

"A holiday! This is a fine time."

"What's wrong with it?"

"What's wrong? Well, there is a little thing like a war on. There's need for everyone to work. And—well——"

58

"Well, what?"

"Oh, you'll be angry."

"How do you know?"

"I do know—but I don't give a damn. Why aren't you in khaki?"

"You sound like a damned recruiting poster. Why should I be?"

"Decency. That's why. To be decent to yourself."

"You sound like Colonel Blimp."

"Why not? We women can get in it. And there's young men like you—well, if I were a man I'd..."

"Fight the war with your mouth probably. I punched a fat chap in the nose the other night for just that line."

"Listen," she said. "There's work to do. If I were a man, I wouldn't hold back because my age hadn't been called, or because I could claim exemption on grounds of essentials of employment. I'd enlist. I'd stand in line to enlist! I'd.."

"Oh, be quiet."

"Are you a conscientious objector?"

"Be quiet. You don't know what you're talking about."

"Then why aren't you in the army?"

"Wa-wa-wa-wa-wa-wa!" he mocked.

"I said, why aren't you in the army?"

"Talk sex again, you make more sense."

"Why aren't you in the army?"

"Oh, for God's sake, be quiet," he said. "I *am* in the army."

"In the army—then what are you doing in civilian clothes?"

"A man can wear civilian clothes if he wants, can't he? I'm on leave. I put on civilian clothes."

"I wouldn't be ashamed to wear my uniform."

"It isn't being ashamed. I want to forget it for a while."

"I know," she said, slowly. "Just as I want to forget the Waffs sometimes."

"Now, we've talked about me," he said. "Shall we go?"

"Not yet. Can't we have another drink?"

"There's just about one apiece left."

"All right. A last toast then—to the two services. The uniform forever!"

"Nuts," he said.

"Please!"

"Sorry. All right, then. To the Buffs, my lass, and a couple of egads! The 1890 port, Clinkers! And damne no heeltaps!"

She passed him the bottle.

"Now I do feel dizzy," she said.

"It would be an awful waste of whisky if you didn't by this time."

"I feel fine."

"You won't in the morning. Now, shall we go?"

"No," she said. "It's very nice here."

She lay back in the hay, and he bent and found her mouth and kissed her. She did not move.

"You make the first advances very nicely," she said.

He sat up.

"Oh, damn it, let's go back," he said. "What are you trying to find out? What are you torturing yourself about?"

She did not answer. She put her hand out to his knee and let it rest there.

"Wait a moment, please," she said. "Just be still a while."

For a long time she lay, quietly. Then she moved.

"Come here," she said.

She pulled his head slowly toward her. Then she kissed him. He cradled her head with one arm. The other hand found her breast.

„Be gentle," she said, very softly. „Be gentle, and I won't be frightened."

He kissed her again. She put a halting hand on his chest. Her voice was a whisper.

"A uniform isn't a very handy thing to make love in," she said. "Wait a second. I've got to take something off."

He did not answer. A few seconds later he felt her arms reaching for him, warmly.

But afterwards she said:

"So it was under a haystack. It is rather common, isn't it?"

"Under a hedge is commoner," he said, coldly.

She lay back quietly.

"I suppose now," she said, "you'll be able to go back to camp and talk about it: the girl from the Waffs you met and—what would your word be for it?"

"A much honester one than you're thinking of," he said. "And you'll have the consolation of knowing you've done so much for one of the boys in khaki. It's all in the name of patriotism. Think how virtuous and self-righteous you'll feel."

He turned his head away. Then he heard a novement and her hand was touching his head.

"Don't," she said. "It isn't right of us to talk like this, is it?"

"It was you..."

"There, there," she said. "Now..."

Her hand stroked his forehead slowly, and he could feel that she was staring out into the blackness. The hand went on and on, moving in a comforting way as if she were suddenly the older and wiser of the two. He began to know only the stillness of night and the oversweet smell of hay. Then, like the turning off of a water tap, time stopped. When it began again, he was sitting up, holding her arm. He heard the tail end of his own words:

"Who? Who is it?"

"Don't," she said. "You hurt. It's me?"

"Of course it is," he said, fully awake.

He leaned forward and rubbed the palms of his hands over his temples.

"Sorry," he said. "I've got an awful headache. Was I dreaming?"

"You must have been. You were asleep a long time, and you began grinding your teeth horribly. When I wakened you, you almost broke my arm."

"Sorry."

"I've got to get back."

He got up and held out his hand. He did not think it curious that she should be expecting it, nor that she should find it unerringly in the dark. He pulled her to her feet. Unspeaking, in a dreamy sort of sleepy peace, they went along the path toward the camp.

CHAPTER VII

THAT week the war had drawn nearer. It was hard to realize it consciously. One always thought of wars as being far away. "The front"—that was always in some other land. Now it was England.

The front—it was becoming all England. London—the counties—it was all the front now; only the battles were fought over the land instead of on it. In the daytime the R.A.F. was shooting down his planes—but at night it was different.

At night the bombers were getting through in ones and twos. But at first one couldn't really believe in the war, even at night. Not even when the air-raid warnings would sound, and pencils of light would leap into the sky and wave back and forth, and, sometimes, anti-aircraft guns would cut loose. It was hard to think of England as the front.

In those August nights people would go into the streets and look up. There was little to see. The guns kept banging away, going like the thump of a trip hammer. The guns sounded loud, but when the shell burst there was only a tiny sound like the popping of a small paper bag. It seemed a silly, weak little noise. There would be just that pop; or sometimes there would be a brief pinprick of light, like a star that was born and lived and died in one second.

In the small towns, when alarms sounded, policemen rode on bicycles and scolded the people in the streets. The people would not take it seriously. It seemed somehow sullying and un-British to scurry away from a danger that couldn't be true. And war right in England couldn't be true.

Even the most sensible people acted much as if the worst that could happen to England was a sort of thunder shower. These people stood in doorways and looked up impassively, or stayed inside and peeped through the curtains occasionally. Somehow they felt quite safe doing that. They were quite protected from this new sort of rain that never came. Most of them had no understanding of high explosives that ripped stone and steel and flesh, that killed people one hundred feet away merely by the concussion that ruptured the cells and fiber of the lungs and left a man unscratched yet dying.

True, some older men who knew this from the last war thought of it—and yet they couldn't make it real. A man could die so in a foreign land—but not here, at home, in Britain.

So children raced in the streets seeking hot shell splinters for souvenirs, and women peeked placidly through the curtains, and the A.R.P. men went about scolding the people for spoiling the blackout. A light from one window, multiplied a hundred times, they said, was enough to show the enemy a whole town.

But when daylight came, it always seemed fantastic and impossible, even to the A.R.P. men themselves. True, there would be news of some bombs dropped. But it was always somewhere else—over the Hampshire border, or far out on the lonesome Downs. That was a long way away.

It always seemed a long way away in daylight, and especially such fine daylight. Such fantastically beautiful weather it was. The wheat was bursting into full ear. There were a lot of tiny, blue butterflies over the south grasslands.

And in the fair sunshine it all seemed silly. The Air Raid Precautions people, the Local Defense Volunteers, the parashots, the auxiliary firemen—they looked like silly badged and armletted and dressed-up figures left over from last night's puppet show. They must have felt it themselves. They looked a little sheepish, wearing their brassards and walking about in broad daylight.

It was all ludicrous in the sunshine—fat men and young lads and meek little clerks and spinster ladies and red-faced old gentlemen tramping around with a dozen strange and makeshift signs of authority. In the daylight. Only at night some people began to feel something. In the blackness they began to feel war, real war, edging nearer and nearer.

Old Hamish felt suddenly merrier as he sat in the park. He had not gone home after all, and he was glad of it. His irritation at London was gone.

The perfection of the greenery, the dappling of afternoon light and shadow, the neatness of the walks, the splashing of colors on the clothes of the children, the uniformed nursemaids—this was as it should be.

This had not changed. London itself had changed—for the worse—had become cheap, tinny. But this was as it had been for as far back as his memory went. And it would be for as long as—as long as——

He put the thought away. You could think and argue pro and con; but Britain would be Britain always. For this was really Britain. And there'd always be parks and little shavers. Therefore, there'd always be Britain.

He felt here was a flaw somewhere in that reasoning, but he liked the comfort of the conclusion, so he turned his mind away from analysis.

He looked sideways at the nursemaid on the bench with him, holding a paper-back novelette. She would read three or four lines and look up. Read three or four lines—look up. It went on regularly, like a conditioned reflex. Reading—then looking to see if the child was all right.

Old Hamish watched the children. They were going round in circles, their hands clenched beside their chests, shuffling their feet and making moaning cries in some incomprehensible sort of game.

They seemed much alike. All nice little shavers. All of

them clean and nicely dressed. All extremely beautiful as only infancy can be when seen through adult eyes.

Old Hamish felt the sun on his face. He half-drowsed. Then he wakened to sound as a boy trotted over. He had a fawn reefer jacket, a blue sailor hat, the incredibly delicate skin of the British child.

"We're playing buzzers," he said.

"What?" the nurse asked.

"Buzzers. I'm the twelve o'clock buzzer."

"That's nice," she said, absently. "Come here."

She wet her handkerchief on her tongue and dabbed briskly at the corner of his mouth.

"There," she said.

The child ran away, and both Hamish and the nurse followed him with their eyes.

Hamish was thinking: Curious—their fingernails. Like the tiny crabs they'd had in the soup at—where—where? Hamish's younger one must be about that size now. Let's see—Munich—Coronation—Abdication crisis—death of the old King—before that—must be five exactly.

"How old is he?" he said.

The nursemaid looked up quickly. Hamish saw her summing up his age, his clothing, his fitness to be spoken to.

"Just turned five, sir."

Hamish nodded delightedly.

"Thought so," he said. "Fine-looking little chap."

"Yes, sir."

She fingered her novelette politely.

"Oh, go on and read. Don't let me disturb you," he said. "I must be getting along."

He got up and marched away sprucely, his cane swinging. Parks, he thought. Wonderful things. A spot of green in a city. You sat a moment, let your senses rest a moment, and there you were.

He went along past the old filled-in trenches of the first

scare. Two girls, gay with lipstick, flounced past—one carrying a bottle of milk. Their voices rose, chattering, high. Hamish swung his stick and marched erectly.

This was like old days. London in the old days. Ah—no tin-pan whinging and pin-ball parlors and that un-British stuff on Oxford Street then. No boop-a-dooping and hot-cha-chaing. The songs they sang now—like the rote songs of savages. In the old days—there had been songs.

"Goodbye My Bluebell!" Lord, how they sang that when they pulled out for Africa. Just to hum the first bar mentally flashed it all back—the rank smell of the Portsmouth mud flats and the odor of tar and the troopship pulling out. The old *Victory* lying there, and over in the harbor the sailors on a warship, standing in rows on the deck, their straw hats flashing in the sunshine, stamping their bare feet as they practiced in unison the cutlass drill. He could hear it now—the voice of the cutlass instructor coming harsh over the water, even over the sounds of the troops on the deck below, bellowing like mad:

> "Goodbye my Bluebell. Farewell to you.
> One last wild look into your eyes of blue.
> Mid camp-fires gleaming; mid shot and shell;
> I will be dreaming of my own—Blue—bell!"*

Ah, days, days. And old songs!

"Under the Bamboo Tree!" Gertie's song. And as fresh as if it had come out yesterday. You could remember the words, which was more than you ever could of any of the things they sang today. Yet it was ten—twenty—thirty—heavens alive, nearly forty years ago. Thirty-six or seven. Just about the time of the Russo-Jap do. That would be 1904. Gertie was twenty-nine then. That made her sixty-five now. Good Lord, Gertie sixty-five. Gertie!

He looked up suddenly and saw a taxi by the Arch. He waved his stick impulsively. The cab circled over.

---

* Copyright renewal 1932, Leo Feist, Inc. Used by permission.

"Do you know Millings Garden Lane?"

"Yes, sir. Off the Millings Road."

"That's it. Number seven. Seven, Millings Garden Lane."

He settled back happily in the cab, gay with a sudden feeling of impetuous adventure. There was the faint odor of leather. His mind turned to hansom cabs.

It wasn't quite the same smell. Then there'd been leather and the good lusty smell of horse sweat mixed in. Saddle soap too, somewhere.

By God, science hadn't done a very good job of it at that. Everyone shouted about the advancements of science; but they hadn't made the world any better. Suppose you were God—with a wipe of your hand you could knock all the jittering gadgets away—sweep the world back to the old days? No motorcars, airplanes, wireless, cinemas, howling tin music in Oxford Street. Think of it!

Why, not even the veriest idiot would hesitate for a moment—wave the hand! Wipe it out!

If you could only bring the old world back! Suppose it! Now at this moment, he'd be able to hear the horse ahead of him clop-clopping on the pavement. There'd be the sweet smell of sweat and leather in the warmth. The busses would be jogging along behind the old plugs. And the brewery lorries—with their teams of enormous shires!

Traps and dogcarts and smart coachmen and a tiger on the box—flowing gowns on the women walking under those plane trees—they'd be holding parasols above their heads—and there'd be that gesture of reaching down and behind to clutch the skirt ankle-high as they stepped from the pavement. How graceful that gesture had been—all woman-hood, sex, everything, in that half-turn of the hips to reach for skirts, to hold ankle-high. Ankles! What were ankles today?

Why, a man would be a howling maniac not to prefer that gentle, slow-paced old-time world to this madhouse.

Of course, there was all this talk of social betterment today. Well—he wasn't rabidly and foamingly anti-Bolshevik as some men were. Dash it all, of course not. He was as ready as the next to look at it as a liberal-minded man should. But, could you say the common people were better off? Could you say their lives were any happier? That was the test. Did they like living any more today than they had then?

No, honestly, you couldn't say they were truly and fundamentally better off. Everyone was happier in the old days, the lower classes included. Servants were servants, and, by God, not ashamed of their calling—proud of doing their jobs well. Happier and prouder. And what was progress if it couldn't make people happier? Making most of the people happier most of the time—that's what civilization was, wasn't it? And all this science hadn't done any good. It had only done harm. Look at wars today, for instance.

Wars had been positively decent things in those days compared to today. They had—well, damn it—good form, in a way. You could mock and scoff at form all you wanted, but where was the scientific substitute for it? Nowhere!

Ah, soldiering in the old days! Tight breeches with the stripe down the leg, and clinking spurs riveted to your heels. The little pillbox hat, and the white stripe down your cheek where the sun hadn't tanned under the chin-strap. Cavalry was cavalry, and the charge was still part of war. The charge at Omdurman! By God, they didn't make wars like that any more.

Of course, people got killed. They weren't *opéra-bouffe* wars. Indeed not! Chaps got killed just as dead then as now. But it seemed to have some sense. Yet—good chaps went.

Carteras with the damned spear right through him—like the snout of a swordfish! Right through him, and riding up and saying: "I never saw him—I never saw him!" And then toppling right out of the saddle. Fine chap. Six-three and a trojan on the polo field. Then—dead! You couldn't realize it. It was hard to realize even now that Carteras wasn't alive. Any moment, you felt, he'd poke his head into the tent and give that great horselaugh. A fine chap! A gallant with the ladies. That time—dancing the cakewalk—Gertie on the table—the bamboo tree!

> If you laka me, lak I laka you
> Then we laka both the same...

It would make Gertie happy to have him drop in. He should have done it long ago—a year—two years! One should remember!

"Hi!"

He tapped on the window with the cane. The driver pulled to the curb, and slid back the window.

"Do we pass a pub on the way?"

"Why, yes, sir. There's several. There's the Tun and Wheel, and the Green Arms and..."

"Any will do. Here. Take this pound note and get me a quart of sloe gin."

"A quart of sloe gin. Yes, sir."

The man took the note and ground the car into gear.

When there was no answer Old Hamish pressed the sneck of the door and walked in.

"Hi," he called. "Hi there!"

He waited, the wrapped-up bottle of gin in his hand. There was no sound. Quietly he walked through the kitchen, which was curiously enough the front room. He went along the hall to the "best room." A fire glowed in the grate.

Then he saw her, asleep, in the rocking chair that was beside a huge brass bed. Her great bulk filled the chair, pressing against the sides that alone seemed to prevent any overflowing. He saw crutches leaning against the fireside. As his eyes took this in, she wakened. She stared, her head half-turned. Terror came into her face until realization overtook it. She blinked. Her eyes were rheumy.

"Gertie," he said. "It's all right. It's me."

There was, for a brief second, no apperception in her face, and then the smile bloomed, going beautifully over her generous features.

"The Captain," she breathed. "Well, bless my soul if it isn't the Captain."

"Of course it's me," he said, as if to a child.

"Come to see Gertie."

"Of course! And look! I've brought you a present!"

"A present!"

She held out her hands and took the parcel. She nursed it without opening it. Then she shook her head.

"Oooh," she said, brightly. "I just dropped off in a nap. Pull up the chair."

He sat beside the hearth, and looked at the crutches. He looked back at her. Then he started. One of her legs was missing.

"My God," he said. "What is it?"

"What?"

She followed his glance, and then she laughed. The merry, bubbling, heedless laughter that had always been her own flooded the small room.

"I had it took off," she said, proudly.

She was fully awake now and bright with liveliness.

"Took off?" he said, vacantly.

"Yes. It was me bad leg, y'know. It wouldn't get better, and always running sores. Nasty things, you know. Not nice, are they?"

"Of course not—no, indeed."

"Oooh, Captain, it got so's I couldn't bear myself. I always was one for being neat and clean—no matter what, you know I always was one for taking pride. And it god so's I couldn't bear myself. And we'd tried this and that and everything else. So the doctor says: 'There's only one thing. It'll have to come off.' 'Then off it comes,' I says, just like that.

"So off I pops into the hospital. And pop! Off comes me leg, just like that."

"But—but why didn't you let me know?" he said.

"Oooh, I didn't want to bother anyone. I says to myself: 'It's your own leg, and your own mind to make up. So have it off.' And glad I am, too. No more sores, and nasty things they are, too—you wouldn't know unless you had some. And it's all sewed up nice and neat. Only six weeks ago, it was, and I feel better already. Never felt better."

She laughed again, the rich, gurgling laugh that Hamish always remembered.

"Outside one thing," she said. She laughed again. "You'll never imagine. I want to scratch the sole of me foot—and it's not there. Imagine! Me foot tickles—and I haven't got any foot!"

She laughed until the ripples spread down her body, and her plumpness quivered all over.

"I know," he said, reprovingly. "But I've always told you, in case of anything, to let me know. Or to get in touch with Mr. Haskell immediately. Why didn't you?"

"Oooh, it wasn't anything, Captain, once I'd made up me mind. And they were that *nice* to me in hospital. The nurses were just lovely. They were so proud of me. You know, they swore up and down that they never had a patient who healed up so fast and so nicely as I did. Never!"

"Yes," he said. "It's just—just a bit of a shock."

"I couldn't help it," she said, almost tearfully.

She bent her head and then remembered the package in her hands.

"It's sloe gin," he said.

"Fancy you remembering," she said quietly, without looking up.

"Now, now," he said. "I haven't been scolding. Would you like a drink."

She looked up, and the sly glance came in her face.

"Well, doctor says I shouldn't. But—there's glasses in the cupboard. I can't get around very well yet. That's why I had me bed brought down here. Would you mind?"

He got one glass and opened the bottle. The clear liquid gurgled. He shuddered at the smell. He held out the glass. Then he sat.

"Cheerio," she said.

"Cheerio."

He settled comfortably in the chair. It was cozy here, he was thinking.

"I can't get over your leg, Gertie," he said.

"Aaah," she sighed. "Well, I can't complain. It did its part for a long time. Danced me along life—what life I've had. A shame in a way."

"That's what I mean. It's hard to think of you—and think of you dancing—and—well, it must be hard on you."

"Oh, Lord loves you, Captain, I can't complain. You can't be young forever. And I did dance while I was at it, didn't I? I *did* dance."

She nodded and went on.

"What I say is, you've got to take life as you find it and make the rough go with the smooth."

She stared in the fire, and then gurgled happily.

"But I did dance, didn't I? And my legs were something to look at then."

Old Hamish did not realize that he was lifting his mustaches with the back of his hand.

"As fine a pair of legs as London ever saw," he said. "You beat Gaby What's-her-name—the French woman. You beat her hollow."

"Why, thank you, Captain. What a nice thing to say. Well, if you ask me, you had a grand leg yourself."

"Oh, come, now."

"Don't be bashful. You did. In them tight trousers with the yellow stripe. Soldiers—they don't wear them no more. More's the pity, I say. Say what you care to, I always liked a man to have good *legs*. And you could see what a man was like them days. Now—well, it's turned around, and you can see what a gel is like. Terrible, I think. Of course, you could us, too, but it was different with a gel in the profession, wasn't it?"

"Oh, yes."

"And we always wore tights. Not half-naked like gels go round on the streets these days. You can't say we ever didn't wear tights—and it looked nicer, if you ask me. Decenter and looked nicer."

Hamish gazed at the fire and nodded.

"Yes," he said. "Women looked better. And they were better—no silly cinema diets then. By the Lord, some of those old principal boys had figures. You did, too."

"Didn't I just!"

She laughed and the sound came warm and almost sexual. Her old frame shook with merriment.

"Oooh, dear. And didn't I *dance*. One and two and... and the cakewalk. Sossidge for tea. Remember? And I Laka You Lak..."

"I was just thinking of that today," Hamish cut in. "It's curious you should mention it."

"Well, it was my song," she said, simply.

He nodded, staring in the fire, and hummed the tune inside himself. It rolled the years back. She stared, lost in her own meanderings. Then she said:

"Remember the parody we had on it. Remember, after Cissie sang it straight, then me and the whole chorus:

> I saw Bill Bailey
>   Kissing a lady
> Under the Bamboo tree.
>   Bill Bailey ran away...

She sang, her voice small and sweet and at strange odds with the jaunty doggerel. He looked up and watched her face, dimpling and shining over the white crocheted collar with its demure clasp pin.

He jogged his mind sternly. It was no use sitting and talking of old times. He ought to be getting along. It had all ended so long ago—Gertie! It was nice to see her settled in her old age. Old age? She was four years younger than he. But of course, age for a man and age for a woman were different.

"I must be going," he said, abruptly.

She stopped humming. When she spoke her voice was small—like that of a forlorn child.

"Will it be three years before you come and see me again?"

"Oh, no. I'll drop past. I don't often get down to London now, you know."

She brooded.

"Please stop a while with Gertie. Look, have tea, it's almost teatime. Please stay."

He stood, perplexed. It was so unusual. That had been the one thing about Gertie. She'd never questioned or pleaded or demanded his time back in the days when—when they were younger. Gertie had shown perfect understanding. But now—crippled, of course. It must make life lonesome for her.

"Look here," he said, briskly. "How do you manage now? I think you ought to have a servant—a maid or a good dependable woman to help you..."

"Oh, I get along so nicely. The little gel from next door comes in. She's such a lovely little thing. She'll be in from school most any time and get us tea. If you'd wait a minute..."

"I must go, Gertie. But I'll look in again. And if there's anything..."

He heard the door slam and the sound of a child's voice, calling.

"That's Alice now!" Gertie said.

He turned and saw the child come rushing into the room. "Oh, Mrs. Tindley. I saw..."

Hamish watched the child halt in mid-speech as she saw him. He smiled.

"What did you see?" he asked.

"The doctor's motorcar bumped a tram," she said, flatly.

She edged quietly to Gertie's side. Gertie put a plump arm around her.

His mind pondered on the "Mrs." Of course, Gertie had to have some standing in her world. But he had never thought of it.

"This is Alice," Gertie was saying, proudly. "She does for me, don't you, dear? Does my bed and makes my tea and everything."

Hamish saw the child leaning half-shyly against Gertie's shoulder. The girl's hair seemed tarnished red in the firelight, and her face, pale above the brown velvet of her dress, seemed brightly intelligent. She was about fourteen—just passing from thin coltishness into the first blossom of nubility. He saw her breasts pushing like fast-growing plants at the flatness of the velvet. He flicked his eyes away.

"Awkward," he thought, "the way one's eyes wander. Hardly quite decent, looking at a child."

He saw that her eyes were fixed on the gold top of his cane.

"Say how-de-do to the Captain, Alice."

"How-de-do," the child said.

She put one foot behind the other and plucked the sides of her dress as she made a quick bob.

Hamish smiled. A pleasant child—and well-brought up. That was the proper way. So few children today had the slightest notion of how to behave. Drop curtsies and what not.

He felt suddenly pleased.

"How do you do," he said.

The child looked up at Gertie.

"Shall I get your tea?"

"Well, now," Gertie said. "We're just trying to get the Captain to stay. Perhaps if we asked nicely..."

"Oh, I might as well stay now," Hamish said. "I *could* do with a spot of tea."

"There," Gertie said, happily. "Now let's give the Captain a real high tea. We'll get something nice at the shop. Just reach me my purse..."

"Here, here!" Hamish protested. He dropped his gloves in his hat and set the cane by the wall. He got a pound note from the folder in his inside pocket, and held it to the girl.

"Now you get lots of nice things," he said. "Lots of them."

"What shall I get?"

"Oh—what you like."

"You just get what you think would be nice for us, dear," Gertie said. "Now you show us how nice you can think up things for tea."

The girl stared at the note in her open hand a moment, then clasped it with a convulsive movement, and ran from the room eagerly.

Hamish and Gertie laughed.

"A nice girl," he said. "Very nice child. Yes."

He settled himself in the chair and stared at the fire. Gertie seemed lost in her thoughts. His mind ambled drowsily.

There was a peace here, sitting in this tiny room, the fire glowing warmly. More than that—a sort of ease of mind. An ease—where one could talk naturally of bad legs

—and old songs. No artificiality. The hard, boop-booping modern world far away outside the walls.

He heard Gertie laughing.

"Oooh, will you ever forget the time I did the dance on the table that New Year's—and that Leftenant Cary-Ford?"

"Yes."

"Ah, now, now. You was always jealous of him. And no reason to be. Because there never was a man you had reason to be jealous of or suspicious of. That's one thing I can always say. Never! Excepting that one particular case, and you-know-who, whose name we won't mention. And we won't speak any more about it. But outside of that, you never had reason to be jealous."

"Why?" he said, suddenly. "Why did you play straight?"

She wrinkled her forehead.

"I don't know," she said. "It's just I have respect for myself, that's all. When a gentleman takes a girl, and does proper by her, why I'd think shame on her if she didn't keep straight."

"I see."

He nodded to the fire.

"Whatever become of that Leftenant Cary-Ford?" she asked. Then she chuckled. "Oooh, he was a one, that chap. A devil if I ever saw one. Laugh! I never saw a chap so full of deviltry—like pouring the champagne in that poor cabby's hat. I often wondered what he does now?"

"Cary-Ford?" he said. "He got killed. He was a brigadier-general. Got it in March, '18."

"He did? Oh, now, isn't that a pity! Such a nice young chap he was—and never a one any fuller of fun than he was. Oh, dear, the war. And now we've got another one."

"Yes," he said. "And it's a bad one."

"Those nasty Germans," she said. "We beat them once and now we have to do it all over again. But I suppose we'll be all right. I have a wireless, you know, and I listen sometimes. The B.B.C. sounds very hopeful. But to tell you the truth, I don't listen very much."

"Why not?"

"I don't know. I can't take this one very seriously, in a manner of speaking. I suppose it's—you know—getting along in years. Wars are for young people. When you get along, you can't take 'em seriously. You get thinking: I may have passed on before it's all over, and then I'll never know how it came out. You couldn't get interested in a play at the theater if you kept thinking you were only going to see the first act."

He shook his head. Then turned.

"Do you mind getting along, Gertie? Does it worry you?"

"Me?" Her laugh pealed brightly. "Lord love you, no. When you're young, age seems just too awful; but the further you get along, the friendlier it seems. Of course, I like to think of what jolly times we had when we were young—and I wouldn't want my life much different. But I wouldn't want it to be like that now. Oh, no. All that helterskelter, and troubles and carryings-on. They're nice when you're young. But now—I like peace. Just sitting here, I'm comfortable."

He nodded.

"Yes," he said. "I understand. It's very comforting here."

He rocked and the room was silent except for the spitting of the fire and the ticking of the cheap clock. He poked the fire, and then lifted a few more pieces of coal on it from the scuttle, setting them neatly with the tongs. He felt somehow that this had included him into the home — as if it now possessed part of him that had been his own before.

He sat back and rocked time away. Then, like a puff of quick, cool air, they heard the sound of Alice returning. Hamish sat up and looked round. They heard her dropping bundles in the kitchen, and coming down the hall. She came in, smiling happily.

"Your change," she said, quietly.

She tumbled the coins into Hamish's hand. They were warm from the tight clutch of her palm. As she turned, he called her back.

"Here, here!" he said.

He looked among the coins and found a half-crown.

"There you are, my girl," he said.

She came forward, shyly, and took the coin. Again she dropped her shy curtsy. He saw her looking at him from under her eyelashes in that second. Then she turned and went as if for protection to Gertie. She opened the palm and showed the coin.

"That's a very good girl," Hamish said.

Gertie stroked the child's hair fondly.

"But you should say thank you, too," she said. "As well as dropping the curtsy."

"That's all right," Hamish said, brightly. "She has very nice manners."

"She has," Gertie said, comfortingly, still stroking the child's hair. "Always watch your manners, and be polite, and keep yourself neat and clean—and watch your figure. And then—some day——"

Her voice lifted dreamily as if she were telling a fairy tale.

"... Some day—you'll have a nice gentleman to call on you for tea, too."

Gertie laughed, throatily. Hamish saw again, in a second, the child's glance come up warm and almost maturely and sexually alive from under her long lashes. He felt that the child must have known it, too, for she ran quickly back to the kitchen.

Hamish avoided Gertie's glance as he turned back to the

fire. It was comfortable, Hamish thought, that was why he had stayed on. What more could a man want than comfort?

Of course, one would soon get tired of it—humble living—this tiny room. Die of claustrophobia. Get to hate the warm, lived-in smell. But—just at this moment of this year of his life, in the city of London—it seemed very comfortable.

CHAPTER VIII

THE pub already was well into the full chorus of evening gabble that would go on until closing time. The low-ceilinged place seemed as if it had been poured full of sound, and one only preserved a small private sanctuary in it a few inches round his own body.

Clive swilled the beer round in his mug and stared at the table. Joe made a movement with his hand, and he looked up. Joe held up a finger. At the same time, the hubbub died and the B.B.C. voice came clearly from the wireless.

The B.B.C. was announcing that bombs had been dropped on the Southeast coast. The R.A.F., however, were shooting down daylight raiders whenever they came over. The army in Somaliland was retiring.

Clive and Joe stared at the table as the mellifluously-accented words went on. When it was over the pub broke into its hubbub like horses starting from the tape. Clive looked toward the door.

"D'ye think we'll beat 'em, Briggs?"

Clive started, and then looked soberly at Joe. He looked carefully, as if seeing for the first time—or for the last—the form and shape of him: the wave of carefully combed hair under the jauntily set-back cap; the regular, good-humored features—small nose, calm eyes, large firm mouth. It was a good-natured, slightly flamboyant, very British face.

"No," he said. "I don't think we will."

Joe looked up quickly, and then drew patterns in the wet table top with his finger.

"Why not? Look at the last war. It looked as bad at times."

"Last war everyone rounded on Germany, Joe. War nowadays is like a gang fight, Joe. A bunch all scrapping—and they end up by all picking on one and beating him down. Like wolves—eating the bloodiest. Last time it was Germany. This time it'll be Britain."

"But if the United States comes in..."

"She won't. That's bad hopeful thinking. She won't fight with and for us. None of them will. They'll all round on us now. We're the fattest picking. There's plenty of plunder for all of them. All the nations of the earth can watch us go down, and there'll be swag enough to make them all happy when we're done."

"We're not going to be done," Joe said, angrily.

"Why not?"

"Well, we're not."

"Well, let's not argue."

Clive rose and looked toward the door.

"Wait a minute, chum. I wanted to tell you. I'm going."

"Going? Where? Joining up?"

"Sort of. A minesweeper. Bill Stafford—you know, skipper of the *Island Queen* I told you about—well, he's going, and he asked me to go along with him."

Clive sat and regarded the table.

"I see," he said. "Well, I can wish you luck. If that's your line, and you're set to go, that's the thing to do."

"That's the way I looked at it," Joe said, happily. "Might as well go for what I know and not wait till they come along and pull me into khaki and set me doing something I don't know."

"That's right. A chap's got to do what he thinks best. But I'll be missing you. When do you go?"

"Well, that's it. I go down to-morrow. And—you know you can take this all right from me?"

"Of course. What?"

"Well, I thought—how about you coming with me? I

saw the skipper last night, and I said I had a chum. And he says, well, the more the merrier. Now you don't have to say anything if you don't want."

Clive looked at the table. Suddenly the noise came into his consciousness again, crowding at him. He wanted to be away—outside. He drew circles with his finger.

"If I say no, Joe, will you understand?"

"Of course, chum. Of course. This is a free country."

"No, you don't see it right."

"But I do."

"No, you don't. I can tell the way you say it."

"No. A man's business is his own. I just thought, like, I'd ask you. There's no harm asking."

"No. That's right. I think—I'll step along, Joe."

"Hold on, Briggs. There's something else, like. Well, I'll be away—and you wouldn't be doing anything to get my old lady in a jam."

Clive sat down again. He looked up at Joe's troubled face.

"What do you think I am?" he said. "I'll pack up and move on."

"No, that's it," Joe said. "I'd like for you to stay—as long as you want. It's a man about. You know what I mean—just having someone around once in a while, then it ain't so lonesome for my old lady. And—after all, renting the room to you does help. Every little bit helps they say, and there's something to it, isn't there? But the only thing is..."

"What?"

"Oh, Jesus Christ. I hate a Nosey Parker, and it's none of my business, but there's the old lady. But—are you a secret service chap?"

Clive looked at Joe's solemn face and laughed, quickly.

"Goodness no," he said. "No."

"Well, I don't give a bugger what you are, chum. Or

what you're up to. If you say it's all right, and doesn't make trouble for my old lady."

"You're a good chap, Joe."

"Oh, hell. It isn't that. Are you—are you in trouble, mate?"

Clive studied the young man before him.

"It's all right. Nothing's wrong. You've treated me well, Joe. So I'll tell you. I'm—I'm a soldier."

Joe nodded.

"That explains those military ration tickets you gave my old lady. But—but why didn't you say you was in the service?"

"Look, Joe, I can't explain. It'd take too long. But I promise you it's all right. I'm on leave. It'll be up soon. A few more days—then I'll move on. Is it all right?"

"I want you to stay as long as you feel like it," Joe said. "You say it's all right—I believe you. It's all right."

Clive smiled.

"All right, Joe. Now let's have a drink on it."

"Yes," Joe said. "Just one—then I'm off. This'll be last night home, you know. And I think I'll spend my last night home. You know how women are. My old lady would like it."

"Yes," Clive said. "That's the best thing to do."

He went and got the beers. He handed the mug to Joe.

"Here's to the war," Joe said. "It's the best bloody one we've got."

Clive lifted his mug.

"And here's to..."

"To what?"

"To you," Clive said. "To you—and to every last bloody one of us—and to—not to the war. To the end of it. To peace!"

"Right. To me and you and all of us and the war and the end of it. Drink up!"

They drank and left the inn. Then they were in the dusk, going through the village with quick step and senses somehow newly tuned to unlighted evenings. At Joe's street they parted.

"I'll take a stroll," Clive said. "Then your mother will have you alone."

"Do you think she'd like it that way, now?"

"I feel sure of it."

They left each other and Clive went on in the dimness, his feet striking the metaled road regularly. It was not until he was almost there that he realized he was by the tree overhanging the wall. He paused in indecision, and then sat on the wall. Detached, in the darkness, from time to time he heard the low voices of passing girls coming from the village. Sometimes there was a quick, uplifted laugh, and sometimes the lower note of a man's voice. Then he heard a voice that he remembered.

"Violet?"

He went into the road.

"I was with Joe Telson—at the concert Saturday night."

"Oh, it's you," she said. "This is my friend, Miss Patsy Acton. Mr.—I forgot your name."

"Briggs," Clive said. He ducked his head at a mass in the blackness which, obviously, was another girl. He heard her voice, metallic in the London way.

"It's really an enormous pleasure to meet you."

She gabbled the syllables as if it were a well-loved phrase.

"Thanks," Clive said. "Look, Violet. You're heading back to camp, aren't you?'

"Well, I was."

"Do something for me, there's a good pal. Tell Prudence I'm here, will you? You remember—the girl I was with Saturday. Ask her if she can come."

"Well, now. I don't know. I can ask her. I don't know whether or not she'll come. She's funny."

"That's all right. Just ask her."

"Well, I will—seeing it's you. But she's—awful uppy."

He heard the girls go away. He went back to the wall and sat, wishing the time away, listening as girls passed. At last there were the foot-steps of one person, coming toward the tree. He jumped to his feet.

"Prudence!"

"No. This is Patsy."

"Patsy?"

"Yes. Patsy Acton. Violet just performed the introduction."

"Oh, yes. What did she say?"

"Prudence? She said she couldn't come. She said to say she was most dreadfully sorry, but she was indisposed with a headache. She says it's *that* bad it's excruciating. That's what she told Violet. Then Violet wouldn't come. She's terrible lazy, is Violet. So I come all alone. I wouldn't have you standing out here all alone. It isn't fair to leave anyone just standing, like that, is it? So I come—all alone. I wouldn't come down here all alone, only I couldn't bear to think..."

"Thank you," Clive said.

He felt the girl waiting. There was a sense of her nearness.

"All right," he said. "It doesn't matter. Will you do something else for me?"

"With extreme pleasure—if I can."

"Tell Prudence—tell her I'll be here to-morrow night. I'll wait here until she comes—if she can. I'd like her to meet me. Tell her that, would you, please?"

The girl yawned, loudly.

"Well, I can tell her. I don't know what she'll say. She's fearful distant and swagnay, that Prudence is."

"She's what?"

"Swagnay. It's French. Well, I'll go all the way back. And alone."

He heard her footsteps drag away. He went back to the wall and sat. A ripening moon came up, and cast faint shadows. There was nothing he desired now so much as to see Prudence. Not being able to see her made it an intense longing.

CHAPTER IX

THE next night it was raining dismally, and he did not expect her to come. But he heard her feet squelching on the road, and heard the rustle of her mackintosh and the slap of rain on the hard fabric. Then he felt her beside him.

He jumped down and they stood, awkwardly and without ease.

"Nice of you to come," he said. "I wouldn't have blamed you if . . ."

"Ghastly weather," she said.

"Fearful. Certainly isn't romantic."

"See here, I shouldn't have come."

"I agree with you. I just said I wouldn't have blamed you if you didn't."

"Not the weather. Just coming at all. Oh—I suppose it's the feminine thing to say. You mustn't if I say useless things, will you? You won't mind, ever?"

"Go on and be feminine," he said. "I didn't mean to be rude."

"No, you're all right."

She stood, waiting.

"Shall we be comfortable—as comfortable as we can?"

They sat on the low wall. The rain slatted and the night was close about them, shutting them in a sort of privacy.

"I suppose there's not much help for these things," she said, slowly.

"What things?"

"You know. Don't crumble the defenses of my phrases."

He did not answer.

"Tell me about you," she said.

"No. You tell me. What do you do? Not in the Waffs—I mean in ordinary life."

"There's almost nothing to tell about me, I'm afraid."

"Now you are speaking phrases. Everyone does something. Everyone's life is full and important and dramatic—to himself at the very least."

"That's so. I studied art."

"Art? What for?"

"You know, that's what I wonder now. I wasn't very good at it, really. It's what you do—study art—it's done. You wander round and wonder what you can do. You don't like bridge, and you don't like doing nothing, and—and you're not the athletic type. So what can you do? You can get a job reading for a publisher through a friend—or start a hat shop with a woman who's having trouble with her husband—or take up social service work—or dedicate your life to having direr illnesses than any of the others you know—or pretend you're having a career. I started a career—art."

"And now you're in the Waffs."

"Yes, and now I'm in the Waffs, sitting on a wall with a strange man—and in idiotic weather."

She spoke the last as a sweep of wind shook the beech tree, sending the gathered rain down in a torrent on their hunched shoulders.

"It is idiotic of me to keep you here," he said. "I'll take you back, eh?"

"We were going to talk about you."

"I'll tell you some other time."

"Yes," she said, slowly. "You shall tell me."

She got down from the wall and they walked along, slowly, in the pelting rain. Their feet dragged as if they wished it to last, this going along the road close together, with the storm making the world lonesome.

"You must leave me here," she said, finally.

"You don't want to be seen walking back with a man?"

"That isn't it. I don't care."

"It is it, and of course you care."

"Yes," she said. "I do care, in a way. You have to get used to things."

They stood waiting.

"Will you see me again, Prudence?"

"Why do you want to see me again?"

"Shall we complicate things by trying to express reasons?"

"It's easier not to, I suppose. But we go through moves of defense—like a chess game—doing it all by instinct. We do it, even when we know there's no defense there. It can't be born in us. It's instilled in us from the time we're little girls."

"Then you'll meet me—not under the tree. Can't I see you sometime—don't you have time off?"

She paused, and then said:

"I could get off to-morrow afternoon."

"Good," he said, brightly. "What would madame like to do?"

"What do you suggest, sir?"

"Far be it from me to be suggestive, madame."

"You do have a sense of humor, don't you?"

"Oh, a very strong one, when it's unbridled. But also I've got a tenacious mind. I still want to know what-where-when about to-morrow. Where do we go?"

"You think it up."

"I'm a stranger here myself, madame. I don't know the ways of the land."

"Well—I'll meet you at two. That's the regular camp routine. Meet you by the bus stop at two."

"Then what's the routine?"

"You ride up to Wythe and you have tea, and then you go to the cinema, and then you come back on the last bus and tell everyone what a fine time you had. That's supposed to be the thing to do."

"Well, far be it from me to upset ordained schedules in these regimented times. I'll see you at two, then, at the Gosley bus stop."

"No, the high road one—it doesn't matter. I'll get on at the high road, and you can get on at Gosley. It will save a walk. Or—no. Please come to the high road and meet me there and we'll get on together."

"That was nice of you," he said. "Good night."

He stood, listening to her go away. Only when he turned about did he become conscious of how wet he was. His shoes squelched with the water.

"It has a High Street, a Main Street, one cinema and a war memorial," she said.

He walked with his eyes ahead.

"And six pubs, one Wythe Community Center and one hotel."

They walked in the sunlight. Now, because they could see each other, they were strangers and somehow uncomfortable.

"We're not very bright, are we?" she said.

He knew what she meant.

"Perhaps I'd better take you back."

She drew in the breath and walked without answering. Then she said:

"It has a nice church and a very pretty graveyard."

He went with his eyes on the pavement.

"It's a very pretty graveyard," she said.

Her voice sounded small. He stopped impulsively, and looked at her face. Then he smiled.

"Is it *very* pretty?"

"Very, very pretty," she said.

He thought she was going to cry.

"Well, if it's very, very pretty—that makes it different," he said.

He looked about him.

"Every teashop looked grimier than the last," he said. "But even if this one is full of flies and corruption, it'll have to do. Wait here."

She stood in the sunlight, watching him go across the cobbled street. They had looked into every teashop in the town, and felt mutually repelled. She shut her eyes, and counted, childishly. At every ten she opened her eyes. She did that until, at the fifth count to ten, when she opened her eyes, he was coming back carrying paper bags.

"Rations ready," he said.

"Was it full of flies?"

"Every kind. House, horse and bluebottle. Now—where's this very, *very* pretty graveyard?"

"This way."

They went along the road from town, past the last shops and a few houses of the suburbia inclination. The lane curved, and there, beneath the wineglass-shaped elms, the church was. The flat-topped wall, the stone green with age, fronted the stone-flagged pavement.

"Now, isn't it nice?"

"Yes," he said, quietly. "It is."

She put a hand on the wall and jumped up quickly, turning so that she sat. He put the parcels on the wall, and then, about to jump, looked up at her face. He smiled and kept looking at her. Now, at last, he was looking frankly at her, there was no more self-consciousness.

He looked at her eyes. They were a fine gray-blue. Her hair, so light that it was almost silvery in texture, was drawn back tightly beneath her cap. Her skin was a blue-white color. Her mouth was somehow square and pugnacious. There were hints of freckles on the nose.

She was much prettier than he had imagined. Pretty? She

was quite beautiful. Certainly one would never dare hope, meeting a girl at random in the darkness, to have any better luck. He was lucky!

"Well," she said, happily.

He knew then that she must have seen gladness in his face.

"So you're the girl I met in the dark," he said.

"Well, what did you expect me to look like?"

"You look exactly like I imagined you."

"You liar. You were afraid I might be cross-eyed, or have a mole on my nose."

"I did not. I knew you had no moles."

"Well, I have."

"Where?"

"I can't show you."

He laughed quickly.

"When you went home last night," she went on, "you suddenly realized that you didn't know what I looked like. And then you drew in your breath, and said: 'My God! She might look like a pan of sour milk.'"

"By God," he said, "I did. How did you know that?"

She put her hands between her knees and leaned back, laughing.

"Because," she said, "I did the same thing."

"Oh," he said, a little ruefully. "I suppose that is so. Well. What did you expect me to be like?"

"Exactly as you are, sir."

"No. Truthfully."

"I'm telling the truth. I expected you to be just as handsome as you are."

"Oh, come."

"You are handsome—a nice sort of face—the nose a little too fine and the mouth a little on the large side. One of your ears sticks out a little more than the other—you know your face is quite lopsided? I can see it now."

"That's enough."

"No. And your eyes are very nice. A good, deep brown. They're a little tired-looking—too late hours, that is. But your eyes are your best feature. Yes, I should say that. Rather tender eyes you have..."

"Tender?"

"And on the whole, it's quite a good face. The lean type. A little too lean, but I'm glad you're not fat-faced. I hate soggy faces, don't you?"

He looked up into her face, without answering.

"Go on," he said. "I don't count in this conversation."

"You're vain—you want me to go on talking about you. All men are vain."

He whistled.

"What a remarkable generalization."

"And you shouldn't wrinkle your forehead so much," she said. "It's a bad habit. Now that's all."

He jumped up on the wall beside her and opened the parcels.

"Ham sandwiches," he said, "guaranteed to taste like damp cardboard. Rock buns—very rocky. And—milk!"

"Very nice, sir."

She took a sandwich and a bottle of milk. He watched her as she ate, her uniformed figure trim. He looked down at her leg, swinging—then he watched her low-heeled shoe. When she turned he looked up. She smiled and looked away again.

"Nice," she said. "We seem to be fated for walls. But it's always nice—away from people."

He nodded and laughed, but did not answer.

"What are you thinking?"

He looked up at her face. He thought: She is quite beautiful.

"It's all funny," he said. "Us. Sitting here. Wondering about each other. Like people newly met. Now we can see each other in daylight—partly shy, partly ill at ease, partly curious. Wondering about everything that happened before we met—and everything that happened after. Wondering about our lives, stretching back with no knowledge of each other, somehow winding tortuously right up to this point where we, two people, should sit on this wall, all full of curiosities and suspicions and defenses."

"Not suspicions," she said.

"Yes. Suspicions, too. Not so much of each other as at circumstance—touching the tentacles of relationship gladly one second, drawing back quickly the next for fear of possession—suspecting that and suspecting captivity."

"Captivity! My goodness. You mustn't think I want to capture you."

"We all do," he said. "We all desire to possess avidly."

He swung about on the wall and stared at a gravestone.

"Don't worry about it," he said. "Listen to this one. 'Jonathan Stanginghorn of the Parish of Wythe. 1739-1818. Look on me as ye pass by; as ye are now so once was I. As I am now so ye shall be. Prepare for God and Eternity.' Cheerful blighter, wasn't he?"

"Ghoulish," she said.

She swung her legs over the wall so that she sat facing the stone with him. He felt curiously pleased that she handled skirts so expertly and neatly. Some women were so clumsy...

"But they liked it that way, I suppose," she said. "They believed in the hereafter and were quite happy about facing it. Made it all very nice for them."

He looked at her, hearing the clarity of her voice. He put his hand on hers.

"You're very nice," he said.

"Please don't start that."

He took his hand away angrily.

"I'm not starting anything. I was just saying you're nice,

that's all. It was a natural thing to say—since I really haven't seen you before."

"What you're trying to say is that I was quite a lucky packet to pick out of the blackout."

"Why do you suddenly talk bitterly like that?"

"Well, I am a lucky packet. And you. You're..."

"It seems to me we've been through this conversation before."

"I know, but it's hard to talk. I was going to say you were handsome, so don't get angry. I couldn't say that though, because it would sound unmaidenly. You wouldn't like to have me unmaidenly, would you?"

"I think you're very nice unmaidenly. You can't be a maid any more."

"That's true. Neither maid, wife, nor widow," she said.

She swung her legs back over the wall.

"It's all right," she said. "I'm one of the Waffs that a soldier took out in the dark. If it's like that there's some honesty somewhere in it, so it's all right to leave it like that."

"It isn't much use talking about it one way or another, if that's what you mean."

"That's what I mean," she said.

He turned, facing the road. They swung their legs. A bus went by, its engine pinging badly. He shuddered at the sound, and crumpled the paper bags. Then he halted, his arm upraised. At last he put the paper in his pocket. She looked at him and smiled.

"Can't strew things around—by a very pretty graveyard, can I?"

"No," she agreed. She touched his knee with her hand. "I'm sorry," she said. "Let's talk. What did you do—before you joined up?"

He sat up, hugging his knee.

"Rotifera," he said.

"For goodness' sake. What's that?"

"Bugs."

"Horrid word. Like bedbugs?"

"Much nicer. You've heard of photomicrography?"

"Emphatically not."

"That's good, because there's photomicrography, and microphotography — which are entirely different things. Now you know all you need to about both, so worry no more about it, and we'll continue up the Ganges to this tiny dot. Well, that's a wonderful beggar named a rotifer. He's a cheerful chap who lives in the marvelously beautiful jungle of slimy water, in which he goes around by turning himself into a paddle wheel. He's the only animal in the world that uses the wheel as part of his body instead of using fins or legs or wings."

"You're not kidding?"

"S'welp me, it's true. He invented the wheel millions of years before man got round to it."

"And what do you do about it?"

"I don't do much. I got a job with an old chap who cuts them up and mounts them on slides. He's a wonderful old chap. The only man in the world who has dissected rotifers properly. But he's after something more important now."

"They're tiny, then."

"Very minute."

"Did you always do that? How did you start?"

"Oh—well, once I was in a secondhand camera repair shop. That's how I picked up the photography part. I'm handy at picking things up—machinery, you know."

"Did you study it?"

"No. Just sort of came naturally—through a long series of fortuitous industrial wanderings. Once I was a dog dietitian."

"No."

"Yes."

"What does a dog dietitian do?"

"Well, it sounds fine. Mostly what it means is driving a delivery truck. Delivering ready-made meals for dogs—chock full of vitamins and stuff, and balanced. We deliver to your door daily. No trouble to you. Have our dog dietitian bring freshly prepared meals of highest quality ingredients for your pet every day. You know—people too thick-headed or lazy to look after their own pets."

"No."

"It's true. Most everyone in cities nowadays is too busy to look after a dog. So it's a mass business. Chopped liver and meal and stuff, all prepared in a dainty frilled paper dish. It's quite a business. You ask anyone in the dog game."

"How on earth did you get into such a business?"

"I could repair the truck. I told you—I'm quite handy with machines."

"But what a curious business."

"That's nothing. Once I was a canary whistler."

She laughed.

"You're fooling. What's canary whistler?"

"Chap who teaches canaries to whistle."

"Why, canaries know how to whistle. It's—it's nature."

"Says you. I take my oath on it. You think canaries sing naturally, well, they don't. Good ones—they have to be taught. They can learn from older birds, or from a canary whistler, or from a machine."

"Oh, come. What machine?"

"A trilling machine. It has compressed air and a water pipe, and it goes on rolling and trilling all day. That's how I got the job. I fixed the chap's machine, and then I stayed on—feeding, you know, and cleaning and caging for market. I stuck at my post and progressed upward to special whistler for fine birds. Listen."

He put a finger on his lower lip, and the sound of a

canary trilling, higher and higher, rolled out over the quietness of the afternoon.

"Good heavens," she said. "How do you do it?"

"It's a secret," he grinned. "And it takes years of practice."

"You're talented!"

"That's nothing. Wait till you see me tap dance."

"Don't tell me you've been an actor. I couldn't stand it."

"Lady, I have my code of decency, strange as it may be. I never fell that low, but I worked in an agency once—you know, that hires actors."

"And you've worked with bugs and dogfood."

"Yes, ma'am."

"And canaries."

"And canaries. Lady, you believe me I worked with canaries. Why, if I ever see another canary—or hear one—or smell one, I'll be sick. Bloody canaries!"

"Well, what did you do it for, then?"

"What did I do it for? Hark to her! Lady, I did it to eat. You know eating?—meals, food? That stuff—you get the bad habit of wanting some two—and very often even three—times a day. Hence the checkered career of employment."

"It has been checkered, I'd say."

"Oh, but you haven't heard anything yet."

"Don't tell me you've had other exploits."

"Oh, dozens. Garage repairman, safety-glass demonstrator, padlock inspector . . ."

"Padlock inspector! You go around inspecting padlocks at night?"

"No. In a factory. A lock factory."

"How do you inspect a padlock? Give a demonstration. You look in the keyhole?"

"No. You have a tray of padlocks. You take a rawhide

mallet. You tap the first padlock in its most ticklish spot. *Voilà*, the hasp flies open! What does that mean?"

"The lock's no good."

"No! That means it's perfect. If you can't rap it open, it's faulty and you reject it."

"What makes it fly open?"

"Lady, my job wasn't to ask questions. It was to rap padlocks on piecework. They said: 'Hit 'em here!' So I hit 'em and didn't worry about the causes—only the results. Like the old chap who hits the train axles with a hammer at the railway stations. He'd been tapping 'em for sixty years and was retired on pension, and they gave him a gold button for his lapel, and shook his hand at a farewell dinner. And he said it was nice of them, after all those years, but one thing—he always wished someone had told him what the hell he was rapping the axles for."

"No. But what do they rap 'em for?"

He glanced up at her.

"You can tell by sound whether a wheel's true or not, or has a crack in it, can't you? Test by resonance."

He held his knee with his clasped hands, and leaned backward slightly. The day was fading to the endless quality of summer evening. The smell of sweetly new dust was in the air, and he heard a thrush singing in the close of the churchyard—saying that the twilight was coming at last.

She wrinkled her nose in thought.

"But you mean you can take a rawhide mallet and go around tapping padlocks and make them fly open without a key?"

"Most common types will."

"Aren't you a dangerous man to be loose?"

"I'm saving the talent for special occasions."

"And you don't know what makes it happen?"

"Of course I do—but it would take too long to explain.

I'd have to explain all about spring locks, and lever tumbler locks, and pin tumbler locks. Would you like a comprehensive dissertation?"

"We'll save it for our old age. Tell me more about you. What else have you done?"

"Lots of things—anything that was a living."

"But where were you educated?"

"I'm not educated, lady."

"But you must be—you are!"

"I'm not. I'm half-educated—like ninety per cent of the people in this country. I know a little more than nothing about a little less than everything."

"But what do you intend to be?"

"Just myself. That's all. It's all I can be. You see, it isn't a case of what you want to be. It's a case of what job a chap can get to make a living, isn't it? You come from a fairly well-off family, don't you?"

"It's all right. What would you be—if you could choose?"

"An undertaker, lady."

"No, seriously."

"I still say an undertaker. It's the only business never has any slack times."

"No, please tell me. Seriously."

"What's the use?" he said. "What's the use of thinking things like that with all this—this mess going on?"

She looked down at her feet.

"How much time have you got left?" she said. "You know—leave?"

"Don't let's talk about it. I hate to count it."

She looked up at him, and their glances were held for a moment. She put her hand to her throat, and then jumped from the wall. She spoke quickly.

"Shouldn't we go?" she said. "It's getting on. If we want to go to the cinema..."

He looked straight ahead.

"Do you want to go to the cinema?"

"It's customary," she said. "Isn't that what we came for?"

"I asked if you wanted to go?"

"What else? What do you want to do, then?"

He did not answer.

"All right," she said, finally. "Let's go find another haystack."

"Good God," he said. "A martyr. No thanks."

"Well, isn't that what you want?"

"Do you have to talk about it like that?"

"How do you expect me to talk about it? That's what you mean, isn't it?"

He got down from the wall and held her arm. Then he lifted his head.

"It's all right," he said. "There's a hundred reasons—you're afraid, and upset, and muddled. You should be. It's all right. Let's go to the cinema."

He lifted her arm over his and started back toward the town. For a while they went in silence. Then she said:

"Will you do something for me?"

"Anything you wish."

"I don't mind, but haystacks, they..."

"Sound a little sordid."

"I didn't say that."

"But you meant it."

"Please, I don't mean it. I mean, talking about it seems a little so. It isn't really itself—when we're there. It's just—planning it."

"So, we go to the cinema."

"No. Will you—take me to the hotel?"

"Then it won't be so sordid?"

"I didn't use that word," she said. "You did."

"I'm helping your thoughts out, that's all. Now we'll go to the cinema if you wish."

She stopped and clenched her fists.

"You're exactly like a woman," she said. "Now will you please decide on something definite and let's not argue. I say, clearly and distinctly, we'll go to the hotel."

He stood a moment, then clasped her hand.

"Forgive me," he said. "You're a little honester and braver than I am."

Arm in arm, walking quickly, they went to the town, and to the Wythe Hotel with its remodeled front, done in pseudo half-timbered style. It was the fake aged fronting set out hopefully to catch the summer tourist trade that now seemed nonexistent. There were no people in the chairs set about the front room. Behind the desk a girl about sixteen sat reading, her toffee-colored hair hanging wispily down toward the magazine. She looked up like a suddenly alarmed animal.

"I want a room—for my wife and myself," Clive said. "Have you a double room?"

"That we 'ave," she said.

She jumped down from the stool and ran toward the back. She called down the three stairs.

"Pa! Pa! There's a lady and gent wants a double!"

She clarioned it, gladly, excitedly. Clive and Prue, standing there, felt suddenly naked and as if hundreds of people were watching them.

They saw the little man come up the steps, wiping his mustache with the back of his hand in a half-finished-meal gesture. They saw, too, the professional smile of welcome on his face drop away as he looked at Prue and saw her uniform.

"What you want?" he said.

"My wife and I—I've come down to visit her. We'd like accommodations."

"You 'ave luggage?"

"I'm sorry, we didn't have time..."

"We don't 'ave no room."

"But the girl said..."

"I don't care what she said. I said, we don't 'ave no room. We don't operate that sort of plyce!"

The little man began to bristle with his own self-righteousness. His voice became more sharply accented.

"D'y'understand? We hoperyte a decent plyce 'ere and.."

"But dirty," Clive said.

Prue began to tug Clive's arm, but he shook her away.

"Now look 'ere," the little man said. "Look 'ere!"

"I have a friend named Joe..." Clive began.

"I don't give a bugger if y'ave."

".... And if he were here, he'd put it all neatly. He'd tell you your place is dirty. You're filthy too. Both you and your place smell. If you'd go in and scrub some of the grime off yourself..."

"Please," Prue said. "Please!"

Clive looked around and she felt as if he were seeing her for the first time. Then, slowly, he smiled.

"Hello," he said. "You're very nice."

He took her arm and put it over his and they left. They went along the street, walking heedlessly, not speaking. He patted her arm, endlessly. They went past the cinema, along the darkening streets. Beyond the town, she drew a deep breath.

"Phew!" she said.

"Think nothing of it," he said.

"But I do feel grimy."

"Don't think of it. I'm sorry—for you."

"No, you were right. Haystacks are—much nicer."

"Cleaner, anyhow."

"And not sordid at all," she said. "Not at all."

He held her arm closely, and they turned a corner going in step.

"You know something?" he said.

"What?"

"You're damned nice."

"Am I?"

"Yes, shall I tell you?"

"I'd like something to cheer me up. I don't want to cry. He was such a grimy little man—it was contagious."

Her voice sounded small and far away. He patted her arm.

"You're real," he said.

"Am I?"

"Yes. You're much nicer than a smack on the lug."

"What does that mean?"

"That's what a chap in my bunch says. Chap named Montague. Old Monty. He's a great chap. He says that when he feels good. You're much better than a smack on the lug."

"Then I'm all right?"

"That and more."

"You know, sometimes you can be very nice and understanding, Mr. Briggs?"

"Thank you, Miss Cathaway. You know, that's a funny name—but pretty, too. At first, it sounded false. But—since I've seen you, it really sounds all right—as if it fits."

"Thank you. It isn't too common, especially down here. I was born in London, but it's a North Country name. My grandfather's place is up there—in Yorkshire."

"Why, I'm Yorkshire myself."

"You are? Our family's place is Oddale—beyond Otley. Do you know it?"

"No. I come from—a more crowded area."

"But you don't sound Yorkshire."

"Oh, you lose it, knocking around. But I can talk it. Eigh lass, tha' knaws us tongues nivver loise it."

She laughed quickly.

"You sound like grandfather when he loses his temper."

She looked up as they turned the corner.

"Oh, we're back by the War Memorial," she said.

"So we are. I don't know how we got back here."

He looked at the silhouette against the western sky—the bulk of carved stone.

"The hen of the British Empire setting on the sun," he said. "I wonder what it will hatch out. Shall we take a bus?"

"If you will. It's been such a nice outing."

"I was glad to show you such a nice time, Miss Cathaway."

They climbed into the bus. Now, jammed among people, they spoke no more. The vehicle went through the darkening day, and their bodies swayed together in the rhythm. After they had left the bus they went along, silently, until they reached the beech tree.

"This is far enough for you, isn't it?"

"I'd—I wouldn't mind if you took me a little further."

They went slowly on the road, their feet kicking ahead of them.

"You've been a good sport about today," he said.

"Don't give it another thought."

After a pause he said:

"Shall I see you again?"

"Do you wish to?"

"My God, the defenses we poor humans have. This fencing!"

She did not answer.

"Prudence."

"Yes?"

"Will you come away with me?"

She stood a moment unmoving in the blackness. Then she said:

"Yes. When?"

"It would have to be—soon."

"How much more leave have you?"

He drew his breath. "Ten more days. Ten, beginning tomorrow. It's up the twenty-fifth."

She stood silently so long he said:

"You don't want to?"

"It isn't that," she said. "There's so many things to figure out. I might get a weekend. Weekend after next."

He considered.

"Now *you* hesitate," she said.

He laughed.

"No—there's things for me to figure out. I promised to meet Old Monty in London on the twentieth and go on a binge. But I could call that off."

"I wouldn't have you do that."

"It's all right."

"No, wait a moment," she said. "I forgot about the most important thing. The end of next week—wouldn't be any good."

"What do you mean, wouldn't be any good?"

"Don't be masculinely dense, please. I mean, I won't be any good."

"Oh."

They stood in silence.

"Can't you get this coming week off?" he asked. "We'd go away somewhere—for a holiday."

"I don't know."

"Couldn't you ask? Have you had leave?"

"Not yet."

"Well, don't you come due for leave—like we do in the army?"

"We're supposed to. I haven't been in service long enough, though. There's other girls ahead of me. But they're very decent. I could ask."

"You'll ask, then?"

"Of course."

"Shall I meet you—by the tree—tomorrow?"

"No. I'll drop you a note."

"That's too long. Couldn't you telephone? Down the pub. The Ram's Head. They have a telephone. I'll be there at eight tomorrow night. I'll be in the bar."

"All right," she said. "I'll telephone."

He touched her with his hands. It was dark at last. He drew her near and kissed her.

They did not speak. Then they parted in the blackness. He stood, listening to her footsteps going away.

CHAPTER X

THE moment he heard her voice he was flooded by a feeling of unreality—as if he had been carried in a strong current to strange places and alien doings and now, suddenly, wondered how he came to be in that place and doing those things.

"Yes, it's me," he said into the telephone.

Her voice sounded high and too frankly full of gladness.

"I got it, darling. It's all right."

In his mood, his mind dwelt on the word "darling." It bound him too closely. He felt uncomfortable in its possessiveness.

"Aren't you pleased?"

He brought his mind back to the conversation.

"Of course."

"You don't sound like it."

"Forgive me. It's just—where I'm talking."

"Yes, there's a fearful row. I can hear it here."

"It's shove-ha'penny. They argue all night over it."

"Can you hear me all right?"

"Yes, I can hear."

"I've got ten days, starting at reveille tomorrow. Say you're glad! I had an awful time wangling it."

"I'm glad."

"Then—where shall we meet?"

He was empty of feeling.

"At the station," he said. "The side going West."

"But I'm supposed to be on the East side. My transportation's made out for London. I didn't know where..."

"It doesn't matter. No one will care what side..."

"But they might. Please let me—be silly."

"Now, if you feel that way..."

"All right," she said. "I'll be on the West side. There's a train—wait till I look. There's one—just after ten. We'll get in the same compartment. If I don't speak to you till we're in—you'll know it's all right."

"What for?"

"I don't know. So many of the girls..."

"What do you care what they think?"

"It isn't what they think. It's what I feel. Don't ask me about it. Be gentle with me, please."

"Of course. You'll be in uniform, will you?"

"Certainly."

"I see. Couldn't you bring some other clothes?"

"I could scrape something together."

"All right."

"I don't guarantee that they'll be very West End."

He wanted it to end.

"You like talking on the telephone, don't you?"

"I like talking to you."

The words, detached from her presence, seemed too arch. She was still talking.

"It's easier to talk this way, darling."

"I know—but I'm in a pub."

"You poor dear. And I'm in a beautiful glass and wood cubicle with the temperature a hundred in the shade and the air a record of every perfume ever used in this camp. I'll ring off. See you about ten tomorrow then. Please say you're excited."

He lashed himself mentally.

"I am, Prudence. Really I am."

"Truly?"

"Of course I am."

"You're not really," she said, quietly. "But we'll pretend you are. Good-by."

"Good-by," he mumbled.

111

As he spoke he heard the telephone click emptily. Then the noise of jumbled voices and the heavy smell of ale and long-dead tobacco smoke struck him keenly.

More than anything else he wanted to run away—to leave this place as he had left Leaford—to start into the night and go, aimlessly, in any direction, anywhere. To go—somewhere else.

CHAPTER XI

Young Hamish saw his brother across the brightly lighted lobby of the hotel. Willfred was taking his hat from the check-girl and inspecting it fore and aft as if he would find, with great joy, that it wasn't his own.

Hamish started away, hesitated, and went back. Willfred saw him.

"Hamish!"

„Hello, Willfred."

The older brother turned to the two men with him. Hamish heard him mentioning their names perfunctorily. Then the four stood in a moment of indecision.

"I'll be getting along," Hamish said.

"No—er..."

Willfred turned to the others.

"I think we've covered everything then, haven't we?"

He did not wait for an answer. He put his hand on Hamish's shoulder.

"Let's pop in the bar."

"But if you're busy, Will?"

"No, we ironed it all out at dinner."

He didn't say what had been ironed out. He propelled Hamish down the steps to the bar, and they found a place at the high counter. The pre-theater rush was in full tide. The people crowded politely in the small space.

"Scotch?"

"Yes."

"Two."

They watched until the drinks came.

"Three cheers!"

"Merry-merry!"

Willfred looked around, happily.

"Quite a crowd."

"Yes."

"What keeps you in so late?"

"Oh..."

Hamish spread his hands and lifted his shoulders.

"Oh, don't let me pry," Willfred laughed.

"You're not prying. In fact, I was just playing with the idea of going to the cinema. That's all."

"Good God, Hamish, what a thing to do! When a man starts going to cinemas, it's an admission of some malaise—loneliness, *welt-schmerz*—some escapism." Willfred said it sententiously.

Hamish, looking up, caught his brother watching him in the mirror behind the bar. As if to defend himself Hamish lifted his glass in a salute, at the same moment.

But Willfred plunged on into his theme.

"Look here, Hamish. What about Iris?"

"Iris? What about her? Oh, you mean being down at Leaford. It'll work itself out."

He thought: I knew that's what he brought me down here for. Iris.

Willfred said: "I'm not trying to pry, Hamish. It's merely that Leaford isn't the best place to have the youngsters."

Quick switch, Hamish thought. But you'll wear me down and get back to it before we're through. And I don't know about Iris myself. My God, I wish I did know.

He said: "Is Leaford really bad?"

Willfred coughed and then picked up a handful of salted nuts. He ate one meticulously, and lowered his voice.

"It—er—looks as if it might be not quite the best place. Probably have to make it a solely military area before we're through, I hear. Nothing definite—you understand how I mean this. Under the rose, and not a word. But it's —being considered."

Hamish pulled the theme to generalities smoothly.

"You mean it looks bad for us?"

"Well—you can draw the conclusion for yourself. There he is, twenty miles away. He's certainly on our front doorstep. Of course, we're shooting down scores of his planes. But the thing is, he can afford to lose planes, we can't. If he can keep it up, we're blinded. And then it'll be—what did they say in the last war? *Il n'y a plus* for us."

"You mean—invasion?"

"Yes."

"But—you're not using that for a political scare, you chaps?"

Willfred smiled benignly, and lowered his voice. "Hamish, there's heads been toppled recently, and there'll be lots more heads to topple, because their owners have been wrong. Well, I don't intend to be wrong. This war—it means our chance. I don't intend to be wrong. I accept invasion as a near-sure probability."

"Good God, no!"

"Good God, yes. You know, there's no special ordinance handed down from heaven that Britain mustn't be invaded. It has been done, quite frequently. Y'know—Caesar, Hengist, Horsa, William—Romans, Norse, Danes, Vikings, Normans and so on."

"I suppose so."

"Well, I just pass it on to you—personally, of course. The South Coast isn't going to be healthy. And if I had any relatives there, I'd get them cleared out now. Yous should insist that Iris . . ."

"It's a bit difficult. You see, she won't come to London, because she thinks it won't be safe. And her father's near a steel works. And she won't . . ."

Willfred nodded. He knew the story, but he listened again. One could always check one report against another.

"It's all silly, her quarrel with father," Willfred said. "You know what it is, don't you?"

"Of course. Some woman of his earlier days, and he has the decency to see she doesn't go destitute in her old age. And that's father's kept woman! I've told Iris, but..."

Willfred laughed.

"If she could see her. She's a plump old thing. Practically senile. Lives way out on the Millings Road."

Hamish stared at Willfred.

"Oh, I looked into it," Willfred laughed. "You know, quietly and on my own. She's—well, like an old retired servant. He used to drop in to see her once in a while—but as far as its meaning anything—you know, physically—there's been nothing to that for the last twenty-five years."

"Well, whatever it is," Hamish said, "I can't see anything sinful about it. Iris is—pretty strait-laced, you know. But—I can see father's side. What could he do? Couldn't chuck the old girl out into the workhouse. I give him that."

"Of course. And it doesn't cost him above three hundred a year," Willfred laughed. "Oh, I looked into it."

Hamish cupped his hands about the glass.

"You know, he's getting along," Willfred said. "Your youngsters would do him no end of good. He just dotes on them. Of course, there's Roger's girl—but she's a girl, after all. And it's boys—grandsons. You know, there's a time in life when suddenly people seem to want children again—and it's way past their own procreative age. He's at it now. Your youngsters'd give him some point in life."

"He's got a point in life right now—getting into the service."

"No, he thinks that's it, Hamish. But..."

Willfred lifted his shoulders.

"They won't take him?" Hamish asked.

"Well, he's seeing Bullyer. Bullyer can't help him. Bullyer can't help himself—not after that Dunkirk mess. Condout —between you and me—is the man. But he wouldn't have any real use for father. I sent out a feeler. Oh, he could get something—local camp command or training depot. But not a real command."

Hamish thought suddenly of his father, sitting in offices, waiting appointments that always seemed to be deferred. He got down from the stool.

"It's hell," he said. "Wanting to go and not being able to. It must be a very private sort of hell."

Willfred got down and followed him. They went to the lobby and out to the street. Without speaking, they turned together and walked along. The black-out kept the city center fairly free from crowds. Their feet sounded on the pavement.

"You can't imagine anything happening—to Old London," Hamish said, moodily.

"Yes, you can't imagine anything fairly well established being disrupted," Willfred said. "It's so in all life. Now marriage..."

Hamish dodged the opening.

"Don't tell me you're thinking of adding marriage to your other successes."

"I wasn't thinking about me. I was thinking about you."

Their feet fell in a slow march.

"What about Iris, Hamish?"

"What about her?"

"Well, the whole business. You see, when a chap and his wife start living at distances—it's going for a break. It's natural. Marriage, I've found, is habit-forming. Some chaps —like me and like Prentiss Saintby—we never get infected..."

"Oh, how's Saintby getting along in the States? Have you heard anything?"

"No." Willfred went back to his theme. "But other chaps, once inoculated—they get used to phases of it."

"Oh, don't worry."

"I don't worry, Hamish. But you're my brother. And I see the signs. Iris staying away. You..."

"There's a taxi," Hamish said.

He whistled, and the car came over through the moon dusk. He stood by the door.

"Can I drop you, Willfred?"

"No, I've still got another conference. Keeps us going these days."

"I suppose so. Well, good night."

"Good night—and..."

Hamish smiled in the darkness.

"Don't worry, Willfred," he said. "However I solve it —I'll do it very decently."

"That's true," Willfred said, crisply. "That's the very comforting thing about your type, Hamish. We can always depend upon you to do everything in such a decent way. Rather routine—but very decent."

Willfred smiled as the taxi ground away.

CHAPTER XII

THE countryside was a moving tapestry of rare perfection. The time of the harvest was near. The unusually glorious summer had brought all green things to a rich fullness.

Already the Land Girls of the new war were getting in the hay harvest. In unmown fields the daisies stood white and the sunlight lay warmly over the land.

The telephone wires dipped and dipped in hypnotic rhythm beyond the window as he watched this wealth of August. Then he heard her voice.

"Please say you're glad to see me," she said.

There was an edge of tears to her tone, but he felt he could not turn his head.

"I am," he said. "You should know I am."

She looked down at the floor of the compartment.

"I'm not being silly," she said. "But I would like you to say something to buck me up. After all, it's upsetting—being sneaky and getting on the wrong train—and I... I..."

His head rang with a curious aching. But he was repelled by his own self-pity. He turned from the window in a surge of anger against himself, and kneeling before her he lifted her chin with his hand.

He looked into her eyes, steadily. Now, close to her, he could see the light, flecked sunflower patterns in the center of the gray-blue irises. The whites of her eyes were unmuddied. He shifted his too-close gaze to her hair. It was smooth, honey-colored. He lifted her cap and set it aside.

"I've never seen you with your cap off before," he said.

Her hair was drawn back simply from a center parting to the knot at the back of her head.

"Honey top," he said.

He touched her hair with his hand.

"Real?" he said.

She nodded, and her eyes were half-tearful.

"In a fake world," he said, "where nearly everything is brittle and false! It's real—and you're real, Prudence. You're very real. So much realer than I am."

"I'm not. I'm a fearful person. And a coward, and so much afraid."

"Now, now," he said. "You're the realest thing—right at this moment, one of the few things I believe in. You mustn't mind if I am often less than you."

"You're not less. I couldn't like you if you were."

"I like you, too."

She nodded, slowly.

"You tell the truth," she said. "And for that—you may kiss me."

Clive took her face between his hands and kissed her. And then, as he knelt there, the door opened with a harsh grating sound. He saw the conductor, a seedy man with mustache adroop as if wet with tea drops.

"Whoops," the conductor said, as if he had stepped into an occupied bathroom. He turned and rapped on the glass.

It was a comedy exit, and they burst into glad laughter.

"It's all right," Clive said. "Come in."

The man came in, averting his eyes exaggeratedly.

"Sorry to interrupt yer, sir. But I've got to punch your tickets."

Clive rose, and they began to fumble for the tickets. The conductor stood, waiting, his eyes lifted to the ceiling.

"And she'd never 'ad 'er ticket punched before," he quoted, quietly, as if to himself, but knowing they could hear him.

He looked down at the tiny squares of cardboard.

"One for Leaford," he chanted. "And one for Pompey! Good old Pompey!"

He handed the tickets back.

"Different objectives, but the same path," he chanted. "Must be friends, eh?"

The cheerful griminess of the man enveloped them.

"Of course. We're very good friends," Prudence said.

He waved his hand at them with a sort of pushing motion.

"I knew it the moment I saw yer," he said.

Clive found a florin and held it out to him.

"Could we keep this compartment?"

The man cocked a finger, half in salute and half in a conspiratorial gesture.

"See what I can do. I'll be right back."

When he came back he knocked at the door. He slid it aside and put a card against the window.

"Private, reserved," he said. "Gainst the rules—but we have so little business these days."

"Well, tell us about business," Clive said. "How is it?"

The man shut himself inside with them and leaned against the door.

"To sum it up in a word, sir..."

"Think of that," Clive said.

The man grinned, appreciatively.

"Well, I'll leave yer," he said. "It's all right—you know, I was in the last war meself. I know how it is."

"How is it?" Clive said.

"Glad you asked me, sir. Since you 'ave, I should say that *amor longa est*, and *tempus fudgits*. Latin, that is, as undoubtedly you both recognize. Used to say that to me old woman when I was on leave. She wasn't me old woman then. Just engaged—that was all."

"Yes."

"Yes, sir. Well, 'ere I stand, wasting your fudgiting tempus. Good-by, sir. And thank you. And—good luck."

"Good luck to you, too," Clive said.

The man paused by the door.

"I'll—pull down your blind," he said, in a sort of mock reproof.

He did so, and then he was gone. Prudence sat on the edge of the seat, looking into infinity. Clive, opposite her, looked up at the pictures above the luggage net. There was a photo of Llandudno, one of the Menai Bridge, one of Fountains Abbey. He cleared his throat, and he saw the focus of her eyes come to him. He smiled.

"You know," he said. "They've had those there for years—ever since I was a kid. They must be permanent—like the Magna Carta or the Dover cliffs."

She did not answer.

"Cheerful bloke, the conductor," he said.

She did not answer, still.

"What's the matter?"

She shook her head.

"Yes," she said. "He was cheerful. Only..."

"Only what?"

"Only—you can't understand. But—this was the first time in my life I've been included in a look of bawdiness."

"Oh, come now. He wasn't bawdy."

"You don't see it. A man couldn't. Only—all my life until now, I've always been looked at as if I were a china vase. Nice to look at—but that's all. And then, all of a sudden, I'm looked at as if I were—what?"

"A thunder mug," he said, curtly.

"You're not helping. No, as if suddenly I'm something utilitarian, hot and alive—and naked—with all my insides visible from the outside. You wouldn't know what I mean, unless you'd been a girl all your life until..."

"Don't let it worry you. He meant to be friendly.'

"I know—but the way he pulled down the blind and shut the door..."

"He meant to be friendly, I tell you. Can't you understand? The warm, gregarious, friendly understanding of the common man—or have you no touch with common man? He meant it generously—his offering to you. Friendliness!"

She put out her hand and touched him.

"You don't see what I mean."

"Well, what do you mean?"

"Don't be angry. It doesn't matter."

She sat back and looked through the window. Then she turned and smiled at him.

"You mustn't mind me. Be a little patient. If I take myself seriously—that's part of me and don't dislike any part of me."

He stared through the window without answering.

"Closing the door," she said. "Don't you see, Clive? There are so many doors shutting behind me just now—and sometimes I want to stop it all for a while. Not to go back, because the doors shut permanently and you can't go back. I know I want to go on—only sometimes I get a bit breathless and I want to say: 'Stop—just a moment. Hold the world still, please—just long enough for me to get a little bit used to being where I am.'"

He wrinkled his forehead and stared at her.

"No," she said. "You'll make lines come."

Slowly he smiled, and then lifted his forefinger.

"Listen," he said.

She lifted her head, and looked from side to side.

"What is it?"

"The world," he said. "It's stopping. And it isn't going to move again until you say: 'I've got my breath. I'm used to being where I am. I'm utterly bored with being where I am. I want it to go on again.'"

She looked at his eyes, and he winked.

"It's wonderful," she said. "That's one of the nice parts about it. I never thought that when you had a man of your own he could say such simple things and make you feel so wonderful inside. That's a part of it I'd never imagined. And you do it so well. Is it because it's really you—or because you know how to handle women?"

He shook his head and put his finger to his lips in dumb motion.

"Everything's stopped," he said. "Even clocks. Even my mouth."

He closed his eyes and lay back, feeling now the gentle rhythm of the train, the swaying, the train-smell, the endless jazz beat of the wheels on the rail joints, and the clacking at the points. He opened his eyes when he heard her laughing.

"It's all over now," she said. "You mustn't mind me. Poor Niobe, weeping over her departed maidenhood."

"You said maidenhood, didn't you?"

"I did."

She came and sat beside him.

"It's over now," she said. "And he was truly a nice man—the conductor. It was nice of him to include me with the living people instead of keeping me out with the china vases. Even if I'm a thunder mug. They're very useful, you know—and much more indispensable than vases—and very human."

"Oh, very."

"He was a nice conductor. I see what you mean now. He made it all human and sad and yet happy—just the opposite of the man at the hotel who made it all grimy."

"Let's keep that smudge out of it."

"It's like vegetable, animal, mineral. All my life until now it's been a useless sort of vegetable life. Now I'm animal. That doesn't sound nice."

"It's all right. When we're planted we'll damned soon take up the mineral phase of existence."

And tempus does fudgit—and the world won't stop and let you examine your fears. So—on to the next door. Because..."

Her eyes went round the compartment.

"... We're getting better at it. At least we have luggage this time, darling."

"You do. All I have is a bag in a hotel at Leaford."

"Is that where we're going?"

"If you like."

"I like."

He looked at her bags.

"You have some other clothes?" he asked.

"Some."

"You could change here," he said. "Then when we get off—you won't be in uniform."

"What's wrong with the uniform?"

"Nothing. But you're a sergeant—and in my army life I'm a lowest private. Every time I see the stripes I feel at a psychological disadvantage."

"That isn't it. Why do you hate the uniform so much?"

"I don't hate it, I tell you. Only—I'd like to think for a few moments, sometimes—that there isn't any war."

"I see," she said, slowly.

She opened a grip. She looked in it, turned to him and then smiled.

"Please don't watch."

"Why not?"

"Well—I'm not used to it. Or—it doesn't matter. You keep your eyes open if you want to. Only I *do* wish I had some nice things."

"What do you want?"

"If you were a woman you'd know."

She took off her tunic and unhooked her skirt.

"Here I go, practically on my honeymoon and ——"

"And what?"

She stepped from the skirt in a flurry of motion.

"All her life a girl wonders and imagines. How it will be, and where it will be, and what it will be. I suppose every girl plans it, and you think of a beautiful lounging robe and—and—well, you know what one would think of. And then, here I am, caught..."

"... With your trousers down."

"What an expression!"

"Do you know, you have very pretty legs, my dear?"

"Thank you, sir. You can say nice things."

He rose from his seat. She clutched the dress toward her and turned, holding out one hand.

"Please—don't."

"You're very pretty, too."

"I know, darling—but—please look out of the window. They say the countryside has never been so beautiful as this year. Look at that."

"Why should I?"

"Oh, I've got no nice underclothes with me, darling. And I'm mad enough to bite a parson, because I have such wonderful ones home, and I left them all behind to be Spartan and businesslike for the duration. Please look out of the window, and then, when I'm dressed, I'll tell you. And you turn round and be no end surprised, and tell me how pretty I look out of uniform."

He stared at her and then smiled.

"All right," he said.

He sat beside the window and looked at the dipping wires. Soon he was caught in an induced hypnosis, and he felt his head nodding in answer to the pattern of movement. His mind seemed very far away when he heard her voice.

"Now, darling."

He turned to look at her. His eyes were dulled by the brightness of the daylight beyond the window. The compartment seemed dark. Then, like a fade-in of the cinema, he saw her emerge—first just a slimness in a dark-blue figured dress. There was a wide-brimmed hat set back from her head. It framed the wash of her hair, and her face beneath was a pale smudge. His mind ricocheted and a fragment of it was thinking: "Laurencin was right. I never saw how she meant it until now."

"Well?" she said.

Her voice wakened him again. He moved his lips. He wanted time to think. This girl—now she was like a stranger—a taller, cooler, slimmer stranger than the girl in the bulk of a uniform.

The train was clicking on. He grasped at a feeling that this was not new. All this had happened, exactly as now, once before. Long, long ago it had been.

Why should one have such odd sensations? Of course it hadn't happened. What quirk of the mind made one feel as if it had? This was the only time it had happened. And yet—there was still the sensation that he was reliving a cycle of incidents all over again. It had happened, exactly like this. She had turned. She had said, in exactly the same tone: "Well?"

And he had said—had said...

"You're—you're very pretty."

"Thank you, sir. You remembered well."

He rose and took her hand.

"You shouldn't have done that," he said. "You shouldn't have asked me to say it, because it's left me nothing to say of my own accord."

She disengaged his hand and sat down by the window. He sat opposite her.

"You're very beautiful," he said, slowly.

"That's nice," she smiled. "Before I've only been pretty; but now I'm beautiful. It's all progressing very nicely, isn't it?"

She sat opposite him, primly like a child in a Sunday-school seat. It was as if, in some feminine-childish way, she was tremendously pleased with herself.

CHAPTER XIII

As they left the train she felt that events had caught her in a trap. The words went in a mental roundelay:

I'm trapped now. There's no escape. I've trapped myself.

She hardly felt the tug of ocean wind at her skirts as she watched the porter putting the luggage in the taxi. It seemed as if everyone were racing with malicious speed: the porter slamming the cab door behind them, the driver whirling the cab through spaces of empty airiness that were seaside resort streets. She had only impressions of bleak, windwashed gray fronts of Victorian houses.

The cab was charging at gleeful speed along a lonesome Esplanade, with monotonous rows of iron lampposts. The lampposts had their backs turned coldly and were gazing out to the crashing sea.

With the telescoped time of a nightmare the cab was at a place. The brass plates said. "Channel Hotel." She had only time to breathe once, to see gray stone walls, a potted palm at each side of the door. and then the uniformed boy had the luggage and was racing with fearful speed up the four steps.

Her heels were clicking on tiles, going soft on carpet, clicking again on tiles. She heard him speaking to the man at the counter. It was a horrible conspiracy of a world of men. She watched a woman come through the door, look at them quickly, and go to the lift. She put out her hand as if for support.

He turned as he felt the touch. He saw the woman with the trim figure standing in the lift. A few days ago, standing here, he had mentally disrobed her.

"All right," he said, curtly. "Let's get the lift. It's waiting."

"No, please. Wait a moment."

He looked at her, and saw her face an ashy splotch in the interior dimness.

"Good Lord," he said. "Aren't you well? Can I get you a drink?"

"Yes," she said. "That's it. Can't we have a drink?"

He took her arm and walked to the lounge. They sat in the chairs. She sat, unfeeling, unmoving, until she saw the glass before her.

"Drink that down," he said.

She drank, and sat on the edge of the chair, staring at the dazzle of light that was the window. She drew a breath and lifted her head.

"All right," she said. "Now."

She rose, and he walked beside her. The lift raced upward. They were walking down a lonesome corridor. The boy was unlocking the door. They were inside alone. She saw him flick his hat toward a bed and hated him for it. She went to the window, turning her back to him and the room, and stared out. She heard his voice.

"Ah, there's my bag. They've been keeping it here for me."

She stared out to the ocean, staring at it but not seeing it. She heard him speaking again.

"It isn't a bad room at all, is it?" he said, casually.

She did not move. She drew a breath and began speaking.

"It's really a very nice room—sunny and everything. And it looks out over the Esplanade, although we *should* be able to get a good room. The place is pratically deserted. And twenty-two shillings a day is high enough for bed and breakfast. Isn't it twenty-two shillings they said? I wonder if he thought I was really your wife. He couldn't have. I didn't have a wedding ring on. I should have got one—at the sixpenny bazaar. You couldn't tell them from real for all intents and purposes..."

He heard only the sound of her voice, gabbling quickly. He blew out his breath and then got up. He went to her and put his hand on her shoulder.

"Stop talking," he said. "What do you really mean behind all those words?"

"I don't mean anything."

"Of course you do."

"All right, I do, then. I'm just wondering."

"What?"

"I'm wondering just what I'm letting myself in for. That's all—and I have a right to wonder it if I want."

"You do. You're a free agent. You have a right to do anything you want."

She did not answer.

"Look here," he said. "I don't want any agony for anyone. If you feel that way about it, we can pack right up and get out again—or you can alone if you wish. If you've changed your mind—just say so, that's all."

"That's cowardly," she said. "Putting it up to me."

"Well, what the hell..."

"I don't want to be asked. I want to be told. You're the man. Take the responsibility of decision!"

"Oh, hell," he said.

He went and sat on the bed. She stood with her back to him, staring from the window. Then at last she came, quietly, and sat beside him.

"You misunderstood me," she said. "I don't want you to say I can go if I want. A woman doesn't want that. I want to be told that everything else in the world could happen, anything in the world—but above everything else you didn't want me to go—wouldn't let me go—couldn't keep the world going round if I did go. That's what I meant."

"One can't say that."

"I suppose not," she said.

Then she laughed and got up quickly.

"How silly of me," she said. "Wondering about being here. And I'm here, aren't I? Shall we unpack?"

"I've nothing much to unpack," he said. "I'll have to buy a few things."

"I see," she said.

She went back to the window.

"Then how about going for a walk? It's such a nice day and..."

He looked up at her. His mind lost itself in indecisions. Then a fragment of memory caught him.

"A *very* nice day?" he asked.

"A very, *very* nice day," she said, turning, slowly.

"Well, if it's a very, *very* nice day," he said. "That's different."

He picked up his hat from the bed, and when he turned he saw that she was smiling. He smiled in answer.

"Shall we explore?"

He held out his arm.

"We'll explore," she said, taking it.

They went along the long, carpeted hall. The place was deathly quiet with the silence of unoccupancy. It seemed, in that quietness, an act of rudeness to ring for the lift.

They went down the steps, and across the lobby. The uniformed boy and the small man behind the desk watched them go. They came into the sunshine, and it made them blink. They marched along the Esplanade, past the ornamental lampposts, past the benches where no one sat.

"I know what it is," she said, suddenly. "It's like being at the seaside in winter—no one here, the Esplanade stretching emptily for a mile, everything all to yourself. Just like winter—only the sun's shining. Have you been at the seaside in winter?"

"No, I haven't. Have you?"

"Oh, yes. It's much the nicest time to be here—although this is very nice. It's much nicer like this—without any crowds."

"Oh, much nicer," he said.

They went along steadily until from the hotel their figures were dots, far up the vanishing perspective of the Esplanade.

That afternoon they walked east, far out to the place where the promenade became a road, to where the road became a path going up to the cliffs. They bent their knees, climbing steadily, up to the top where the breeze blew strongly and evenly.

They spoke about the smell of the sea—the strong odor of rotting kelp and spray. They sat by the cliff edge, watching how the waves below in the bay came like tiny eddies, creeping with a synthetic sort of time and space of their own.

Only faintly, up there, could they hear the boom of the waves as they struck the looming chalk face. As humans they became small and chastened by the vastness of far horizons.

She hugged her knees and spoke, her voice small in the great spaces.

"I'm sorry I was so ratty," she said.

"There's no need to be upset," he told her.

"Not really—only—you see, I ran into my aunt."

"You what?"

"My aunt."

"Your aunt! Where?"

"At the hotel. Did you see the woman in the lift—she went up alone when we went to get the drink."

He stared at her.

"You mean to say that woman—the rather trim one in the tailored suit—that's your aunt?"

She nodded.

"Isn't it incredible, that of all the places we could pick, she's at the same place for some unearthly reason?"

"No, it isn't incredible," he said. "It's strangely just and trite, that's all. I never knew of anyone who—who went away for a secret holiday—as we have, who didn't run into someone he knew. It never fails."

She nodded, slowly.

"Well, I say," he said. "Did she see you?"

"Oh, yes."

"Perhaps she didn't."

"She did."

"Well—by God. We can't go back there, then."

She lifted her head.

"Why not? I'm not going to run away from Iris or anyone else!"

"But if you meet..."

"We won't. I know Iris. She'll move immediately and pretend she hasn't seen me, and save it all up for some opportune occasion."

"But if you *do* meet, what'll she think?"

She lifted her head.

"Iris," she said, "has no right to assume anything wrong about my conduct, no matter what the circumstances are, or what the exterior evidences might lead anyone to conclude."

He looked at her, sitting proudly and calmly. Then he thumped his knee in laughter.

"Oh, my Lord God," he said. "I never heard anything so beautifully illogical in my life. So beautifully and proudly and magnificently illogical. Let us return to the hotel with those brave banners going on before."

He took her arm and they walked back to the town. They had dinner at the hotel. They were the only ones in the dining room. The old waiter stood at attention near

133

their table. The place was so silent that there was a self-consciousness to talking.

They could feel only the lonesomeness of the place, the emptiness of the room, the forlornness of themselves.

After dinner they sat on a bench on the deserted Esplanade, and watched the clear light drift away.

The sunlight that had left the place went marching across wide oceans to new shores, going west, across a new continent, over far plains, into ranges of mountains and dry, sun-baked lands.

CHAPTER XIV

THE trouble with it was, Prentiss Saintby thought, you always felt as if America were a holiday world. It wasn't really, he reasoned. It was only because of its foreignness. Foreign lands always seemed to be living in perpetual holidays. Probably because ordinarily it was only during holidays that one went to foreign lands.

He docketed the thought neatly, and looked from the car window. The town looked like a horrible jumble of purpose: a too-new skyscraper with modernistic coffee shop under its lee, then ramshackle, wooden-fronted shops within a stone's-throw; motorcars that gleamed smugly like this one, then rusty rattletraps with mudguards tied up with baling wire, and driven by people who wore that unending clothing of blue overall-ish stuff.

That blue seemed like the uniform of the working class in this land. Funny, somebody had that once in a story—Wells, that was it—writing about a future world. Workers all in blue garb, nobles in something else—probably purple.

But it was quite gay in a way, that blue—deep color of new ones, then all the varying degrees of lighter blue that came from repeated launderings. The people seemed quite happy and well-fed, though.

He grasped at another thought. It was like a mixture of New York and the cowboy cinemas he'd watched when a boy. That was it. A lot of people still wore those very large cowboy hats. It made the city look a little masqueradish—but the men didn't seem to be at all self-conscious about wearing them.

He turned his eyes ahead. There was the bullethead of the Negro chauffeur. The hair was cropped, but you could see the spots where the kinky whorls would grow if it were longer.

That was another part of America. Negroes. They seemed quite jolly chaps—interesting servants. He had heard they were somewhat of a problem. They didn't seem like a problem to him, the ones he'd seen—the porters on the train coming west.

His eyes went beyond to the road. There was a tangle of streetcar tracks and paving bricks. Yet the car flowed over them with the same milk-smooth motion. He smiled and looked at the man beside him.

"It rides beautifully, Mr. Lachran," he said.

The man nodded, energetically and gladly.

"You can't get a better one," he said. "It's a British car, you know."

"Oh, yes? I hadn't noticed."

That was another part of America—being lost in the moves of conversation. Back home, in England, you could understand the words a man said, unterstand what he meant behind the words, and understand what he thought behind his meaning. Here, you had to listen so carefully to the pronunciation that you only understood the words. You lost everything else concentrating on that.

And people were different. That was a thing you had to understand. For instance, when he'd said the car rode nicely—you couldn't expect that such a remark would bring a delight so obvious to the other man. Yet it had—a childish sort of delight. Lachran was quite childish in many ways —an open sort of aged childishness.

On the other hand, that might be one of the things hard to understand about America. It might be a mask. It could well be. The man wasn't an idiot. No man got to Lachran's power—a real czar in his own field—by being an idiot.

Saintby sighed. He wished fervently that Lachran were

a Britisher, and then he could unterstand him really, see the real man behind all the exteriors.

"Yes," Lachran said, slowly. "We can turn out stuff on a line; but we can't touch you chaps when it comes to a handmade job."

"Perhaps that is true," Saintby said, carefully.

"It *is* true," Lachran grated. "And its your strength—and your weakness. You don't seem to have the mind for mass production—and you're going to have to learn it if you want to exist—in this war, you are."

"I suppose that is true."

"You're darned right it's true. It's all right making something good when you've got all the time in the world in which to make it—and all the time in the world in which to use it. But what's the use handfinishing a thing you're going to send out to be blown up maybe next week? Huh?"

"Perhaps it's our national temperament to do our best always, no matter what we're doing," Saintby said, a little stiffly.

"Sure you do. Sure. That's what we like about you Britishers. But you can't do it with everything."

Lachran turned away, and leaned forward to tap on the glass. The car was gliding through formal shrubbery to a low, wooden building.

"Right in there! Right in there!" he shouted, irascibly.

"Mr. Lachran, it say..."

"God dammit, I said right in there!"

The Negro grinned happily and nosed the car into a vacant space among the others. As Saintby got out he saw its bonnet almost touched the sign that said: "No Parking. Bureau of Police."

"Oh, I say," he said. "You're in a forbidden space."

Lachran turned, almost in surprise.

137

"That?" he said. "We don't pay any attention to those things."

They went up the steps into the wooden building. In the large hall the attendants came forward quickly, like acolytes. Lachran greeted them happily.

"How do you like this?" he asked.

Saintby stared about him. The place was like a hunting lodge. Heads of strange antlered animals studded the walls. There was a dark gloominess to the room.

"Very nice," he said.

"I thought you'd like it," Lachran said, happily. "It was built on the idea of an old Scotch hunting lodge—something of that sort. Everyone says its quite British, anyway."

"Oh, distinctly," Saintby said.

They went from the hall through dark doors to a veranda, and then Saintby drew his breath. Coming from the gloominess, with the mixed impressions of the city still touching his mood, he was struck by the new scene. What he saw was like another world. A gay, crowded world. There was the seclusion of the veranda, with its white napery and silver. Below were people on lawns of immaculate turf, sitting at tables under gay striped umbrellas. To the left was a blue-tiled swimming pool. To the right, tennis courts. Farther beyond, a polo field. Beyond that, granite mountains rising jagged to blue heights.

"Oh, I say," Prentiss said. "This is a spot!"

Lachran breathed deeply and happily.

"Yes, it's pretty good," he said. "Does it remind you of the old country?"

Prentiss Saintby drew a deep breath. You could say the place was Monte Carlo, Hurlingham, Switzerland and an unbelievable Hollywood musical comedy all in one. But the man seemed to be waiting his answer with almost pathetic anxiety.

"Why, yes," he said. "It's just like home."

Lachran went happily to his seat. As he followed, Prentiss Saintby justified the outrageousness of his lie. If the man expected him to say it, why not give him the pleasure? And it was unimportant. The business—that was the thing. If he could only get the man to hard tacks—but he seemed exasperatingly determined to put off everything as long as he could. That's why he'd been sent to the West.

Prentiss sat at the table and looked out over the scene. It was a vibration of color—flowered walks, strange blossoming bushes, the striped umbrellas, the dresses of the women, the assorted hues of bathing suits at the pool, the white of tennis flannels, the moving red and yellow spots of the shirts on the polo field.

He saw color first—and then he saw youth; a world of youth. Every-one seemed young. It was almost unbelievable. As far as he could see there was not a person who wasn't young. It was almost a heaven of youth—sun-tanned, well-fed, handsome youth. He—and Lachran—who looked down on it, were the only unyoung ones. It was fitting that they should be detached, isolated.

"You know," Lachran said, conversationally, "my father started this club."

"Oh, indeed?" Prentiss encouraged.

"Yeh. There were a lot of Johnny Bulls here then. Younger sons of lords and dukes and so on. They came out here for hunting and what not, and stayed on. Why, they used to call this town Little England."

"Oh, indeed?"

"Yeh. That's why there's so many things of English character round here. You'd enjoy staying here."

Prentiss fingered the fork before him.

"It's tremendously pleasant," he said. "And it would be nice to stay here. Except that—well, this is wartime for us, you know. And there's nothing I'd like better than to stay here—except of course to get business done. Now if you could give me any idea of a basis of..."

"Now don't worry," Lachran said, almost impatiently. "Don't worry. You saw how things are. They're working on it, and I'm turning it over in my mind, and when I get it all set—it won't be a basis of discussion. It'll be something that'll just make you happy."

"But of course, there's an element of time..."

"That's all right. This isn't a case of hand to mouth. You fellows have got plenty for this year. It's a steady supply for one year, two years from now you want. And I can give it to you. But just don't push me! Don't push me!"

Saintby looked at the table. Suddenly, now, he knew the hardness of this man behind the bluff friendliness. There was stubbornness in the last words—almost a pugnacious belligerence. Lachran had spoken almost as one would to a servant. And he—he was the British Government.

Then it was as if Lachran himself had recognized the hardness of his words and tone. For he was smiling.

"Besides," he said, laughingly, "I like you. I like to have you round. If I came over to your country, wouldn't you want to be hospitable to me?"

"I rather suppose so."

"Well, there you are. You're in my country. You mustn't begrudge me the chance to show you round. You know— when you're here, you're in the best goddam part of all these United States. You can travel high and low, north and south, but you're never going to find a finer part of these United States than right here. They talk of God's country. Well, this is God's country."

"Yes, indeed."

Prentiss sank into his thoughts. Obviously it was no use trying to nudge the old man along—he wouldn't be hurried.

And you had to treat him with gloves. He was too powerful to be antagonized.

And it had been a false move trying to talk business before lunch. Almost elemental, that. Wait until a man was fed before talking business.

Prentiss looked up, and found Lachran smiling at him—his heavylined old face suddenly shrewd and wise.

"So you've decided not to try to hurry me any more," he said.

Prentiss drew in his breath. It was as if the old man had been able to see all the tickings and workings of his mind. He opened his mouth to speak, and then saw the funniness of it. He began laughing. Lachran's face broke into a wide beam.

"Am I so transparent?" Prentiss said.

Lachran shook his finger in a gesture of warmth.

"I've got you Johnny Bulls' number every time," he said, happily.

"Have you really?"

"Yes. And you know what? That's why I like you. You take a Dago or a Dutchman. I wouldn't trust 'em any further than I could throw an elephant—and I wouldn't give 'em the smell off my shirt. But you Britishers—you make me laugh."

"Laugh?"

Lachran waved his hand in a gesture. Looking at the old, smiling face, Prentiss suddenly felt like a schoolboy.

"Let's have lunch—and just put your mind on that," Lachran said. "And when we're set to do business, I'll let *you* know. How's that?"

"All right," Prentiss smiled.

"That's fine. Where in the hell is that—hey! Maurice!"

"Here, sir."

The waiter came quietly from the doorway. Prentiss freed his mind from a sort of conscience that forbade him to enjoy anything in America while Britain was at war, and settled to the contentment of a good lunch. There was a fine chowder—wonderful name, chowder. And excellent trout.

Lachran chatted on, happily. Prentiss found him easy to listen to.

"There's all the trout you want in those mountains," Lachran said. "If you like to fish..."

"I wish I had time."

"Well, if you like to."

Lachran gazed at the mountains silently for a time. Then he nodded his head. He waved his hand.

"You know," he said. "In my time, I've climbed over those goddam mountains from end to end—and sometimes my belly flat as a griddlecake."

"Yes?"

"Yeh! Look, you see that peak up there—the far one beyond the saddle?"

Prentiss looked into the clear air to where the finger pointed in the blue range.

"My mother cooked up in a lumber camp there."

"Yes."

Lachran paused, and Prentiss did not answer. The old man seemed to be far away. He went on again.

"And the only woman for two hundred and fifty miles around. She come out here as a school teacher from Kansas to marry a feller. They got married and he died o' lungs a year later. But she didn't sit down and she didn't go back. By God, she up and hunted a job. They were starting lumbering up there, and she went as cook.

"'Why,' the boss said. 'This isn't no place for a lady like you.' 'I need the job,' she said. He says: "I mean with all these men around. They're a tough bunch.' 'You just give me a tent,' she says, 'and I won't have a minute's trouble with any man on the job.'

"And, by God, she didn't. Not in all the two years she was up there. She used to say afterwards, though, she began to get a bit worried. Got so's she wasn't sure whether it was because of the inherent nobility of lumberjacks, or because she was so homely she didn't inspire anyone to make a leer at her. Of course, that was kidding. Then she met my father up there.

"He hauled lumber down—made a fortune before he was thirty and lost it again. He lost it when they hit gold up there. He went back to lumbering—hauling to the mines. There was no steel then. All wood shoring. He made another fortune and lost it by the time he was forty. Made two fortunes and lost 'em both before he was forty. The railroad, the second time. Railroads cleaned him out. When I was seventeen, we were flat broke—we lived up in a shack right up there where the foothill boulevard is now. And by the time I was twenty—I had half his fortune back. By God, I did. I cleaned some of *them* out, too. By God, I made some o' them say yessir and nosir before I was through!"

Lachran nodded as if he were dozing. Prentiss felt a moment of mental clarity—as if for a brief moment he was seeing behind the outrageous façade of this country club in the too-clear sunshine, seeing behind the man's American veil of accent and speech and manner, to something vital and real and truly American. Although what "truly American" was he didn't know. Only it was something that—that wasn't pseudo-British. It was something very different from British. It was curious, he thought, that he should like and understand Americans much better when they had this "different" American quality than when they were so much like a bad imitation of Britishers.

He looked at the old man, musing. It was a hard face —almost a cruel face. Lined and discolored as if from years of hard living, hard drinking—pouched eyes, coarse stubbly steel-gray hair. Yet there was an engaging quality to the man that was almost childish in substance.

Prentiss looked up at the blue mountains, beyond the polo field with its fringe of artificial-looking trees.

"What was it like," he said, "in the old days?"

Lachran looked up. Then he grinned, in a grim sort of way. He flung out his hand toward the mountains.

"There was the whole goddam country," he said. "The whole—goddam—country."

He stopped, as if that explained it all.

"Yes?" Prentiss said, with rising inflexion.

Lachran looked up at him, almost astonished.

"Well," he said, impatiently, "that meant everything. Millions! There was millions in it—just waiting. Waiting for anyone smart enough and tough enough to come and take it. And a man took what he wanted..."

Then he shook his head, slowly.

"... But he only held what he was able. You took what you wanted —but you only held what you was able. *That's* how it was."

"And you were able to hold it, eh?"

"I held it. And I licked some of the sons o' bitches that had it coming to them."

"In the gold fields?"

"In anything. There was money in anything those days —if you were tough. And I was tough. Why look—right up there. I remember coming over that ridge one day, and there was four of 'em, sitting on their horses there waiting. I knew I couldn't run, so I had to go forward. I was only twenty-two then. But I went right up and said: 'What the hell do you want?' And they said: 'Lachran. You're putting a flume in up there, and we don't like it. We want that water.'

"And there they sat, with their hands on their guns. So I just says: 'Get the hell off of here before I run you off!'

They looked at me like they thought I was crazy. One of 'em says: 'Lachran, I don't know whether you're crazy or just plain tough.' So I sat there with my hands crossed on the pommel, and I says: 'Start figuring that out for yourselves, and figure it quick.' And they just turned round and hauled out of there."

The old man laughed, and looked up at Prentiss.

"So they must have figured I was tough, eh?"

"I should say so," Prentiss said. "Four of them with pistols."

Lachran laughed.

"Ah, I *was* tough then. I could lick anything in this valley—and then haul him up one side of the mountains and throw him down the other. I was tough."

He nodded to himself, and then looked up quickly at Prentiss.

"You ought to see some of that country, Mr. Saintby. It's real scenery for you. Do you like hunting?"

"I do—but I feel at this time..."

"Oh, don't give that a thought."

Lachran halted and, his face suddenly beaming, he waved his hand agitatedly to a girl below. The girl swung a tennis racket in each hand in greeting.

"That's Mary," Lachran said. "My brother's granddaughter."

He looked up at the steward.

"Sure coffee," he said. "And Mr. Saintby—or he'll probably take tea."

"Well, tea..."

"I feel sure that you'll like *our* tea, sir," the steward said. "We don't—boil linen bags with it."

"That's right," Lachran said. "Maurice is a Britisher, too. Aren't you, Maurice?"

"Yes, sir," the steward said. "From Chichester."

"Oh, indeed," Prentiss said. "Beautiful place."

"Thank you, sir. Then I may make you some tea?"

Prentiss thought of the processions of evil tea—at hotels, on trains, that he'd had in America. Always prepared so that one tasted the inevitable linen sack in which Americans kept doles of tea.

"If I could have a good cup..."

"Yes, sir."

Lachran looked up, slyly.

"If you like tea—I've got a Chinese cook up on the ranch. If you like tea, you're his friend for life. He'll spend half his waking hours making tea for you."

"Indeed?"

"Well, you might as well. You cantn't do anything till I'm set. You've got to wait around here until I do get set. You might as well be up there as at that hotel. You know, some day I'll do something about that. I've been saying we need a good hotel for the last six years. I'll do it, too."

Lachran stopped suddenly and grinned.

"Hello, Mary!"

"Hi!"

The girl came onto the veranda, lifting one of the rackets in salutation.

"This is Mr. Saintby, Mary. He's a Britisher—over here on business."

Prentiss looked up. She was a striking young woman. Like all the others below, she seemed youth and health gloriously triumphant. As if their bodies were leaping up to the sun—tall, sunburned. The white of her tennis clothes made the tan seem more deeply golden. A curious sort of white jockey cap held in her black hair.

"Hello."

She turned away, as if ignoring him.

"Did you eat?" Lachran began.

"Long ago. I had a date with the pro, and that Cecil

Hawkins is still taking a lesson. She knows it's time, but she's just doing it to make me mad. She's a pill."

Prentiss noted a juvenile quality in the young woman's petulance.

"You're coming up to the ranch tomorrow, aren't you? You know, that Hawkins girl and her mother are coming."

"Oh, gosh, what do you want to ask her mother for? She's worse than Cecil."

"Well, it'll give you a chance to trim the tar out of her again."

"That'll be nothing new," the girl said.

"Then I'll see you. Mr. Saintby, here. He's coming up for a while, too."

The girl turned, quickly.

"Do you play tennis??"

Prentiss wondered why he didn't deny his acquiescence to Lachran's invitation.

"Well, I have played," he said. He felt the need for something better. "I played in the tournament at Nice two years ago."

The young woman's eyes lightened.

"You did? Nice? That's fine. There's Johnny now—I'll have to run. See you again, then."

"Yes," Prentiss said.

He was adjusting his mind quickly. There seemed something wicked, somehow, in playing tennis while all this ghastly war went on—as if a man were carousing on a grave. And yet, as Lachran said, it was merely a question of waiting, and one might just as well wait in comfort as go through days of dragging disagreeableness.

He looked up. He saw Lachran looking at him with a smile that was either one of great age and wisdom—or one of childishness.

CHAPTER XV

THAT first morning when he woke Clive saw her sitting by the window, looking out at the sea. He came up into full waking and lay looking at her. The edge of the sun came slot-wise through the window and touched into shouting light the edges of the white peignoir she wore. He waited, knowing she had heard him stir; but she did not move.

"Hi," he said, finally.

She looked around quickly, and smiled to reassure him. Then she turned back to the window.

"Didn't you sleep well?"

"All right,' she said.

"Or maybe," he said, "you're one of those who can't be talked to before breakfast. Do you bite or snarl before breakfast? Do you curse the cat and kick the maid?"

"It was all right. You ground your teeth, horribly—so I got up. I'll telephone for breakfast. What will you have?"

"Anything."

She looked at him a moment. Then she picked up the telephone.

"Breakfasts, please," she said. "Two of grapefruit, two bacon and eggs, two toasts, two teas, that's all."

She turned to him as she hung up.

"That's for being mentally lazy—you'll eat what I do."

He watched her move back to the window. He got up and sat on the edge of the bed.

"I'm sorry," he said. "I'm sorry you didn't sleep well."

"You ground your teeth horribly. It was ghastly."

"The unromantic aspects that aren't mentioned in the love stories," he said, trying to please her. "Some people snore. It's never mentioned in the songs. You never get adore, implore, bedroom door, and snore. You get moon, June and spoon and then it stops. It never gets on to the part about how he ground his teeth horribly."

She smiled.

"It's hard to do that so early, especially with a headache," he said.

"Have you a headache?"

"It's nothing. Seriously, though," he said, "you should have wakened me. I didn't know I did that."

"No, it was interesting. You see, you talked, too."

"Talked? What on earth did I say?"

"I won't tell you."

"Oh, don't be coy. What did I say? Did I mention any names?"

"No, you gave commands."

"I did?"

"Yes—ou were drilling a whole army, I should fancy—and using language."

"What language? Fancy?"

"Very fancy language."

"Very, *very* fancy?"

She nodded her head slowly and then turned from the window and smiled.

"That was nice," she said. "Yes. Very, *very* fancy."

"Well, if it was very, *very* fancy—that's different."

"It was different. You used words I'd never heard before."

"Oh, perhaps you aren't up on words."

"Is that so! Then perhaps you've never been around art students and studios."

He swung his legs and lit a cigarette.

"I thought in art circles they talked art."

"That's a misconception."

"What do they talk about?"

"About food," she said. "The best food you never ate is talked in artstudent circles."

"Food will be here soon," he said. "I'd better bathe—and I'm exhausted by trying to be bright before breakfast."

"Don't make too much effort," she said. "Can I call for a Seidlitz Powder?"

"No. I have aspirins. I'll bathe."

"Don't hurry. It looks as if it will cloud over. Rain probably."

"I prefer the indoor sort of showers."

He put on his mackintosh as a dressing gown and rang the bath bell. He heard her suddenly laughing and turned.

"What's so funny?"

"I can't tell you," she said.

"That's all right. You have a right to your own life, too."

He sat on the bed until the knock on the door told him the bath was ready. He started to follow the old woman down the hall. Then he came back and poked his head in the door.

"Be happy," he said. "You are glad you're here, aren't you?"

She smiled quickly.

"Of course I am."

He looked at her and then spoke slowly.

"You're not," he said. "But it was quite decent of you to say you were."

The rain fell steadily after breakfast. They sat in the hotel room, feeling imprisoned. At noon they ordered lunch, and kept wandering to the window to look at the drabness of the rain-wet promenade.

"Oh, damnation," he said finally, his pent-up irritation rasping in his voice. "Let's go out anyhow."

They put on raincoats and went out to the Esplanade, going quickly. There was no incentive to talk. Going in step they came to the end of the promenade, and kept on up the hill.

"It's nice to have low heels on again," she said. "I got so used to them in the Waffs I'd forgotten how high heels could be uncomfortable."

"Is that so?" he said.

"Yes."

They went on climbing to the cliff-top. There the wind and rain came with more force, driving almost parallel to the ground. At last, by the cliff edge, they stopped. He put his arm about her.

"This is better," she said, finally. "It isn't good for us to quarrel."

"Quarrel? You mean my explosion at the weather? I wasn't quarreling."

"I see. Shall we go back?"

He turned and looked at her, at her face with hard highlights from the rain-wetness. A wisp of hair hung straggling. She saw his eyes on it, and brushed it back angrily. He wanted to speak comfortingly, but she had started away. They went down from the cliff to the promenade. Almost at the hotel he touched her arm.

"Look, I'm sorry," he said. "Sorry for my picayune tempers. You must forgive me."

"Of course," she said. "You're much like my father. I understand."

"I don't mean to be nasty."

"Neither of us do," she said. "Only there's a frustration—we're—I don't know—empty in some way. Shut off from each other."

"Do you want to call it all off?" he said.

"Do you?"

"I certainly do if you do."

"Then it's all right for my part," she said.

He lifted his head.

"All right. I'll take the decision."

They stalked back to the hotel.

"I'll tell them," he said.

She went on to the lift. He stopped by the desk. The little polite man looked up hopefully.

"Yes, Mr. Briggs? Anything I can do?"

"Yes, You can get the bill ready—we're leaving."

"Oh, but..."

"And don't call in Mrs. Whosis. Everything's all right—it's just that—we're leaving."

The assistant manager stood with pen poised.

"Are you going back to London, sir?"

"No. Just—well, probably back to London."

"I'm sorry you're leaving. And such nasty weather to travel. It seems a pity you couldn't stay until tomorrow—since you have to pay whether you stay or not."

Clive stood in thought. Just where were they going? Suddenly he laughed.

"That's sensible. But—I'm afraid we're moving on."

He went upstairs. Prue was sitting by the window, still wearing her mackintosh.

He sat on the bed, and in the silence sought for some hinge of speaking. Suddenly she sneezed.

"Here, here," he said. "You mustn't catch cold."

"I'm not catching cold," she said into her handkerchief.

They sat in silence again, until once more she sneezed.

"You know, you *are* catching cold," he said.

"No."

Then, suddenly, she went into one of her bursts of laughter. It was a quiet laugh, soaring into a bubbling note.

"Tell me, if it's funny," he said. "I'd like to laugh just about now."

"It is funny. I just realized what it is. It's a honeymoon cold. I've often heard father speak of it. And now I've got it."

"A honeymoon cold?"

"Yes. Didn't you know? About ninety per cent of people on their honeymoons—well, they get awful colds."

"They should be careful to shut the windows."

"Yes," she said, laughing.

"I like you," he said.

He saw her face, puzzled and almost childlike in the deepening light. It contorted, and she sneezed again.

"Look," he said. "This is foolish. We can't travel with you getting a cold.

"It really isn't a cold."

"It is. Now for God's sake don't let's start a quarrel over that. I say it is one. You should stay over."

"But," she said. "You've just told them at the desk we're leaving. And they'll have the bill..."

"That's all right. It won't make any difference to them. I have to pay for us anyhow for a second day—giving notice after twelve noon makes it another day."

"I see."

"So we might as well stay tonight. Then we can pack off tomorrow."

"That does sound sensible," she said.

There was a silence that became too noticeable. He got up and walked the room.

"Well," he said. "That's decided. Now, we might as well eat. Shall we eat here—or downstairs?"

"I couldn't stand either."

"I see."

He paced the room. Then he sneezed.

She laughed irrepressibly.

"You've got one, too."

"Perhaps your father was right," he said. "It doesn't matter."

He paced the room again, and then snapped his fingers.

"I've got an idea. Let's go out and have a good drink.

We need a good slug of something—it'll be good for the colds. It's no use our going different ways with the same cold. We'll have a drink—and then a good dinner. A farewell dinner. We'll find a place somewhere..."

"It might be a good idea," she said.

She got up and they went down the stairs. Almost at the entrance they heard the clerk.

"Mr. Briggs!"

He came hurrying over.

"Your bill—and if your luggage is ready."

"Luggage?" Clive said. His mind had been far away. "Oh yes. Well—never mind the luggage now. We've decided to stay over tonight."

"Then you won't..."

"That's right. Send the bill up tomorrow morning, and we'll take care of it then."

The little man ducked away, his forehead wrinkled.

"Funny little man," Prue said. "Now, where are we going?"

"We'll find a good place. There's got to be one good place in this town."

The inn was low-ceilinged, dimly lit, with highlights glowing softly on the age-polished wood.

Clive stood at the door and lifted his hands and looked at Prue in an expression that said: "Isn't it simple?"

"I think this *is* the place," Prue said.

"A good place to spend your reclining years," he said.

They stood by the door, watching the plump, white-aproned man bustling to the fire. He lifted the blaze in the high-hobbed hearth into a good glow. He put on more coal with a small pair of tongs. Then he turned to a table by the hearth and spread his hands in invitation. He did all this without speaking.

As they sat, he waited, his back to the fire.

"Now," he said, finally. "What shall it be?"

"Well, something to take the chill off," Clive said. "We've got post-hymeneal colds."

"What's them?"

"It doesn't matter. A medical name."

"I see. How about a hot mulled special?"

"What's that?"

"Ah, now, sir. You just leave that to me. It'll have you warmed up in no time."

Clive watched him bumble away down the steps to the bar.

"Obliging cove," he said.

"He's sweet," Prue said. "Like mine host."

"That's it. Probably read it in a book."

"No. Give human nature credit for being human."

"I do. What I mean is that he's merely conforming subconsciously to the popular imagination of what he is. We all do that."

"Do we?"

"Of course we do. That's the trouble."

He stared into the fire, feeling comfortable and happy at last.

"You know, Prue," he said, "we're all living under the chains of conformity. Conforming to what popular imagination say's we should be. Take a young doctor. He knows what popular imagination says he should be; how he should walk, talk, dress, act. He conforms and soon isn't what he really is, but a sort of walking, composite creature of what mass imagination fostered by novels and cinemas and plays says he should be."

"Don't wrinkle your forehead, darling."

"All right. It's the same with everyone—ministers, policemen, actresses, waiters—all of us. We're all supposed to be something. We desert ourselves, and live a fake life. And really—that's not us."

"It makes the world smoother perhaps. You're wrinkling again."

"All right. I don't think it does. I don't mean this silly thing called self-expressionism. It's something truer. We live too many ready-made things. In childhood we start with: a boy is this, and a girl is that. Well, a boy isn't this and a girl isn't that."

"Then what on earth are they, darling?"

"Now don't fool. I almost have something."

"I wouldn't fool. You're so wonderful when you get serious. And you do have good ideas. You've got a very fine mind."

"Stop it. What I mean is—we're always peering through a false front of what we pretend to be and know we're not. A Briton is supposed to be this, and a Protestant is that, and a Lancashireman is always something, and an Englishman never does this, and a workman always should do the other thing. Popular imagination, lumping us and crowding us and molding us."

"Sometimes for our good."

"Yes, but too often for bad. Suppose some morning, millions of us should wake and be free. A real revolution —a revolution of self . . ."

He pursued the thought—it was like a chase after a fox. The shape and form of what he was racing after couldn't be seen. But if he could catch the thought, he might know —might know something important.

"If all mankind arose and said, I am not a lay figure. I am me. I am not a *brave* Briton, a *reserved* Englishman, a *stubborn* Yorkshireman, a *cold* Protestant, a *sober* workman . . ."

"Then what are you? A *cowardly* Briton, a *garrulous* Englishman . . ."

"No, by the Lord Harry, no. Because I am not one thing, I am not necessarily the reverse. Nationality means nothing, anyhow. Take the British. In France a Briton is perfidious, in America he's a silly ass with a monocle, in Italy a gaunt, chill, cold-blooded aristocrat, in Germany a bony pipe-sucking child-starver. And we're not those things, either."

"Then what are we?"

"Don't you see—we're all things. Each person is everything in the world if he could only recognize it and admit it. If each man could only say: 'I'm brave one moment, a coward the next; I'm reserved in parts of me, yet childishly friendly; I'm hot and cold about religion as the fears and hopes of the day move me. I am all things. Each one of us is just me—everything—humanity.' "

"Yes, darling. Here comes the man with the drinks."

Clive shook his head. He had suddenly understood something—yet his words hadn't said it. He left thoughts regretfully. The man was saluting him.

"Here you are, doctor. And madame. If you'll try that."

The man watched them as they sipped. Then he rubbed his hands.

"Good?" he asked Prudence.

"My, yes."

She looked at Clive.

"It does warm you up," he said.

"Makes you tingle all over."

"We'll have another," he said.

"Yes, doctor."

The man took the glasses, still clouded with steam, and bumbled away.

"He thinks you're a doctor," Prue said, "because you said posthymeneal cold was a medical term."

"That's why. You know, I almost had something—about popular imagination. Only I didn't get it out—express it right."

She put out her hand.

"What worries you, Clive?"

"Worries me? Nothing."

"It's all right if you don't want to tell me. But I know there is."

"No there isn't. Tell me about you. What do you think of it all?"

"What all?"

"Everything. Life—war—love."

She shook her head.

"Have you ever been in love?" he asked.

"Oh, constantly. From childhood up."

"No. I mean with a man?"

"I don't know."

"What do you mean, you don't know?"

"I mean—what did Robin say to Makyn: 'I wot not what is love.' I wondered whether I had any capacity for it. I grew up—matured—slowly—but ... I was engaged once."

"But not now?"

"No. We broke it off."

"Why?"

She looked at her hands, and spread the fingers. Then she lifted her head.

"It's curious that I don't mind telling you. It seems so empty of emotion now. We'd known each other a long time—oh, since before he went up to Oxford. It died and went up and down, and then when he came down from university, it got very serious and we got engaged. Then we had a fight and ended it."

"Perhaps you'll patch it up."

She put her hand out to the fire, and shook her head.

"You might," he said.

"I couldn't. It's curious, I don't mind talking about it now. I thought I'd never get used to it. You see, he was a C.O., and we quarreled dreadfully over it."

"You shouldn't have."

"What, at a time like this? You can't see a man—when things are like this—not being willing to fight. We've got to fight, that's all. Everyone! It's—something bigger than personal feelings."

"So in place of him you joined up."

"Not at all."

"Yes. He wouldn't go—so you did."

"I don't think so—or perhaps that's true."

"To put him to shame."

"He put himself to shame."

"I don't think he did."

"You're a soldier—and you can say that?"

"Let's not argue, then. I'm sorry—if you feel hurt about it."

"I don't."

"You do—but don't feel too bad. I'm sorry I made you talk."

"It's all right."

She looked at his face, sober and too grim. She laughed, quickly.

"Don't you worry about it, then," she said. "I don't. It isn't the end of the world. You can rationalize it that way. There'll be other loves—common sense tells me that."

"Yes," he said, slowly. "It's just that the first one is always hardest."

"That wasn't my first," she said.

"Don't try to be sophisticated. I can tell. You always can."

She looked at him, staring in the fire. The place was dim and in its emptiness somehow conveyed lonesomeness. She smiled to herself.

"Cheer up," she said. "I've had lots of other experiences."

"I'll bet."

"I have, really. In Paris."

"You in Paris!"

"Yes, me," she said. "I had a very daring experience in Paris."

"Very, *very* daring?"

"Yes, very, *very* daring. Do you want to hear about it?"

"If you care to tell me."

"You do want to hear, only popular imagination says a man mustn't be curious."

"*Touché*—as the chap with the ax said when King Charles' head rolled into the basket. I'm all agog. I never was agogger, in fact. What is agog?"

"I don't know. That was in Paris when I was fourteen. It's very important in my subsequent development.

"Fourteen. Precocious!"

"Yes. I was walking by the fountain of the Observatoire one day, up beside the Bal Bullier—you know where the Closerie de Lilas is?"

"Don't dazzle me. I don't know Paris."

"Oh, well. It doesn't matter. I was walking, and a man came up behind me."

"Thank you. That's a very exciting story."

"Wait. I haven't finished yet. I was just trying to see how I could phrase it politely."

"Oh, don't stand on ceremony to me."

"You can't say it politely, anyhow. You see, this man, suddenly, he pinched my bottom."

"The rascal. A bottom-pincher!"

"Yes, and it was a real hard pinch, too."

"Ah, wonderful nation, the French. Good old nation of bottom-pinchers. Little-girl bottom-pinchers."

"But why do they do it?"

"Just an expression of their good old Gallic courtesy. All Frenchmen are bottom-pinchers at heart."

"Oh, but isn't that popular imagination? You just said. ."

"Of course it is, but the French believe it, too. Popular

imagination says the Frenchman isn't dull and phlegmatic like the Briton. He is always sexually alert. That's the popular view. The Frenchman believes it, and tries to live up to it. Maybe he's overdone it. Maybe that's why his birthrate is falling."

"Sort of overtrained?"

"That's it. Look, the Latin nations are supposed to be perpetually amorous cockerels. I doubt whether they're any more sexually fervent than any other race. I'll bet that there are plenty of cold-blooded Englishmen who are calm in the daylight. But once the lights are out—they'll give a head start to any hot-blooded Latin."

"And the lights are always out these days."

"That's right. Look for a birth increase here in a year. They won't be war babies this time. They'll call 'em blackout babies. Twenty years from now there'll be a crop of youngsters—all about the same age. They'll say: 'Oh, I was a blackout baby.'"

'You think long dark evenings help?"

"Couldn't be otherwise. In the wintertime there is no fishing."

"Maybe that's why..."

"Please. No discussion of present parties."

"Why, it never entered my head."

"Then don't let it."

She smiled to herself.

"You know, I never thought I'd talk like this. It's quite wicked, talking vulgarity."

"It's very natural—and when it's natural it can't be vulgarity any more. Let's talk very properly, then. Do you still think we should play Wagnerian operas during wartime?"

"Silly," she said. "Here's Mine Host."

The plump man set the new glasses before them, and watched them as they sipped.

"What's in this?" Clive asked.

The man glowed appreciatively.

"Ah, some of this, and a little of that."

"It's red wine—with some spices."

"Some spices," laughed the man. His double chin began to shake. "Tha's a good 'un, that is. Some spices!"

Shaking his head he waddled away. Clive sniffed and turned to Prue.

"He's seen someone do that on the stage," he said. "Secretive cove stuff."

"Perhaps it is an old family recipe—been in the family for centuries."

"Yes. It was revealed to his great-great-grandfather by an Indian chieftain out of gratitude for saving the chief's daughter from an attack of chills and ague."

"Where did you get that?"

"From a bottle. When I was a kid my mother used to make me take some stuff called swamp-root elixir, and that's what it said on the bottle."

"What did it cure?"

"Everything. Corns, warts, bunions, scars, scarlet fever, tic, rheumatism, sciatica, gout, lumbago, chills and ague."

"But that's just it. If the Indian had such a wonderful recipe for curing chills and ague, why didn't he cure his own daughter?"

"Ah, that's it. He saveth others, but himself he cannot save. Anyhow, it's an important question. I think it should be asked in Parliament."

"I feel very happy."

"That's fine. So do I."

"I like this place. It's good luck to us. We don't quarrel here."

"Quarrel? We don't quarrel. We merely differ."

"All right," she said. "Just we don't differ here, then.

Did you take your medicine like a good little boy when you were small?"

"I knew I'd better—or I'd get my bottom smacked."

"Your bottom. You know this man..."

"What man?"

"The man in Paris—by the Bal Bullier."

"Oh, the bottom-pincher. Is he in again? He seems to have been important in your life."

"I've led a very exemplary life."

"Until now."

She smiled, and stared at the fire.

"Poke it up a bit," she said.

He got up and stirred the coals. They sat silently, sipping the hot wine.

"There was one curious thing I haven't told you about," she said.

"I thought so. Well, go on. Confess."

"Well, this man..."

"Which one is this?"

"The same one."

"The bottom-pincher? Persistent duck. Won't keep out of our lives. Go on."

"Well, this man..."

"You met him again, eh?"

"No, this was the same time. You're making it hard for me."

"If you were a man you wouldn't make gauche remarks like that. Better get back to the story."

"Well," she said. "After he pinched me, I turned around, and he—he had his trousers open."

"Right by the Bal Bullier?"

"Yes. Right in daylight."

"Well, the old showoff! What did he do then?"

"He—I don't know how to phrase it. He made—lewd and lascivious gestures. Is that right?"

"Perfect phrasing. So what did you do?"

"Well, when he nipped me, of course, I jumped. Then when I whirled round, and saw he was ——"

"Revealing all?"

"That's it. Well, I got so angry, I swore and shouted at him..."

"You must have had a good command of French at fourteen."

"No. I shouted in English."

"How insular."

"Well, I was so stunned, I couldn't be bothered to think in French."

"But he wouldn't understand you."

"Oh, but didn't he just. He understood all right, because I punched him right in the face."

"I see, *entente cordiale* stuff. Then what?"

"Then he ran."

"Without buttoning his trousers?"

"Without waiting for anything. He ran just as fast as his legs would carry him, and I ran after him, just shouting at the top of my voice, and telling him just what I thought of him. It was a terrible scene—going right down through the little park of the Observatoire, and nursemaids and people passing..."

He bowed himself in his chair, and began choking.

"I did," she said. "It's true."

"My God," he said. "It's too marvelous. There should be a painting of it to symbolize the relationship between the two nations. Youthful British virginity incarnate, outraged, and chasing one fearful little Frenchman through the streets of the city of boulevard, art, and life. Going with her pigtails flying—and all the good French nursemaids staring in total incomprehension as they see only a foreign young hussy so avid for one of their fine French men that she chases him in open daylight through the streets. His clothing is disarrayed showing how she'd forcibly attacked him in broad daylight."

She shook her head.

"I suppose it must have looked very funny."

"I suppose so. Well, here's to good old British womanhood. Drink up. How do you feel?"

"Very, very pleasant."

"We're very nice people," he said.

He stretched his feet to the fire, feeling warmly happy.

"Clive," she said, finally.

"Yes?"

"What do you think made him do it? I've always wanted to ask someone."

"Who?"

"You know. The bottom-pincher."

"My God, is that fellow in again? What about him now?"

"What makes people do that? It's all right to laugh, but there's something quite terrible about it. I tried to look it up in father's books—I told you, he's a doctor. But I couldn't find anything..."

"Maybe you got the wrong book."

"Yes. And you can't really talk about it to anyone."

"That's right. It's perversion. You're not supposed to talk about it in mixed company."

"I know. But the thing is, one is supposed to know. And we don't know. We go on—girls like me, you know—pretending we know, and all the time we don't."

"None of us do, really," he said. "We're all sophisticated and hand-painted exteriors wrapped around a quivering sort of frightened curiosity about life. Everyone is."

"That's true. But what makes people suddenly do such frightful things? What happens in a man's mind to make him suddenly become so outrageous?"

"I don't know. They have a name for it. Not exhi-

165

bitionism. Something else. The name doesn't matter. Being performed by a human being—it's human. Perhaps he was hungry—for love, physical love. He was fighting for it as blindly as a sperm rushes at an ovum. He was a warped poet, repelled by nature's falling below his imagination. It doesn't matter. All that matters is that he's human."

"It's terrible, though."

"No, it isn't terrible. It's in all of us. Good and bad, right and wrong—all mixed in every one of us. All the evil in the world lives in me. And all the good, too. The potentialities of all the world are wrapped in each one of us. They're all there, in this vessel of ourselves—and they lie there always, waiting to see what circumstances and life will evoke. Give us a fair life, and the fairness of us will come forth. Give us a bad set of circumstances, and all the evil and cruelty can come rushing forth, to go marching on to pillage and rapine and bombing cities and slaughtering innocents in a manner that seemed impossible. Cruelty, evil, perversion—it lies in all of us, waiting for opportunity to become dominant."

"I'm glad normality's dominant in me, right now."

"May I not say, madame, that I'm awfully glad you're normal, too."

"Thank you for handing out compliments."

"Do you like them?"

"Should I answer?"

"I'll give you another, then. I'll give you all the compliments in the world, wrapped in one compliment. I hereby give you words, and words, and words, and words."

"What does that mean?"

"It means these drinks are good."

"Nothing else?"

"Lady, it also means that I mean that those words are the symbols of all the things the poets of all the ages have tried to put into all their poems. Only they didn't dare come out and speak plainly, because they're poets. So they veiled the truth behind these words which have certain rounds and rhymes. I give you the things over the words and under the words, and now you have everything—a better poem than was ever written."

"It sounds mixed up. I still think a lady would rather have a poem."

"Poems are no good—not love poems. Nobody writes a true love poem."

"Why not?"

"Because no one dares to. There's a curious dishonesty in life and art, and poetry is built on dishonesty. You know what all the love poems in the world tried to say and didn't? The poets tried to tell one eternal truth and got lost in their medium."

"What is this eternal poetic truth, master?"

"A simple truth. That of all things on earth, God has made no more noble, nor beautiful, nor poetic, nor exultant thing than a man and woman who truly love each other in bed together.

"If we could only say that clearly, and understand it, and teach children it—we'd clear out all this wickedness of present morality—our cinemas and songs and novelettes could no longer warp mass minds with their smirking behind barrages of leers and smut and false immoralities.

"And that's what all the poets of the world have tried to say—and have never said."

"My," she said. "These must be wonderful drinks."

He smiled slowly.

"I get deeply philosophical, and you blame it on the drinks."

"No," she said. "I'm fighting for time in face of a rather big idea. You really, underneath the kidding, believe all that, don't you? About poetry—and two people making love?"

"It's one of the things I believe."

"You think it's true?"

"Yes. It's true—if two people are very, very lucky."

She stared at her glass.

"Clive."

"Yes?"

"Are we—very, very lucky?"

"You can't tell at first. I think in that way we are. But I don't know you. I can only tell my part. Do you think —we're lucky?"

She looked at her hands, and sought for words.

"I think it's true what you said—about poetry," she said, slowly. "It's hard to understand—the whole thing is, isn't it?"

"Yes. Thinking about it doesn't help sometimes. Let's not worry about it. I'll do the worrying for two."

"Clive."

"Yes?"

"What is worrying you?"

He looked up from the fire quickly.

"Nothing," he said. "Nothing's worrying me. Let's have another drink—this time just the two of us."

"Who's the tertium quid??"

"Jean Jacques Pince-Derrière. Let's keep him out of this."

"All right. But we'll drink to him."

"That's right. To absent friends. I'll order another drink."

"But we ought to eat, too."

"One drink, and we'll go eat."

"Clive, let's not go back to that hotel. Ask him if he can give us something to eat here. It's so comfortable."

"That's an idea."

"Bang on the table."

He thumped his glass, but the place sounded empty.

"I'll go find him," he said.

He went over the stone-flagged room. She watched him go, and then stared at the fire. She started abruptly, then pulled the seams of her stockings straight. She crossed her legs and folded her hands on her lap and waited.

Clive came back.

"He can do it. He said, just leave it to him. Competent cove."

"Yes," she said. "Clive, are you married?"

"Just like that. You should give warning."

"Are you married, or something?"

"Neither. I'm not married, nor I'm not or something."

"That's nice. You know what I've been planning?"

"To learn to play a trombone."

"No. I've decided to buy you a dressing gown. You know, you do need one."

"I can't think of anything I need less."

"Oh, but you do. You can't go round wearing that mackintosh for a dressing gown forever."

"Mine Host was in the war. He was telling me. Has the Mons Star."

"With your bare legs sticking out. You looked so funny, this morning, following the old crone out with your upper part so military and smart in a mackintosh, and then your bare legs sticking out below. I see now why men wear long trousers—male legs certainly aren't the handsomest part of them."

"Nor deligthteth he in the shape of any man's legs. That's the Bible. But you note, it doesn't say what God thinks of female legs. Which shows that the Bible is a purely male creation."

"I'm still going to buy you a dressing gown. A nice one. Then you can parade down the hall like a thing of masculine beauty."

169

"My God, it is a parade, too. If I were in full pack I'd call it a fair route march."

"Oh, and that bathroom. It's so big it feels like taking a bath in Covent Garden or Crystal Palace or something."

"You could do the backstroke in the tub."

"It's funny. Bathrooms should be small, shouldn't they. Why?"

"Conditioned reflexes or something. False morality."

"A blue robe—that's your color. Just to set off your liquid brown eyes. A very pretty blue."

"If I pass a man in the hall he'll tip his hat to me."

"There's no danger of that. You won't pass anyone in that hall."

"By God, yes. That hotel's empty—except for auntie."

"Let's forget her, too," she said. "The whole town's empty. It's all empty. As if everyone's hiding silently in the cellars, waiting for something to happen. And we're strange sinners who walk around on top, alone."

He fell suddenly silent.

"What's the matter?" she said. "Did I say something to upset you?"

He looked up, and his face cleared and he smiled.

"Eh? It's all right," he said. "I wish he'd hurry that food."

She turned her chair slightly so that they both faced the fire, and they sat in silence.

He sat up in the blackness, feeling someone near, and then realized she had been shaking him.

"What it is?"

"The teeth," she said. "You were making that horrible noise. I'm sorry. You told me to wake you."

He lay stiffly, listening to her go back to her own bed. He heard the whisper of bedclothes and the sound of her lying down. He lay, looking upwards into the dark, listening to her breathing. He wondered if she were going back to sleep. Then he heard her speak, softly, as one does when not sure whether the other is awake or not.

"Clive!"

"What's wrong?"

"Nothing's wrong. I just wondered—are you sleepy?"

"I don't know. Just breathe steadily and you'll go back to sleep."

He lay quietly, and now his wide-open eyes began to see shapes of the room, the dim angles of the wall, the line of the dresser, the curtains at the window. He heard her breathing, but he knew she was awake, and he knew she would speak again. He waited with the mounting minutes. And then it came:

"Darling."

"Yes?"

„Are you sleepy?"

"No. What is it?"

"Tell me about you."

"I've told you."

"No. Other things. You're in the army—and you're on leave?"

"That's right."

"Why didn't you go home for leave?"

"Home? I haven't a home."

"But your people. Haven't you any people? You must..."

"I don't. My mother died several years ago."

"I'm sorry. Is your father dead, too."

"Oh yes. He's dead."

"Oh, bad luck. What did you do in the army?"

"I told you. I'm a rear rank private. The rearest and the rankest."

"Why aren't you something higher? You could be, you know."

"I didn't want to be. I liked it where I was. You meet a better class of people."

"What were you in?"

"Infantry."

"What regiment?"

"Oh, what does it matter? Why the cross-examination?"

"Don't get angry, darling. Only I know so little about you—and—I get wondering. All your life stretching back, and it's a long road of mystery. I begin to wonder what made you and why."

"I'm not angry. Go on and ask."

"I won't if you don't like it. Only I wonder. What did you come down here on leave for if your home's up North?"

"This is as good as any other place, when you've no relatives, isn't it?"

"Oh, yes."

She lay quietly for a while.

"Clive."

"Yes?"

"You won't get very angry if I ask you a question, will you?"

"How can I tell till I hear the question?"

"Well—I've got to ask you. Are you a coward, Clive?"

He laughed suddenly, and the spasm held him. He laughed until the bed shook.

"Good God, woman," he said. "What a schoolgirl question."

"Well, are you?"

"Of course I am. Every man's a coward. Why do you ask?"

"Oh, nothing."

"It must have been something."

"Well, just the things you mumble and groan when you're asleep. And you shout."

"What?"

"Oh, all sorts of things. You were saying: 'Come on. Come on! You don't want to die here!' That's one thing you say. And then: 'There aren't any more. There aren't any more!' That's what you say. Any more what, Clive?"

"How can I tell? I don't know what I'm doing in my dreams, do I?"

"But you keep on saying it. Any more *what*?"

She could hear his breathing.

"Bombs," he said. „Bombs."

"You mean air raids? Is that what you dream about?"

"No. Not that kind of bombs. Hand grenades."

"Oh, I see. Are you a bomber?"

"No. Monty is."

"Oh, the chap you're going to meet in London."

"Yes. I've told you about him."

"But why do you keep saying there are no more?"

"Because there weren't."

She lay still a while. Then she said:

"Were you in France?"

"Hell, I'm on leave," he said. "I came here to forget the army for a while. Now let's have a little peace."

He lay quietly and listened to her breathing. He could not tell whether she was sleeping. He listened, carefully, through the long, dark time. His ears heard her breathing. Beyond that sound was the rush and thump of the sea, so ever-present that the ear ignored it unless consciously prompted. Near by was his wrist watch, ticking furiously on the lamp table between their beds. Beyond that was a faint droning. He lay quietly a long time, and then his mind began sifting gently away. But it leaped back to awareness, and he knew he had heard a sound that meant she was sitting up.

"What now?" he said, angrily.

"Hush," she said. "Planes!"

"Oh, go to sleep," he said. "I heard them long ago. They're ours."

"How do you know?"

"By the sound."

"But how can you tell all different kinds of planes...?"

"You can, that's all. You can hear his and hear ours. You get to know."

"You *were* in France," she said. "I knew it. Why didn't you tell me?"

"Oh, go find somebody who likes to get hemorrhage of the mouth about it. Now let's get some sleep."

She lay listening, as the drone of the planes came nearer. There was a sweet throatiness in their song of unison. The planes passed overhead, and then droned away inland.

"They're on their way home," she said.

"That's so. Now you can go to sleep."

She lay quietly a long time, and then she said:

"It's very funny."

"What is?"

"Well, those planes. Suppose it had really been a raid. Supposed I'd been killed—in a hotel under an assumed name with a man. Then what?"

"Then we'd be dead and we wouldn't give a damn."

"That's true," she said. "Do you like double beds?"

"They're all right. Double beds for the double life."

"I think a big bed is much nicer than twin beds."

"We must go into it all some day when we've more time. We'll discuss wallpapers, too. And our tastes in carpets."

"Don't be sarcastic, dear."

He sighed, and turned on his side. He waited with mounting tension for her to speak again. Then he heard her voice, going rather quickly.

"I don't want to be a nuisance, darling. But—please! Let's move the beds together."

He threw back the clothes, feeling a mounting hysteria of laughter.

"Stay there," he said. "I'll shift the lamp table and push mine over to yours."

He began unplugging the lamp from the socket. Suddenly he stopped in the dark.

"By the Lord Jesus Christ," he said. "I've done some balmy things in my life. But I've never got up and moved furniture around in a hotel at three in the morning."

"It can't be three, yet."

"It's long after three."

"Well, no one will hear us."

"That's one thing you can bet on. By God, there isn't another soul in this blasted edifice. Now! Is that better?"

He got back into bed. He felt her outstretched hand reaching across on the covers.

"Now," she said, happily. "We can go to sleep, and if you get dreaming bad—well, I won't let you."

"Ah, nuts," he said.

"Don't be rude, darling."

"Then go to sleep."

"I will, now. Truly. You're very patient with me."

"Go to sleep."

"You are. Beautifully patient. I appreciate it."

He did not answer. She lay, listening, until his breathing came evenly and steadily.

CHAPTER XVI

There was a clean, washed feeling to the air that came even into the lobby of the hotel, and the morning had a feeling of cheerfulness.

He looked up, hearing the sound of the lift door opening. She came to him, smiling. She glanced toward the desk and nodded, and then took his arm. They swung gladly onto the street.

"What makes you so happy?" she said.

"Nothing. I haven't a headache this morning for a change."

"You sneaked into the bar and had a drink, you mean."

"I didn't. I had one from the bottle before I came down. I was just laughing at the little twirp behind the desk. He was really so upset."

"About us?"

"Yes. About the bill. He said: 'It's all ready, Mr. Hanley.' He seemed so damned tickled about it. Then I told him we'd stay another day—and you'd think I'd ruined a work of art. He was quite upset."

"Oh, that's so. We told him we were leaving this morning. I forgot all about it."

"You liar," he said. "You didn't forget any more than I did."

"Of course," she said. "Unpleasant things—you just put them off hoping something happens to forestall them."

"Mental laziness," he said.

"Well, it's very comfortable—and it often works. In this case it did."

"Well, we were idiots—to get angry and say we'd do it."

"That's right," she said. "We won't get angry at each other any more. Now, where do we go?"

"Well—we can go on the clifftop!"

"That's nice," she said. "We'll sit up there, and then afterwards we'll go down to Mine Host."

They walked along, feeling a sudden sort of holiday aura about the deserted town. The wind came in from the sea, bringing torn swatches of clouds that hurried along, making the sea and land an unfolding quilt of occasional shadow and sunshine. The day was warm. Seagulls strutted calmly on the edge of the forsaken sands.

On the clifftop there were tiny, pearl-shelled snails on the grass stems, and many blue butterflies. The larks lifted themselves and sang from their hiding places of height, and the sounds of their song came clearly above the background of surf cannonading against the chalk faces below. They walked far over the cliffs to a slope that looked seaward, and there they lay in the thick, dry grass. He lay with his head on his clasped hands and looked upward, and she sat, looking over the Channel.

"It's nice," she said. "We're very lucky."

"This is my idea of a holiday," he said. "Eat, drink, sleep."

"Nothing else?"

"Now who's getting a bawdy mind?"

She laughed in a sort of happy embarrassment.

"You said last night it was poetry," she said.

"So it is. But talking about it isn't—not always."

She lay quietly for a while, and then turned and studied his face.

"You're wrinkling again," she said.

"It's force of habit."

She moved a finger across his forehead.

"Clive."

"Yes?"

"Will you tell me about something?"

"What about?"

"About the war. About being in France."

"Oh, hell, let's forget it."

He turned over, face down. She looked at him, studying the line of the nape of his neck.

"You see," she said. "I want to know about you."

"That's feminine possessiveness."

"Well, if I'd been at the front, and seen how it was, I'd tell anyone who asked me."

"Yes. You'd be a big-mouthed hero."

"There's a difference between boasting and telling. What was it like?"

"Oh, Jesus, you won't be satisfied until you pry it out of me. It was a bloody do. Now that's it. It was a damned, bloody do. Now you know."

"Were you in it?"

"What the hell do you think I was doing? Taking tea with the general staff?"

"Whereabouts were you?"

"All over. All over."

"Where?"

"How the hell should I know?"

"Well, if you were there..."

"You don't know. You're too bloody tired to know or give a damn whether you do or not. At first you knew, but afterwards you didn't. You didn't know anything except that you wanted to go some place and sleep for ten days straight."

"Where did you start from?"

He raised himself on his elbows, and looked at her.

"All right," he said angrily. "You won't be satisfied until you have it out of me. I'll tell you. If you want to know, I'll tell you, and then you'll have it. You'll have all I've got."

He looked down at the grass, and plucked the stems, carefully.

"This is all there was to it, and nothing more. We were at a place called Hersin. We'd been there months, waiting. They sounded fall in, full pack, and we lined up and started off. Monty said the Corporal told him the Sergeant-major had heard the Captain telling the Lieutenant that Jerry was coming through Holland and Belgium.

"So much for the tactical situation. Three cheers were nobly given by our enthusiastic troops who were fed up with waiting, and off we went.

"We marched. We got on a train somewhere. We rode. At two in the morning, we got off. We ate. We got in motor lorries, all except the transport. That was to follow by road.

"We went in the lorries through places called, I think, Quivrain and Quivrechain. Anyhow, it was a pottery district. Then we were in Belgium. You could tell it by the flags. The people hung them out. They were very happy. Everyone was happy. The chaps in the lorries sang: ‚Adolf, you've bitten off much more than you can chew.' That's how happy they were.

"That was all right. I won't mock. We'd been waiting too long. We'd done our part in the ranks. We were tired of waiting. We were glad it had come.

"We rode till about noon and got out. We waited there. We got hungry. The transport was supposed to catch up with us—cookers and things like that. I don't know. Anyhow it didn't come. So we ate iron ration and lined up and marched. After that—let's see—oh, busses came back some time about then and picked us up again. We rode till about midnight. No one was singing any more. We got out and flopped down. My platoon was in a barn somewhere. The farmer gave us hell for taking his straw to sleep on.

"Next morning when we got up—it was a village. The refugees had started coming. One of our cookers got up and we had hot tea. The others never found us. The refugees were too heavy on the road. That's what they say.

"We marched again that day. We could hardly get through the refugees. They came down the road with push-carts and wheelbarrows and perambulators—anything on wheels. The damned upper classes were coming through in motorcars, and honking like hell to get the others over to the side of the road.

"We had a hell of a time getting through. You can't push them off the road—there were kids and sick people on pushcarts. Even when you want to march you can't shove them into the ditch. So we went in the ditches, sometimes Indian file. We just kept on slogging that day. About dark we stopped at a place and dug in. Then we marched back about ten kilometers in the night, and we dug in again.

"We got dug in by about daylight, so then they sounded fall-in again, and we started up the road once more.

"The refugees were saying: '*Allemandes toute suite.*' We said: '*Bonnes nouvelles.*' We went past the first place we'd dug in, then they told us to dig in again. The one cooker kept coming right with us and made some hot stew. That cook was a good man. He kept up with us somehow.

"Then the dive bombers showed up and left souvenirs. Chaps picked up splinters. They were quite hot. But most of us fell asleep. Old Monty had dug a sort of tunnel into a bank and we crawled in there. He said it was going to be worse later.

"He was right. We woke up in the afternoon, and Monty and I went down by the road. The last of the refugees were going past. Some of them had been hit. Jerry was strafing the road with his dive bombers. They were saying: '*Les sales boches.*' One woman was carrying a dead kid with its arm torn off. They said they couldn't get it away from her and that she'd gone balmy. I think she was.

"We stayed there all that day and nothing happened. That night we stood to—two hours on, four off — and nothing happened. About ten in the morning a bunch of the Guards came back down the road.

"We knew they'd been through it. You could tell—the way they looked—their clothes and their faces and the walking wounded. When they saw us, the officer called them to attention, and they went down the road, stepping right along and eyes straight to the front. They were wounded and filthy but they went past us as if we were dirt, like the Guards always do.

"After that everything was quiet. No more refugees.

"Monty and I went in his funk hole. We were sitting nice till the dive bombers came again. Then Captain Allen came down and found Monty—they were both in the last war together. He said someone had to go back and try to find the cookers and guide them up. He had a Sergeant, but because Monty was an old-timer, he thought Monty could look after the Sergeant. He detailed us to go with the Sergeant, and he winked and said: 'And we want food.'

"So we went back, and walked over about half of Belgium. We lost the Sergeant and a kid named Baker. We were supposed to meet at a crossroad later, but we never saw them again. Then Monty swiped a wagon and we got some grub. God, it was funny. It was getting almost dark, and I was ready to lie down and die. Monty said: 'I'll be damned if we go back without food.'

"And by God, we didn't. He saw a wagon by a picket line of the Engineers, and just walked in and harnessed up the wagon, and started to drive away. As we were coming out, a sentry said: 'Where you going?' And Monty says: 'General orders,' and while the kid was puzzling it out, we were down the road and going hell for breakfast. Some time—oh, long after dark—we found a ration dump. We didn't have any requisition, and we had a hell of a time. Monty said we were from brigade headquarters, and if we didn't get any food he'd like to have a chit from the Captain explaining why we'd been refused. The Captain went in to call up somebody, and while we were waiting, we loaded the wagon with anything—a Sergeant came along and helped us—he thought we were all right. We put on everything—cheese, jam, bread, sides of bacon. Anything. Then we jumped up and rode away as if hell was after us.

"After that we went damn near all over all the part of Belgium we hadn't covered already, trying to find our way back. Just after daybreak we saw a spire, and Monty said it had been to the right of us. I thought it had been to the left. But Monty was right, and we found the place, but they'd pulled out and there was no one there. So we headed for the village where the spire was, and that was empty, too. It was like dead. We drove down the main street—all the stuff was in the shops, but there was no one there. And then suddenly a Lieutenant of the Coldstreamers came marching down the street. He had his gloves on and had a walking stick, and he said:

" 'Hello, by God, get that jolly thing out of here quick.'

"So we turned round and left him alone in his village with his gloves and cane complete. Monty said it looked pretty obvious that the front had moved back, so we started back, and about noon we found the outfit at a new place where they'd dug in.

"We turned over the grub and went to sleep. After that we went back about ten kilos more, and dug in again.

"Jerry didn't give us much time and the Stukas came over again. This time they did it right. After dark we piled the wounded in the wagon we'd foraged, and started them back. About midnight, maybe, we got a stand-to, and we moved back again and dug in. There was about a foot of topsoil, and after that, chalk. It was bad going.

"Stukas found us bright and early, and the leader would tip his wings over, and dive—and then the next one right after him—a whole line of them. They'd let us have it, and then right back for home to load up honey again. We couldn't get our casualties out.

"Old Monty found a machine gun and set it on a post and tried to pot them as they came down, but we didn't get any. But three of our Bristols came over, and the Jerries cleared away like magic. Then the minute the Bristols were gone, the Stukas were back again until dark. Then we pulled out again and went back further. We were supposed to dig in again, but no one did much digging. A chap would be standing beside you, digging, and all of a sudden you'd hear: Clunk! Like a whole ironmongery shop falling —from his equipment. Just go: Clunk! And he'd be out. They'd be asleep before they hit the ground. They'd just groan a bit and then lie there. You could kick 'em, or drag 'em out of your way, but you couldn't wake 'em.

"We couldn't dig in, so they put out pickets. Captain Allen picked on us. I had to laugh. He said: 'I'm sorry you're for it, Monty, but they don't seem to make them like they did in the old days, Monty. They get sleepy.' Monty said: 'Captain—did you ever see a dream walking? Well, I did—and it's me.' We got posted in a barn and took turns falling asleep.

"After that—well, we went back some more. By God, we went back—clear on through the Guards that had gone through us before. So this time we treated them like dirt, and went right back through without looking at them.

"After that—oh, what the hell. You get the general idea. Much the same, and more so."

Clive looked at a piece of grass he was shredding. He threw it aside and looked out over the ocean.

"No, go on and tell me," she said, quietly. "You might as well go on now."

He laughed quickly.

"Yes," he said. "Now you've got me doing it, too—fighting the war with my mouth. No—it's no use talking."

"Please," she said. "Go on, now. It might be good for you if you told someone all about it—then you might get rid of it."

He turned and looked suddenly at her, looking steadily as if he were seeing a stranger. Then he laughed.

"I've told you. We dug in and marched back and dug in and marched back—till finally, till finally we'd marched clean to hell out of France."

He looked up and saw her with her lips curiously parted.

"Didn't we ever hold him?" she said.

Her tone sounded so plaintive. He looked down at his hands, and laughed quickly. Then he said:

"Oh, I suppose we gave him a crack once in a while. They did at Douai. The Guards cracked him at Douai. We were on the flank. They said the French were coming up fast to help us. You could hear the Guards yelling over on our left—like a crowd at a football match. When they were going over—rushing some strong point.

"We kicked him to hell out of Douai and kept on going way beyond and had him running, and, Jesus, you began to think that at last it was the miracle and we were going to have another first battle of the Marne all over again.

"But first thing you know they're ordering us to retreat to the town again, to try to link up with our chaps in Arras—and next thing we know it's hang on to Douai in a defensive action—and finally it's hold Douai in a rear-guard action—hold it to the last man! Die at your posts, boys! The chaps at Arras were trying to fight their way through to the north, and we had to hold Douai to keep a road open for 'em.

"I had to laugh. Captain Allen came crawling up—we were down behind the brick part of what had been a hothouse in a back garden—and he said the orders were no one was to retreat—for the honor of the regiment. Then he said: 'Here's your chance for a cross, Monty.'

"Monty says: 'Victoria or wooden?'

"'What do you care?' Allen says. 'You've got to die to get either.'

"It's curious how you remember odd bits that people say.

"'Well, old soldiers never die,' Monty says. 'And you can't tell. Maybe those frog bastards will break through to us.'

"'You mustn't call them those frog bastards,' the Captain said. 'In future they are to be referred to at all times as our gallant allies.' Then they both laughed—it was an old joke—about the orders in the last war or something.

"So—we were the glorious rear-guard boys."

He sat, fraying the piece of grass.

"And what then?" she asked.

"And what then?" he said. "Oh, after Douai we cleared out of—oh, a hell of a lot of places—all the way up to Dunkirk, and then we got to hell out of that. That's all."

"But," she said, "but—why did you leave Douai if they told you to stay to the last man? How did you...?"

"I ran to hell out! What the hell did you want me to do? Stay there and get shot to hell as I sang: 'Oh' let me like a soldier fall'? Stay and be nice fertilizer for some French farmer? Not me!"

She listened to his voice, lifted angrily in the great space of the flat land on the cliff top.

"I meant," she said, softly, "what happened to you at Douai? Did you lose a lot of men?"

"What the hell! You don't expect a rear guard to come marching out on parade front with the regimental band playing, do you?"

"Don't get angry, Clive. You should be proud, not angry."

"Proud—angry! That's got nothing to do with it."

"Well, then you mustn't feel badly. There's nothing wrong with an army retreating when it has to. In a way it was even glorious—a victory in defeat..."

"Oh, don't talk like a newspaper editorial page. That's got nothing to do with it."

"Then what has got anything to do with it?"

"Nothing. It won't do any good talking about it."

"Why not?"

"It won't, that's all. You wouldn't understand it."

"I'm capable of understanding, Clive. I'm not—not weak-minded."

"It's nothing to do with your brain."

"Well, what has it got to do with?"

"It's more than the brain. It's—it's everything—your background."

"There's nothing abnormal about my background. It wouldn't stop me from..."

"It's middle class—that's all."

She looked at him quickly.

"And you're lower class," she said coldly.

"You pay me a compliment when you call me lower class. You pay me a compliment."

"I'm glad you appreciate it."

"Well, I'd sooner be out-and-out lower class than a smug, complacent, crass middle classer. The backbone of the nation! The overgrown appendices—the ossified gallstones of a nation!"

"You're vulgar."

"It's the lower class coming out in me."

She sat silently, looking out at the cloud-patched ocean. Then she regarded him, steadily. She said, quietly:

"You're not really lower class, Clive."

"By, God, I am," he said. "I say it distinctly. Don't think you're complimenting me by trying to include me among the pompous, blind, self-centered bastards who..."

"You *are* lower class," she said. "Very low!"

She got up quickly and turned away, waiting. He rose slowly and stood beside her.

"All right," he said. "All right. You won't have to stick my lowerclass vulgarity very long. Only a couple more days—or you can end it now if you like."

"It suits me if it ends now," she said.

"Then it certainly suits me," he said. "Let's go back to the hotel and get cleared out."

"All right."

Unspeaking, they strode back to the hotel, aware of themselves only as two isolated figures in the empty town. He stopped by the desk and told the clerk they were leaving.

"You mean, in the morning, sir?"

Clive looked at the little, misshapen face.

"Of course," he said. "In the morning. First thing. Have the bill ready."

That night the planes came over. They were very high, and the sound was so faint that the more you listened the less you were able to tell whether it was a sound or the strain of listening that made the hum.

Clive lay stiffly in his bed, lifting his head slightly to keep both his ears from the pillow. He lay like that a long time until the strain on his neck destroyed all power of hearing.

He lay back again, and then he could hear only the near sounds: the sound of his own breathing, and of his heart beating; the watch ticking and her breathing, and beyond that the steady flow of the wind and the shattering of the sea at high tide against the Esplanade wall. Then above that he could hear again the humming—so faint, yet clear enough so that one could not deny it. When he lifted his head again she spoke, and her voice seemed suddenly much too loud.

"Darling."

"Yes?" he said.

"Do you hear something."

"No. Go to sleep."

"There is something," she said. "I can hear planes."

"Oh, go to sleep."

She was silent a moment. Then she said, calmly.

"There are planes. Is it an air raid?"

"No. They're ours," he said. "Now go to sleep."

He lay back again, his eyes open to the blackness. He tried to empty his mind, but now he could not stop listening. Every sound seemed to clamor for recognition. He could hear her breathing, stifled against the pillow. The sound came in gasps. For a long time he tried to shut himself away from the noise. At last he gave up. He leaned on his side.

"Are you crying?" he said.

"No."

She said it as a woman will when there is no denial of it.

"You are," he said. "What's the matter?"

"I'm afraid, Clive."

"Afraid. I've told you, they're our planes. They're probably coming home. If there's a raid..."

"It isn't that."

"Well, what is it?"

"It's me, darling. I'm afraid. I'm no good."

"Oh, now—you're all right. What's there to be afraid of?"

"Of me—of everything. All I'm doing. Being here—in this dark room—in a hotel I don't know—with a strange man."

"I'm not strange, am I?"

"Not in the daytime, darling. Then everything seems all right. I can see you, and know who we are. But—we quarrel—and then in the dark, I wonder what I'm doing, and why I'm doing it—and I'm afraid."

He waited, and the sound of the planes seemed more distinct. He began talking.

"I'm still me in the dark, Prudence," he said. "In fact, I'm a better man in the dark than in the daylight. At least, I don't fight in the dark—and I don't argue with you—and I don't get evil-tempered and..."

"I don't mind, darling. You don't mean to be, really. You can't help being short-tempered, can you?"

"Of course I can help it, I don't mean to, at the time. Afterwards, I'm sorry about it. I shouldn't get so nasty—to you of all people. You're so very patient, and nice..."

"I'm not. I'm no good."

"Oh, yes, you are. You're a fine girl."

"I'm not, really. You'd find that out if you knew me very long."

"I wish they were all as good as you."

"All? Who else do you mean?"

"No one," he said. "I say, let's have a drink. That's what you need. It'll quiet you down."

She sat up and drew a breath.

"That's a clever way to duck the conversation," she said.

She listened to his feet slapping on the floor.

"Close the blinds before..."

"I can do it in the dark," he said. "I know where the bottle is."

She lay, listening to the plop of the cork, and the tinkle of glass, and then the gurgle of pouring. He came back to her in the dark, and put the glass in her hand.

"Straight," he said. "Three cheers."

"Three cheers to you, too," she said.

She drank and then shuddered, and held the glass out at random. His hand found it.

"Now you'll feel better," he said.

He set the glasses on the floor, and his hand found her face. He stroked her forehead.

"Now you'll be able to go to sleep."

She sighed.

"That feels so good," she said. "It's nice—but you'll get cold sitting there."

"Oh, no I won't."

"Oh, yes-you-will."

"I'm warm enough."

"Look, Clive. Let's move the beds together again. Then I'll feel better—and you can keep warm..."

"Oh, my God," he said. "The Midnight Movers once more. Holy Jesus!"

He got up and moved the lamp table and dragged his bed to hers. He got into bed and put out his hand. She moved over and rested her head on his arm. Then she laughed.

"Now I know you—even in the dark. And I like this room, too. It's very nice."

"Very, *very* nice?"

"Yes," she said. "Very, *very* nice. That makes it different, doesn't it?"

"Indeed," he said. "Comfortable?"

"Yes. Is your arm tired?"

"No. I don't get tired. Not in the arms, anyhow."

"They are pretty steely," she said. "I'm glad. It would have been awful if I'd got here with you and you'd turned out to be—flabby. Don't you hate flabby men?"

"Of course," he said.

He lay there, and the sound of the planes seemed to be closer.

"I used to be pretty spindly as a kid," he said, quickly.

"I used to read all the strength advertisements. You know —our patent grip dumbbells will turn you from this—to this! Picture of a gent with lightning bolts coming from his biceps. I used to admire those things."

"Did you try one?"

"No. Never saved enough."

"But you got strong anyhow."

"Yes."

"Your biceps are all right. Triceps too. Pectoral muscles like iron."

"You know anatomy."

"I told you, my father's a doctor. I was the kind of kid that pried into books. How did you develop your arms finally?"

"Work. A job I had."

"What job was this. Hammering locks?"

"No. A carpetbeater."

"Oh, you haven't told me about that one. Tell me about it. Then I'll go to sleep. You mean, you went out bright and early every morning, and knocked at the doors, and said: 'Have you any...'"

"No. This was in a fabrics mill. It was very boring."

"But I'd like to hear about it. Then that will be something else I know about you. You see, that's what's frightening. All your years stretching back when you didn't know me, and all mine stretching back when I didn't know you. Why, we might have actually passed one another on the street."

"It's quite probable we did," he said.

"Tell me about carpet beating, then."

In the pause he heard the planes. He began, quickly.

"Well, it's piled fabrics," he said. "You know what piles are. Not the medical kind. The nap on heavy textiles like carpets or plush or velvets and velveteens. Well, after they're woven, they go to shearing machines—they have spiral blades round a cylinder going about three thousand revs a minute, and that cuts the pile off evenly—and a few fingers once in a while..."

"Oh, no."

"Oh, yes. You can get a percentage figure on it—it's quite a normal figure. Industrial hazard number so-and-so. Anyhow, when the carpets are sheared, then they come to you, and you beat them."

"What for?"

"Make the pile stand out, get rid of all the fine bits of dust and pile that adhere."

"You just do that all day? Why don't they have a machine?"

"Hand beating's best, I suppose. And when you have a job you don't start wishing for a machine to come and take it away from you. Besides, a machine can't inspect for cuts."

"But it could. It could beat, and have a photoelectric cell to check defects, couldn't it?"

"I suppose it could. But I was just working there. I wasn't the mill owner."

"But if you'd invented a machine they'd..."

"They'd have taken it under the employment contract saying all inventions made by the undersigned employee are the property of his employer. Then they'd install the machine, say thank you, and lay you off."

"They wouldn't. They'd promote you and..."

"You've been reading soppy stories, my girl. I know. Look, once when I was a kid, I invented a machine. Well, it wasn't a machine—it was so simple that it was better than a machine. I was working on an assembly belt. Electrical equipment. The stuff came from the stamper, and they had to have a kid or somebody on the belt, just turning the stuff round for it to go into a drilling outfit. Well, at first I picked each piece up and turned it round. Then I found by sticking my finger out and holding it in exactly one spot, as the stuff came down it bumped my finger and turned in exactly the right position. Well, I did that, but my finger started to get sore. Then I got a bit of machine steel, and I held that. But I couldn't hold it perfectly steady. So at noontime, I got an old clamp from the scrap pile, and rigged it up with the machine steel in it, and after dinner I horsed it round until I had it set exactly. So there I was, and there was the piece of steel doing all my work for me, and all I had to do was sit there reading and see that nothing slipped.

"But when the foreman came round, and saw it! God you'd have thought I was a criminal—that I'd been drawing wages under false pretenses. So they left the jigger there to do the job—or they rigged a proper one up, and the next Saturday I joined the ranks of the ungainfully unemployed."

"But you'd created something."

"Oh, yes. Have you ever tried eating a bowl of creative soup?"

"But—in the fabrics mill, didn't you get tired? How did you beat the stuff? With carpetbeaters—just like women use?"

"No. You have a stick in each hand. The stuff's on a sort of roll-up drum. You just stand there and wallop."

"All day?"

"Of course, all day."

"You beat steadily for eight hours?"

"No. Ten."

"Ten hours? But I'd think your arms would drop off."

"No, they stay on all right."

"But don't you get horribly tired?"

"Lady, you do—you do!"

"What do you do then?"

"You go right on beating—you have to. The drum is still turning. After a while, your arms build up and you hardly notice it."

"But how boring."

"No, it isn't in one way. You see, it makes no demand whatsoever on your mind, so your mind's free to go where it will—just as if you were sitting before a fire in a comfortable chair. So your mind goes to other things."

"What things?"

"Oh, payday, and how you'll get drunk, and the girl you're going to make advances to."

"No."

"Why not?"

"You couldn't think of that ten hours a day."

"No. You do turn to other things."

"What?"

"Oh, best is complicated things—try to do mathematical problems in your head. I once read about two Russian prisoners of war who used to play whole games of chess in their heads. They hadn't any chessmen, so they just did it all mentally. So I tried that."

"Could you do it?"

"No. Only for about ten moves—until I'd get slinging knights about. Once I got to about twenty moves. But the trouble is I knew what each side was after, so I'd have to start gypping one side to let the other win. So I used to call one side me, and the other side the foreman. The foreman's side was very dense. My side would get all sorts of brilliant plays going, and the foreman wouldn't see it until it was too late."

"Didn't he ever win?"

"No one ever won. I couldn't carry it that far. But he certainly was in some awful messes when I left him."

"What else did you think about?"

"Oh, everything. Politics, economics, who held the heavyweight title from Sullivan down, the books of the Bible..."

"The Bible?"

"Oh yes. I used to recite it. You see, in my Sunday-school

days I had a flypaper memory. Everything stuck to it. And it's pretty goodsounding stuff to shout out loud against the roar of machines. Like: For God so loved the world that he gave his only begotten Son that whosoever believeth in him should not perish, but have everlasting life. John, three-sixteen—our promise of eternal life. And poetry, too. Reams of it. But let me tell thee now another tale, for Bleys our Merlin's master as they say, died but of late, and when Uther in Tintagil passed away, wailing and moaning for an heir—I can do about a half hour straight of that—the Birth of Arthur."

"Go on with it."

"No. It's not good poetry. I only used it for a time counter. See how fast I could do it. Once I did it in three lengths of material—that's about eighteen minutes."

"What else did you do besides gabble poetry for speed records."

"Oh—sing."

"Sing? I've never heard you sing."

"That shows you what luck you have."

"I'll bet you sing very nicely, darling."

"Like a raven. But that's one thing about singing in a factory. You hardly hear yourself above the noise. And it passes time. Around three in the afternoon is when everyone sings."

"That sounds the nicest way yet to pass the time."

"It isn't nice. It's very terrible."

"Terrible?"

"You see, it isn't singing over your work. You're singing against it. You sing when the hours drag and it seems they'll never end. You sing when stopping time seems miles away. You sing when boredom nearly kills you. The girls start to sing, and everyone picks it up—and it's rather terrible to hear in a way."

"The girls? Were there many girls employed there?"

"Very many. There's a high percentage of female labor in textiles."

"What were they like, Clive?"

"Like? They were—girls, that's all. Like your girls at camp—the Waffs. Just like everyone else."

"Did you ever make love to them?"

"No."

"Truly?"

"I'd say truly if I had, and I'd say truly if I hadn't. But I didn't."

"Why not?"

"I don't know. I think I was—frightened."

"Frightened? Of girls?"

"In a way."

"Why?"

"Oh, many things."

"But you're not frightened of me?"

"No. That's different."

"But I'm just the same as a mill girl—for making love to."

"In essentials, I suppose you are. But not in nonessentials."

"In what nonessentials are they different?"

"They're not very gentle, to begin with. They can be pretty tough. That's the way it seemed to me when I was young. They can be tough on a new youngster."

"How?"

"They gang up on him, and sun him."

"Sun him? What's that?"

"Rush him and knock him flat and then sit on him and take his pants down. Take a look to see how big he is, and then get an oil can and oil him up good and rub it in—and then let him go."

"Oh, Clive, they wouldn't."

"All right."

"You're making it up."

"All right, I'm making it up. But I'm just telling you,

196

that's the way they are. They're not supposed to be. Nobody ever writes about them like that. They're either supposed to be unwashed riffraff, or patient, oppressed heroines—whichever side of the fence you're on. They do work hard, and they are patient. But living has made them tough, too. I'm just telling you the way they are. It's like—like tribal co-ordination.

"My God, I have to laugh. People get up expeditions and lug cameras thousands of miles to Africa to film the so-called esoteric and secret rites of jungle tribes—initiating the boys into manhood. I saw one—there was a hell of a hullabalo about how exciting it was. If ever anyone wanted a grain of truth, and they had the skill, they could go into any mill in any industrial town in Britain—or in any other country for all I know—and film rites and customs that are exactly as set and dark and ignorant as Africa's. It's the same everywhere I've worked. When people work together in one place, and spend most of their working hours together, they get a sort of code of customs and prejudices, like a tribe. In textiles it's worse, because the people live and are brought up in tougher surroundings. They don't mean to be vicious—although sometimes they kill people."

"They kill them! Oh, come!"

"All right. Believe what you want. I've seen a boy that was killed."

"Killed? How? By girls?"

"No. By men—and very unpleasantly."

"How?"

"I told you. Unpleasantly."

"But how?"

"In a machine shop. They put the air pressure hose in his anus and turned the air on. In two seconds they'd ruptured his entire internal system, and he died screaming and in dreadful agony. You could hear him screaming all over the plant. That's how we knew. We went over to see."

"Clive!"

"I shouldn't have told you. It isn't pretty, it is? But don't misunderstand. They weren't vicious or brutal. They were ignorant. It was the machine age bringing new toys to old customs, and they did no worse with them than mankind has done with airplanes and bomb mechanisms. It was just that they had no conception of the force of an air pressure hose and the relative fragility of human tissue. They were profoundly shocked when they found out. Now, shall we talk about something else?"

She was quiet a moment, and his ears seemed to ring as he listened above the sea sound and the wind sound.

"Clive," she said, finally, "were you ever initiated?"

"No. Never."

"I'm glad. But why not?"

"Because I've always been fairly active and strong and I can take care of myself."

"But when you're small—what do you do?"

"It doesn't matter. You must fight. You fight back desperately—and you find strength somewhere. And then—well, they learn to let you alone. It's exactly the same as anywhere else in life. Nobody picks on a chap who can fight back. They learn to leave him alone."

She lay quietly, and then she said, suddenly:

"Clive, do you think we're going to lose this war?"

"No," he said, slowly. "No."

"You're not saying that just to comfort me. I'd like to know. You've been in it. Are we going to lose it?"

"It isn't the war," he said. "It's something bigger than that—and we've lost that already."

"What?"

"I don't know. I wish I were wise enough to know. I try to puzzle it out, but I can't. But I do know we've lost it."

"But we'll win the war?"

"No," he said. "We won't win it. I don't think we'll lose it; but I know we're not going to win it."

"Why not?"

"Because we've lost the other thing."

"But what is the other thing?"

"That's what I don't exactly know."

She lay quiet, and then he said:

"Oh, pay no attention. One's never optimistic at this time of the night."

"That's true," she said. "But it's nearly morning. Look, you can see the room getting gray."

He listened, intently. There was no sound of planes. He could be sure of it now.

"You'll be gray if you don't get some sleep. Now go to sleep. Get back on your own pillow."

He drew his arm away, and heard her settling herself. Then he lay still, listening to her breathing. He thought she was asleep at last, and he began to analyze the strange pleasure he felt in being awake and knowing that she was asleep.

But she lifted her head and spoke.

"It was terribly nice of you to talk me through it, because I was awfully afraid just at first—and they were German planes this time weren't they?"

"Oh, for Christ's sake," he said. "Will you go to sleep!"

CHAPTER XVII

PRENTISS SAINTBY rocked contentedly in the sun. There was a smell of heat-baked boards of the porch—and the smell of burning piñon wood that drifted up among the pines. The air coming down from the jagged juniper-dotted montains was like cold wine, but the sun was unexpectedly warm.

He laughed to himself. So this, he thought, was ranch life!

Somehow he had expected it to be a place of dust and roughing it. Something like the cinema—low shacks and a few cowboys sitting on a tumble-down fence. Instead, there was this—this heaven: the great log château looming up on the green-wooded grounds; the individual guest houses among the pines, complete with sitting room, bedroom, bathroom of gay orange tile—the knotty pine walls, stone fireplaces, vacuum ice flasks and whisky-and-soda siphon on the table, the chintz curtains, and the sprays of fresh flowers in the vases. This was really roughing it—right down to the monogrammed towels in the bathroom and the menservants to tend the log fires.

He looked at the everlasting wonder of the mountains, and rocked time away. He only wakened from his half-doze when he heard foot-steps on the porch. It was the manservant.

"Yes?"

"Miss Mary, Mr. Saintby. She asked me to tell you about tennis."

"Oh, yes. I'll change and be right down."

The man followed him into the bedroom.

"There are flannels in this closet, sir. Or if you wish, I put some shorts down here in the bureau."

"Oh, fine. Flannels."

"Yes, sir. Mr. Lachran said you were traveling light, so I thought..."

"Good. I'll be right along."

The man lingered, half-apologetically. Prentiss looked up.

"Is there anything..."

"Well, sir—if you'll pardon me. But—how are things at home?"

"At home?"

"Yes, sir. In England. You see, I'm British, too—a Suffolk man. I understand that you're just over, sir."

"Oh, yes. Yes. Why, we're quite all right. Quite. You get the news, don't you?"

"Oh, yes, sir. On the radio. But I wondered how things *really* were. How we're getting along."

"Oh, we're coming along. You know—after a slow start. We're always a bit slow getting started."

"Yes, sir. That's what—if you'll pardon me—I don't like."

The man went slowly to the door.

"If you wish anything else, sir—the bell, there."

Prentiss wrinkled his forehead and changed slowly. He was beginning to get used to it—people asking him about England as if the real truth weren't being told, as if Britain were hiding something, instead of being open and honest about all news—that is, of course, about all news of nonmilitary importance. You couldn't expect anyone to give out news that would be of service to the other chap—or that would be detrimental to the public morale. Yet everyone here seemed to think Britain was hiding something.

He finished dressing, and went slowly down the path through the scented pines, over the rustic footbridge across a needle-carpeted gully, along the more formal path beside a great lake. By the boathouse he saw Lachran, playing with two small children. The old man looked up happily and waved.

"Getting everything you want?"

"Oh, quite."

"Good. These are my great-grandchildren," Lachran said, proudly. "We're running a shipping line."

He held up the water-soaked toy yacht.

Prentiss stared at the two youngsters. They were ash blond, fair-skinned, with delicate features—so physically unlike old Lachran himself in every way. They were—were aristocratic. That was it. It was inconceivable that in four generations the rough frontier blood could produce a flesh-and-blood aristocracy. Incredible.

"How do you like it here?" Lachran prompted.

Prentiss looked at the lake, its surface a mixture of cool blues and vivid sun-struck greens from the mountains and the near-by willows and sycamores.

"Magnificent. How did you manage to find such a heavenly spot?"

Lachran beamed with pleasure.

"Well, it wasn't exactly like this always. When I first came up here—I'll bet not more than fifty white men had ever been up this canyon. It's been fixed up quite a bit. This lake wasn't here. I put that in."

"You put the lake in?"

"Sure."

Lachran rose. He waved his hand and a uniformed nursemaid came from the boathouse and took the children. It was utterly incongruous—the nursemaid with bonnet right out of a London park, walking under the towering tapestry of the Wild West mountains. Lachran was waving his hand expansively.

"See, we dammed up there, then we dammed the stream

about a mile up the canyon and piped it in—fourteen-inch cast-iron pipe."

"Good heavens," Prentiss said.

Lachran laughed gladly at his wonder.

"Yeh. Then I put the bridge in. You remember where you came in, up Horseneck Gulch. I spent seventy thousand putting that bridge in. You remember it, don't you? About twelve miles down the canyon."

"Oh, yes," Prentiss said. He did not remember, but it seemed impolite to say so. His mind was hanging on the thought of the miles. You mean, your ranch extends all the way down there?"

Lachran could not have been happier.

"Why, we start a couple of miles before that. This isn't your little island, you know. This is America—the West. Why, we go further up the other way over the divide there. Then back this way, over the other side of those Sangre de Dios foothills, and round the other side of the Sombrero Mountains. Big Sombrero and Little Sombrero. They're both my mountains."

"Your mountains!" Prentiss echoed.

"Yeh. Then we built this new ranch house here. We had an old ranch, and Mary liked to come up here. That was my wife. So I fixed it all up. Had an architect come here from California and remodel it. When it was done, Mary didn't like it. So we tore the whole damn thing out, and I got another architect, and told him Mary was going to stand over him and tell him how she wanted it. And she had it all done in logs, like the old place. She had good taste.

"Then we built the guest houses. It's nicer that way. I figure people enjoy themselves more if they have privacy— that's the British idea, too, isn't it?"

"Oh, yes," Prentiss assured him.

"Yeh, I've often heard that. And I think it's a good

idea. You can get together for rides, and so on. If you like to ride, we'll pack a lunch and go up Big Sombrero some time."

"I'd like that, very much—if I have time."

"Ah, you'll have time," Lachran said, emphatically. He turned his head. "Ah, Mary!"

Prentiss saw the girl waving her racket almost angrily from lower down on the path.

He smiled at Lachran and hurried along toward her.

After the match Prentiss sat on the stone-flagged portico overlooking the court. He tried to appear bright as people spoke to him; but they seemed just a half-real maze of other guests. He was intent upon his own utter exhaustion.

Truly, he decided, one was a fool to try to play tennis like that when he'd turned the forty-year mark. He shouldn't have let them drive him to it.

That was the trouble with Americans—no love of the game itself—only this intense emphasis on victory. Games weren't a social pastime to them; they were a means to that end of winning. They played every point with something akin to vicious possessiveness.

He leaned his head on his hands.

Yet, perhaps there was a merit to it. Undoubtedly that's why they won so much at the Olympics. On the other hand, they burned themselves out here. Youth, burning itself out in a brief flash of super-excellence instead of spending a long life at standard goodness. Wars—they could ignore wars and yet play tennis games as if more than nations depended upon the outcome.

And there was a sort of belt-fed mass-production air about even the young athletes. The two girls—they were exactly alike. They had stood on the base-line, pumping their pro-taught shots with mechanical regularity—forehand, backhand, cross-court, base-line—exactly the same.

Like two mechanical dolls from among thousands turned out by the same machine. Same motions, same form. Mass produced.

"Well, partner. How about changing, and then a swim?"

Mary was standing before him. More than anything else he wanted to rest there, but he found himself jumping up.

"Righto."

Mary linked her arm in his, and they went past the chairs. She smiled and called to the others.

"Good-by, Mrs. Hawkins—so long, Cecil—better luck!"

Unspeaking they went from the court until they rounded the fringe of conifers. Then, suddenly, she drew him into the thicket, and danced a war-dance. She jigged in a kind of ecstasy and peered through the bushes.

"Oh, boy! Did we trim them! After dropping the first set; then pulling up—4-6, 7-5, 6-2. Look at Old Lady Pieface Hawkins—wouldn't that sour smile etch a piece of copper. She knows Cecil never will beat me singles, and she'd have had a pup if she'd beat me even in doubles."

Prentiss stared in amazement at the girl, gloating. It was some silly rivalry—the girls always meeting in the finals of the state championships and Mary always winning.

"You shouldn't gloat," he reproved, as if to a child. "It isn't sporting."

"Sporting? Was it sporting of her to pull in Jackson as her partner? Why, he's too good. That's all the old lady brought him up for—slipping him in as Cecil's partner so's they could give me a trimming. But it didn't work. Oh, partner, you were really fine. I could kiss you."

She turned to him, her face glowing. And then, suddenly and unreasonably, in the seclusion of the shrubbery, he found himself flooded by a sensation he hadn't experienced for years—the sense of the nearness of a woman. As if a transparent curtain had rolled up, he became instantly aware of her physical being. There was the brown warmth of her forearms and neck, the warm smell of perspiration, the scent of hair.

He was so amazed at his own response, so shocked at himself, that he reproved his own senses Puritanically. It was unthinkable...

"Well, we can shake hands," he said, stiffly.

Instead of dispelling the tension, his answer seemed only to communicate it to the young woman. Her face seemed to glow more warmly.

"Yes," she said.

She held out her hand and he shook it. She turned quickly and went past him to the path, and then waved.

"See you at the boathouse in five minutes," she said, and hurried away without waiting for him.

Prentiss went to his bungalow. In the lower drawer of the bureau he found swimming trunks—three pairs. He took a blue pair with white belt, and changed quickly. By the door of the bathroom he glanced into the full-length mirror, and there he halted. With satisfaction he noted that he was lean enough. Forty-three hadn't brought him a protruding midriff. His stomach still showed the ridge line of muscles—from crewrowing, twenty years ago.

He looked at his face. It was still unseamed—no pouches beneath the eyes. Only a slight crinkle line. His mustache had a few gray hairs. But then his mustache was lighter than his dark-brown hair, and in the bargain it was cropped Guardee fashion, and the gray hardly showed.

Suddenly he turned away with a feeling of such distaste as he might have had if he'd caught another man staring at himself in the looking glass. He felt a little—a little unclean.

He put on his robe and sandals, and went down the path to the boathouse. She was there on the dock, dabbling her feet in the water. Her white sharkskin bathing suit was almost blindingly white in the sun.

"Hello," he said, casually

"Hi," she said.

He sat beside her and they were silent. As if this were unbearable, she jumped up.

"I'll get the canoe," she said. "Let's paddle."

He got up to aid her, but she was pulling it along more dextrously than he could have done, and he was aware of it. She leaned down from the dock and held it for him. He stepped in, feeling the insecurity of the craft. Then she followed him and pushed off. He took the paddle. After all, he thought, it wasn't more fragile than a rowing shell.

He slipped the gown from his shoulders, and paddled, intently. He found that his eyes were focused on the breasts of Mary's bathing suit where the nipples showed in relief through the fabric. Quickly he looked up at the mountains.

"This is good fun," he said.

"Yes," she said. "But you'll get awful sunburned. You'd better pull over in the shade there—down by those willows."

He paddled over, and she caught the overhead branches and held the canoe steady. She looked at him in appraisal.

"My, your skin's white," she said, frankly.

He looked down at the blue-whiteness of his body. Somehow he felt a little ashamed. There was an unhealthy look to white skin—among all these dark-bronze Indian-like creatures—like the body of a snail pulled from its shell.

"Why, yes," he said. "You see, in England we don't have as much sun as you do. More rain—and fog, you know."

"I wouldn't like that," she said. "Of course, I'd like England, I think. We were going over, and then they had to start this war."

She spoke as if it were a personal irritation—something done just to spite her. A fringe of guilt touched his mind. That he should be lolling in a canoe on a lake, when back home there was war—it didn't seem right. She was speaking again.

"You know, you were awfully good on the court. You're a good player—you've got funny form, but you're a good player."

"I used to play quite a lot when I was young."

"Young? You're not old. I don't think anyone is old until—oh—until they're past forty."

"I've turned forty," he said.

"Oh. Why—you only look about thirty. You look awfully young. Just nicely sort of grown up, I mean. You know..."

"Well, thank you. I didn't feel awfully young on the court. In that first set I thought my lungs would burst."

"Oh, that's nothing," she assured him, quickly. "That's just the altitude. Didn't you know? You see, we're more than a mile high here. I don't notice it much, but lots of people, why, they can hardly walk up the front steps without resting to get their breath. But if you keep on, I always think it passes soon. That's what you did. You kept on, and afterwards it wasn't so bad. That's the British way, isn't it?"

"Oh, I don't know."

"I think it is. You British, you always keep at it. That's what I like about Englismen. They don't quit. Now, you kept on going, and we came back and outlasted them. Really we shouldn't have beat Jackson, not on tennis. But we did on guts. You were getting stronger and he was all pooped out."

She stretched her arms.

"Oh, it's nice here, isn't it?"

"Yes," he said. "It's too nice."

"Too nice?"

He assayed his own thoughts.

"You see, over home—there's a war on. One feels terribly guilty, lolling here, taking things easy."

"Well, somebody has to come over here and buy supplies," she said, complacently. "And since you've got to wait, you might as well wait comfortably here as in that smelly hotel. I hate it."

"That's true, I suppose," he smiled.

She looked up at her hand and arm, holding to the green translucence of the overhead willows. Then she dropped her head and looked at him from under her eyelashes.

"You know," she said. "You're an awfully good sport."

"Am I? What about?"

"Oh, you are. I can always tell. So, I'm going to tell you something. You're trying to get a contract or something from Uncle Mickey, aren't you?"

"Well, we're discussing..."

"I know. It's all supposed to be quiet, I imagine. But that's what you'd be here for. Well, you're a good sport, so I'll tell you something. You want to get a good contract, don't you?"

"Not for me—for my Government, of course."

"I know, but if you got a good contract for your Government, that would help you—and help your reputation."

He stared at the girl, trying to adjust his mind to her utterly realistic way of looking at his life.

"The contract's the primary thing,' he said, stiffly. "My personal part in it is incidental."

"I know. That's the British way of putting it. But all the same, no matter what, it's because—well—because I like you that I'll tell you."

She looked about as if for eavesdroppers, and then bent forward.

"If you want a good contract, just don't try to hurry Uncle Mickey. If you try to hurry him, he gets hard to deal with—in everything. Just don't bring it up. All you do, is stay here, and every chance you get—tell him how wonderful you think it is on the ranch—and how much you like the West.

"Tell him you don't like the East, but if you had your way, you'd live the rest of your life out West. Tell him you'd even leave England, perhaps—although with regret. Tell him England and this part of the country are just alike, and you love them both..."

"But, my dear young lady, I could'nt do that. I've already told him the ranch is magnificent. And it is."

"Well, that's fine. Now he likes you—or he wouldn't ask you up here, not to stay. You're all right if you told him you like it here—and said it really convincingly. Because—you know what?"

"What?"

"He's funny about this place—my great-aunt Mary—I'm named after her—well, she designed it, see? And if anybody says anything about it!

"Once he heard someone laugh about the glassed porch. And he was so mad. And sometimes—well, I'll tell you. Sometimes when people are coming up here—even big businessmen and so on—he sometimes puts on blue jeans and an old hat and shirt, and goes puttering round like he's a workman, and listens to what they say. And if anybody says anything about Aunt Mary's ranch house he doesn't like—well, when they get back to the guest house, their bags are all packed and there's a note telling them the chauffeur's waiting with the car."

"No, you're making it up."

"All right. But all the same, if you want a good contract, you just stay here as if you never wanted to leave, and don't hurry him, and first he'll give you a hat and then, when he gets round to it, he'll give you a business deal you couldn't pry of him any other way."

"A hat?"

"Yes—when he likes anyone, he gives them a Stetson—a ten-gallon one!"

Prentiss stared at the young woman. Sometimes she was

so wrapped in dignity, and then, oddly, she often became so absurdly childish in her ways. He smiled to himself.

"I thank you, at any rate, for trying to help me."

"That's all right," she said. "That's because I like you."

She said it so openly that he found nothing to do except to smile in what he hoped was an avuncular manner—the adult to the child.

Just as he was beginning to suspect that the smile might look more fatuous than avuncular, she pulled the branches and sent the canoe out into the open water. She began snapping on a white bathing cap. She buttoned the strap under her chin, and became a white-helmeted Indian.

"Swim," she said.

She rolled overboard and began swimming away, leaving him sitting in the canoe, undecided as to what to do.

He paddled the canoe slowly after her. Her arms were going in the crooked uplift of the crawl. Behind her the beating feet left a trail like the wake of a ship. It was machine-perfect swimming. Like everything else—standardized and mass-produced.

And yet—yet he was aware of the comparative ineffectiveness of his own old-fashioned trudgeon stroke. He decided not to swim—just to paddle the canoe after her.

CHAPTER XVIII

THE South Coast of England had never had such fine weather. The weather stayed fine and the mid-August sun shone and the clouds seemed very high up in the air.

In that fine weather the German planes came over the Channel by day and by night. But by day the R.A.F. was going up in Hurricanes and Spitfires and knocking them down at four to one—getting nearly a hundred a day that week.

People looking up to that rare sky, seeing the dogfights on the coast, began to grow confident. They began to think of the R.A.F. pilots as young demigods, who joyfully charged up into a Valhalla of blue, gladly calling "Tally-ho" to each other through their microphones when they sighted squadrons two, three, four times their own number.

People were proud and got confidence back. If that was all war was—gay adventure for young men far up in the sky—then war wasn't so bad. The sky was vast and remote, and the land was never so fair-faced as in this glorious weather.

Only the old soldiers hated the weather and thought of invasion and what might come when the enemy organized his bases twenty miles away. And they grew to hate the sunshine and longed for fog, rain, bad weather. For they knew from the last war what bad weather could do to an offensive. They knew what it could do to stop horses and men and machines.

They remembered mud in Flanders, and how the passage of a single division could so churn up a road that caissons and guns and limbers and trucks would start sinking in the ooze. They remembered how, in those days, men even muddier than the machines would pry and sweat and swear one whole day just to get a truck from a ditch onto the *pavé*. Cars were bad. Trucks worse. Horses—they were the worst of all, somehow worse than men.

For you soon got used to seeing humans in gray uniforms dead, and humans in khaki uniforms dead, and learned to pass them with no feeling about death and no curiosity about what the men had been—unless it was to go through the pockets. For they might have something—some possession—that could no longer serve them, being dead, but might well serve the living.

That way you felt about dead humans; but it did not seem fair that horses should die, and so you fought harder to save them. The horses would plunge and struggle in the mud. The men would pry under their bellies with timbers, and shout and lash and spur them. The animals would leap and bucket in strange spurts of energy. Then, suddenly, they would stop.

After that you knew no shouting, no lashing, no spurring, would make them move any more. They had given up. They would rest there, their bellies going deeper in the mud. Their eyes would be softly calm then, for they had made a peace with war and mankind.

When they got like that, nothing was any use. The man who had driven them, who had groomed them and polished their harness for the divisional transport horse shows, would keep going around to the other men, asking them to get shovels and try digging them out. But everyone knew it was no use and finally someone always took his Lee-Enfield and shot them. Sometimes the driver would beg for help until only the neck and head of the horse showed above the mud and he would hold on to the bridle, holding the head high to prevent the horse from drowning; but in the end it was the same. Someone always shot those horses.

They were better off that way—far better off than men

who got into the mud. Better off than the men who got hit in pushes like Passchendaele, where if you fell off the duckboards you began drowning in mud.

That's why the Passchendaele push was made with such "a remarkably low figure of wounded." The wounded didn't live.

The first waves went in carrying slatted wooden duckboards to lay down in the mud, and if a man got hit and fell off the duckboards, he just drowned slowly in the mud and never got to a dressing station.

Or sometimes the wounded got off the duckboards of their own accord. The Canadian Colonel who was hit mortally saw the men piling up behind him, waiting to get past. So he said to the major: "Shove me over and take 'em past. We can't hold up the whole bloody regiment for one man." So they rolled him off and he drowned in the mud, too, watching his regiment go by.

Afterwards those things sound impossible, or they sound artificial and bad; but at the time they were real and hard and brave. For no man wants to die, especially slowly in mud that grips like a thousand suction cups. Yet that was the way they died, knowing the stretcher-bearers couldn't get them back down the duckwalks without holding up the whole advance.

So in a way, the horses were better off. You could shoot the horses; but it tears the intestines out of you to shoot your own wounded. You can talk of it easily, or read it easily in a story; but when it comes to doing it, you know you are cursed and are doing something that you are going to remember every night as you go to sleep or at inexplicable moments: as you lift a glass to say "Cheer-oh" to someone, or as you stand in a crowded elevator, or as you open your mouth at a party to say "Double two spades." All the rest of your life—if you are lucky enough to get out and have any more life.

So if you possibly could, you did something easier and simpler and more cowardly. You would turn your head the other way.

That's the way you did it if you could. You went on, turning your head so that you could pretend you didn't see them. And you would pretend you couldn't hear them.

But you could hear them. They would call: "Chum! Chum! Hey—please! Please, chum! For Christ's sake—please!"

You would go on just exactly the same as you do in a city when a begger tries to stop you and you don't want to argue with him or give in to him. You would go on, merely saying to yourself that it would all be the same in the end. Death would get everyone sooner or later. Even if the war did end, death would come some time—a few more years. So you couldn't really help them.

But you wished to hell they would die and get it over with and not linger there to put any more mental strain on you. You had enough to do as it was; fighting in the war and trying to keep alive. You wished to hell all men had the decency to drown quickly in the mud and stop calling. Because, in the end, it would all be the same.

That was the way it was in a bad weather push, and the old soldiers who came out alive, to live among civilians and yet be forever shut apart from them, remembered it.

And so, when people felt that the war was a sad thing, but after all, far away, and said: "But a least, we've got beautiful weather," the old soldiers would say inside themselves: "Oh, Christ—they don't know what they're going to be in for yet. They don't know! He's twenty miles away! If it would only rain—cats, dogs, and corruption! If it would only rain!"

But the weather stayed beautiful and the blessed gardens of England were never more perfect.

And there were only the youngsters of the R.A.F., going

up against triple their own force, to prove to the enemy that no matter what their leaders had been, the common man was not decadent or soft.

So while Britain was still re-arming, the R.A.F. shot German planes out of the sky from the Thames to Lands End and back again.

That was the way the invasion of England was stopped. The enemy was forced to think up new plans for softening Britain. But no one knew that then, and the R.A.F. kept on knocking him out of the faultless sky all along that aged, sleepy, green South Coast.

They lay on their backs on the cliff top, almost drugged with the warm sun, and only half-awake when the tiny sound, as of a far-off, slow rending of cloth came.

"It's funny, you hear so plainly—yet you can't see them," she said.

He did not open his eyes.

"Sound travels," he said. "Watch for when they bank. You'll see the sun glint on their wings."

They were quiet, until, with a quickly rising roar, a V-shaped flight of Hurricanes snarled low over the cliff, swung out over the sea, and moved in a great climbing arc.

"It's magnificent—what they're doing," she said.

He laughed quickly.

"Well, isn't it? They're shooting them down four for one."

"I didn't say they're not, did I?"

"The way you laughed—you'd think we weren't. And we are."

"Are we?"

"The B.B.C. says so."

"Then we're doing fine."

"Well, what do you want us to do?"

"You figure it out," he said. "You figure it out. Now let's drop the war."

"You say something and then want to drop the subject. What on earth do you want us to do?"

"I'm not the general staff. Ask them."

"I ask you. Don't you think we're doing all we can?"

"No," he said. "I don't. We're not even awake. We're running around gabbling in a nightmare. We're still doing what we've been doing for years—hoping something will happen that will let us forget the whole business and go back to the comfortable way we were.

"We're hoping the French will revolt and fight again. We're hoping Jerry will let the war sink into stagnation so that we can settle down to a nice war of attrition where no one suffers much—except the poorer classes of people who usually develop malnutrition and kindred resultant diseases from blockades. But they usually develop them during peace conditions, too, so they should be quite used to it and content about it.

"Or we're hoping the Germans will run short of petrol—or that they'll read in history books that the British Isles really mustn't be attacked or invaded. Or we're hoping Hitler will fall and break his neck—or get assassinated by someone—or die of apoplexy—or eat a can of bad meat and die of ptomaine, or pick some toadstools instead of mushrooms..."

"Don't be silly."

"It's true. It's true. For years the British Government has been a Micawber Government—hoping—oh, hoping so badly—that something would turn up to stop Hitler. That's been our policy. And nothing has turned up. It won't turn up. I don't know where our country's going, but Hitler's people know where he's going. Because he's written it in a book for them—and us to read. He always said where he's going and he's on his way. God bless the Micawbers of Britain, he's on his way."

"Why do you talk like that?"

"Why not? You asked me. I told you."

She did not answer. For a long time they lay, staring up, feeling they were as far apart as the expanse of sky. Then she said, softly:

"Clive."

"Yes?"

"Don't you think Churchill is good?"

"Yes. He's good. That's why they've kept him out of power for all these years. But I don't think he can pull us through now, until all the others understand."

"What others?"

"The Cabinet and the staff. Our military staff has no more idea of what it's about than you, my innocent young woman."

"Our staff doesn't know anything about it—but you—you do?"

"Alright, I do."

"You know more than our general staff?"

"Strangely enough, I do."

He rolled over and shook his finger at her.

"Come right down to it, I do! And I'll tell you why. It's because Hitler's a guttersnipe. And we've got a Government and a general staff that was educated at Eton and Sandhurst—and they're still thinking in terms of 'Sporting, old man!' and 'That's not cricket, what?' Well, Hitler isn't interested in sport or cricket. It isn't even a question of a war as our generals and statesmen have been bred to conceive it. It's a world idea. And it's a guttersnipe's world idea. And our jolly old gentry will never understand it, nor even realize it—until he teaches them. And I don't know what the lesson will be—but I do know that lesson will be paid for by thousands of our lives.

"Yes. I have a better chance of understanding Hitler than all your blue bloods in the world. I ought to, because I'm what they're not. I'm a guttersnipe myself."

"Clive!"

"Well, I am. I'm one of the lower classes, you know. You pointed that out to me."

"I didn't say you were."

"You did, the day before yesterday."

"Well, I don't keep bringing it up. You do. It's an obsession with you. Why is it?"

He did not answer. She put her hand to his face.

"Clive. You've got a sort of a complex about it. And you shouldn't have. No matter how you were born, you've risen above it—made yourself into something—fought your way up. Why, you're educated—far more truly educated than thousands of men and women who've been to universities and colleges. A man can rise above his background."

"How nice," he said. "You say it just like a Victorian novel. Rising above my background—and how decent you're being to admit it. The assets of democracy. I hate my own petty attitude in having brought the matter up—and I hate more your smug attitude in trying to put it down."

She drew in her breath.

"You know," she said, tensely, "I often wonder why I came here with you. Why, of all the people in the world, it should be you that I picked."

"You know why," he said.

"No, I swear I don't. Or I do—and that's it. That's what we came for. That's the only real contact we have—getting into bed together. That's all the good I am."

"Oh, for Christ's sake," he said.

He stared down at the ground, but she was silent so long, and sat so still, that at last he looked up, and saw she was crying. All he felt was surprise that a face, normally so beautiful, should become so ugly and contorted by tears. He looked down at the ground so that he should not see.

"Why?" she said. "Why? You mustn't do it. We mustn't do it. I know you're not torturing me—it's hitting at yourself through me. When we don't do this, we're so happy."

"Well," he said. "It's our last afternoon. Let's go down and eat and get packed up—and tomorrow it'll be over."

He held out his hand to her without looking at her, and they went down from the cliff toward the town.

Afterwards, in Mine Host's, he looked at her suddenly and put out his hand.

"Prue," he said. "It's no use talking about it. But..."

"I know," she said. "Don't talk. I know. It was just that I wanted it to be nice—our last afternoon together.."

He got up impulsively, and went to her. He cupped her face in his hands and bent and kissed her.

"You're sweet," he said.

"No. I'm all ugly. Wait until I fix my face."

He watched her dabbing with the powder, bowing her head and turning it from side to side as a woman does when trying to see herself in a tiny compact mirror. When she was done, she looked up and smiled.

"Now I feel better," she said. "Am I all right?"

He stood with his back to the fireplace and cocked his head on one side.

"You're beautiful," he said.

"No, I'm not."

"Listen, That's one thing I don't lie about. To me, you look beautiful. Very beautiful, in fact. Really, don't you think you're beautiful? I mean—can't you see it?"

"No," she said. "I only know that my face is my face,

and I'm not entirely satisfied with it. Of course, I know I'm not ugly—you can tell—what people say and—and the way men look."

"That's so," he said. "I wish he'd hurry the dinner."

He teetered on his toes by the fireplace.

"It's nice here," she said. "Do you know, we never argue here?"

"We don't argue," he said. "Only when we talk war. Let's not mention it again for the rest of the time."

"All right," she said. "But there's so little time. Only about twelve more hours."

"It went fast," he said. "What'll you do, Prue—with the rest of your leave?"

"Oh, go home and spend it with the family."

"Well, we could go up on the same train."

"Where are you meeting Monty?"

"Oh—a pub we know. The Britannia."

"We could take the same train. I ought to be back in uniform for my grand entry home again."

"Change in the train again."

"Go in a civilian, come out one of His Majesty's forces."

"That's right."

"How about you? You know, I've never seen you in uniform. You'd be so handsome."

"Terrific!"

"You would."

"You should hear the dainty patter of my ammunition boots."

He stretched himself.

"O, hell," he said. "In a way, I wish I hadn't promised Monty—but he's a great chap, and I couldn't let him down."

"Of course not."

"Look, couldn't I call you up in London—we could get together."

"I don't know. If I got home, the family would grab me, and I'd never have a minute."

"Oh, I see."

"Please, now don't start anything, darling. I just meant that—it isn't I wouldn't be glad to see you, but families are the devil. They'd arrange for every minute of my time."

"How many in your family?"

"Just me—father, mother, me."

"I see. Oh, well, at that you'll have a better time with them than you would here with me."

"I never want to quarrel with you, darling. And really, truly, you don't want to quarrel with me, do you?"

He stood by the fire, his face blank. Then, slowly, he passed his hand over his face.

"What is it?" she said. "What's the matter?"

He looked at her in astonishment.

"Nothing," he said. "I just said, we won't quarrel any more. That's all."

CHAPTER XIX

IRIS CATHAWAY looked from the cottage window at the rolling Somerset land. The evening light was gathering under the pendulous branches of the apple orchard beyond the quiet lane.

Suddenly, perhaps because of some influence of the dying day, she felt weak, hopeless. There was no one to lean on. She felt the world was unfair to her.

She heard Mills come in. The woman must have sensed her mood. She spoke less crisply than usual.

"It's nothing to worry about, ma'am. Probably only the excitement of moving. A single degree of fluctuation in temperature in a child is nothing."

Iris looked up at Mills, knowing what she would see rather than seeing it. The nurse was the tall, rawboned, toothy type—angular and efficient and seemingly cold.

"I wonder if it's good for them here," she said.

"It's perfectly healthy, if that's what you mean."

Mills said it primly.

"You don't like it here, do you?" Iris said.

"It's all right, ma'am. But it certainly is better than Leaford. Everything there was—so deserted."

As if she had committed herself too much, Mills stalked back to the children's room. Iris sat in the dimming light, and was slowly re-enveloped by her mood. She felt dreadfully lonely. She pitied herself in her loneliness, and sought justification for it.

She sat, unmoving in the chair, recounting to herself the myriad minute justifications of the case—the little incidents marching back over the last three years. It was as if she were arguing a case at law.

The slowly mounting bits of grievances against Hamish began to fit into a pattern. She began to feel warm and satisfied again. The pattern of her own grievances wrapped about her like a shawl and she found comfort in them, and rested in them as before a fire.

Suddenly she started. But—suppose a court gave him the children! She made a sound of exasperation. The thought had destroyed the warm satisfaction her own arguments had given her. She sat in thought a long time, wrinkling her brow. Then she rose. With many sounds of exasperation she lit the old-fashioned oil lamp. She got paper and pen from the leather writing set in her bedroom, and began writing:

Dear Prentiss:

How do you like America, and how do you do with the Yankees? Things are dull here. As you see, I am now in Somerset with the children.

I wonder if you could tell me about things in the United States. Is it livable there? Is the climate as severe as reputed? One hears constantly of floods, cyclones, hurricanes, earthquakes, and so on. Yet newspapers constantly exaggerate most things—so why not these?

I might, if I can, run across there with the children. It would be safe for the duration. There have been desultory bombings here—the papers say mostly in open fields. If one can believe newspapers. I hardly think there will be much more than that, and if so, it seems logical that it will be on military objectives. That is why I am here. There are no places of military importance near by. But really it is quite ghastly—the cottage is most primitive—and you've no idea how people in these quieter rural districts have taken advantage of the situation with regard to rents. One feels fortunate in getting even such a primitive place as this. In fact, I write this by light of an oil lamp.

At all events, let me hear from you. I suppose Clipper service will get this across fairly promptly.

My best to you.

—Iris

She sat back and stared through the patch of light. She felt better satisfied now.

At least, it was a feeler. An iron in the fire. There were so many reasons why America sounded good. It was safe —for the children. And then—if anything *did* happen between her and Hamish—if by any chance it should—the children would be safe in another sense. She had always heard that the British law was so unfairly prejudiced in favor of the father in cases concerning children.

But in America—that built a set of entirely new circumstances.

Not, of course, that she was going to America to get the children beyond Hamish's legal control. It was for their safety—but if the other matter did come up ...

She took up her letter again and added a postscript:

P.S.—Tell me all about America. What it's like. I would like to see it for myself, and now seems like a good time. Could you help get me over there now?

She re-read the letter and then added:

The children, too, of course.

CHAPTER XX

He lay in the bed, watching her move about the room.

"You really ought to get up, darling," Prudence said. "Or *we'll* miss the train, and *you'll* miss your date with Monty."

He put his hands behind his head.

"No, we won't. There's no hurry."

"I'm almost dressed."

"So I see."

She went to the window, and looked out.

"It's a beautiful day. Do men like to watch women?"

"I'm not watching women. I'm watching you."

"Why do you watch me? That's what I don't understand."

"You charm my eye. You're pretty—and very beautifully built."

"Thank you. You feel happy this morning, don't you?"

She sat on the bed.

"You know," she said. "I suppose that's been said so many times before. As long as life has gone on. Millions of years. Millions of times. The same speech: 'You're very pretty,' and so on."

"But each time it sounds all right. You like to hear it, don't you?"

"Of course. But when you think how long it's been going on, it makes you feel a bit insignificant."

"Thinking of eternity always does. Eternity and a Stuka bomb are two things that shrink the ego."

"But going on so many ages—millions of years."

"Yes, sex is pretty old—it keeps on happening. Maybe the first words ever spoken were: 'Will you?'"

"No, probably they didn't ask. They just—well, it began."

"Cave man stuff. All right. The same thing without trimmings."

She sat a moment, and then jumped up.

"Do get up. We're late now."

He stretched his arms and lay comfortably. She sat inspecting a stocking.

"Clive."

"Yes?"

"You said I was beautifully built."

"You are. You want to hear it again?"

"It isn't that. How do you know?"

"Anyone can see it."

"Yes, but how do *you* know. You have to have—well, a basis of comparison."

"What you're trying to find out is: how many other women I've seen *au naturel*?"

"Well, more or less. That's putting it baldly but very nicely."

"Baldly is correct."

"Well?"

"Well, what?"

"Oh, don't be difficult. You know—have you seen a lot of women—to know?"

"Hundreds."

"Hundreds! Isn't that a lot?"

"No."

"But wouldn't it be rather wearisome?"

"Perhaps so."

"I should think so. And it must have taken so much time."

"No."

"Well, it must—hundreds..."

"It serves you right. I saw them on the stage, in choruses,

in the cinema. That's one thing about cinema. You can always count on either the girl taking a bath during the story for the masculine trade—or the hero taking a shower to give the girl fans a thrill. But just see what that's done to mass standards. Set new levels to aim at. In the old days a man had to work on rather small personal experience. Now everyone knows what all Hollywood looks like in a nightie or less. And see what that does! In old days, a man was content with what he had. He might get a girl with a shape like a sack of sawdust tied in the middle, and accept her as Aphrodite. Now he knows different. He measures her up to the standards of the screen sirens. Thus the whole standard of feminine form is raised."

"You talked out of that nicely."

"Oh, do you want details? Did I ever tell you about the seraglio I was in—in Marseilles?"

"You've never been to Marseilles."

"What'll you bet?"

"Did you see anyone—nicer than me?"

"Not a one. You're Venus, Galatea, Lady Godiva, Sappho..."

"How nice. Just why am I—beautifully built?"

"Well, you're pretty sound in the pelvis yet you're not fat in the rump, and your legs are slim, and your thighs aren't cushioned with lard, and you don't have pneumatic tires on your stomach, and your muscles aren't broken on your breasts—although they're a little on the teacup size—but the nipples are nicely placed in the rosettes and..."

"Please. I'm embarrassed. You can't have noticed all that."

"It is a bit embarrassing, isn't it. Yet it's silly that it should be."

"I'll try and get used to the idea. Tell me some more."

"No, that's enough before breakfast."

"Look, darling. You must get up. We'll never catch

the ten o'clock if you don't. We've only twenty-five minutes."

"If we miss it we miss it. I've got to bathe yet."

"That'll take you hours."

"Well, it's a half-hour route march to the bathroom. And half-hour back..."

"But you'll look so pretty in your new dressing gown."

"Pretty! You don't say a man looks pretty. You say he's handsome, manly, dashing, virile, appealing, masculine, well-tubbed, well-groomed, curried or mucked out. But *not* pretty. Maybe I'm devastating, or godlike..."

"You're all of them, darling, except your legs. If you'll only..."

"Then I'll stay in bed."

"No, darling. Even your legs are handsome. Here's your gown. I'll order breakfast for when you come back."

The sun was striking hard down on the napery and silver when he came back. He stood at the door, looking at the way the refracted and reflected lights burnished her face in the shade. She lifted the teapot and smiled. Without speaking he went and sat by the table at the window. Because he was silent she said:

"You must get your hair cut, darling."

"You won't be seeing it," he said. "It's short enough."

She ignored the first part of what he'd said.

"Yes, but just at the back," she said, quickly. "It should be clean there—because you've a very nice back to your neck."

"I'll try to keep it toward you, then. How's that?"

"No. Do eat. We've missed the first train now."

"Then why hurry?"

"Oh," she said. "Because—I like to get unpleasant things done when you have to do them."

He put down his cup.

"You mean that, don't you?"

"Of course," she said.

He held his cup and stared down from his window at the dancing sun spots on the sea.

"We've lot's of time," he said.

"Well, let's get something definite. What time do you have to meet your friend?"

"Monty? Oh, some time."

"Don't be exasperating, Clive. What time?"

"Oh, no time. I just said I'd drop in the Britannia threeish. But he'll be around and wait if I'm not there."

"But we'll miss the eleven, too, Clive. And the next good one is after two. That won't get you there in time and..."

"Then I'll telegraph him and say I'll be late. Now is that all right?"

"That would be better, I suppose."

"All right, then. Now I'll get dressed, and if we make the eleven o'clock train, all right. And if we don't—I'll telegraph."

"All right, eat your breakfast and hurry."

The clerk looked over the desk in a minor panic.

"I'll have it done in a moment, sir," he said.

"But we're trying to catch a train," Prudence said.

"Yes, ma'am."

"I told you last night we'd be leaving this morning," Clive said.

The clerk put down his pen.

"Mr. Briggs," he said. "Every night since you've been here, you've come and told me you were leaving in the morning. And every morning you've ignored what you've told me. And every time I've had the statement prepared and ready. Until this time. One cannot cry wolf all the time, Mr. Briggs! Not all the time!"

Prudence and Clive stared at the little man. It was as if all the resentment in his soul had erupted and colored the tone of his voice. Yet his outburst was unexpected—as if a caterpillar had started to lead a revolt.

Clive began to laugh; but Prudence stopped.

"You shouldn't laugh," she said. She turned to the clerk. "You're perfectly right. And we're sorry. Now we can't catch the train, so we'll go out and take luncheon, and then come back for the statement and catch a later train."

The clerk looked at her tearfully.

"I'm sorry I spoke like that, madam, but you understand how..."

"Of course," she said.

She pulled Clive's arm.

"You shouldn't laugh," she said, as they went out into the sunlight. "I suppose we've driven him mad."

Clive did not answer. He walked along, laughing. She shook his arm angrily, and then she laughed, too.

At Mine Host's they sat in the booth.

"Shouldn't we order lunch?" she said.

"We just had lunch."

"That was breakfast, darling."

"It was so late it felt like lunch. I'm not hungry—unless you are."

"I'm not hungry either."

"Let's just have another drink, then," he said.

"I haven't started this one yet."

"Then let's start conversation. Did you know conversation was a lost art? Answer quickly."

She bowed her head and traced with her forefinger on the dampness outside her glass.

"Come on," he said. "That's easy. You should say: ,Who lost it and where?'"

"Should I?"

"Oh, yes. Then I tell you it's a lost art—like tempering bronze and cutting stone with obsidian and constructing dew ponds and building Stonehenge and why."

She did not answer.

"Come on," he said. "Can't you even make conversation about making conversation?"

She looked up quickly.

"You see, you *are* educated, Clive. You know so much. How did you learn all that if you have no formal education?"

"Miraculous faculty for absorbing useless information—Tit-Bits, Comic Cuts—read everything."

She looked up through the window beside her. She lifted her hand and ran a knuckle round the whorl in the old glass.

"I suppose you know how they got these things in old glass, too," she said.

"I have an idea. They didn't mean to get them in. Just happened when they poured it. They didn't know how to roll panes then. I suppose that's it."

She nodded her head.

"How many more days have you, Clive?"

"I don't count them."

"Of course you do."

"You know—five more. To-morrow, Thursday, Friday, Saturday, Sunday."

"It went fast, didn't it?"

"It flew."

She was quiet and he looked at her suddenly. Then he reached out and took her hand.

"Look here, Prue—you're not sorry? Sorry you came?"

"No," she said. "You know that. I'm glad it happened."

"All but for my temper. What I mean to say is—I'm sorry I quarreled. You didn't mind much, did you?"

"It wasn't anything, really. We got over it. Why, we

haven't quarreled all day today. People have—have to make adjustments."

"I should have been a bit more of an adjuster."

"Do you think it was because we were getting more used to each other? Do you think people grow closer, and then finally don't quarrel at all?"

"That may be true."

She looked through the window.

"Another beautiful day," she said. "A very nice day. Very, *very* nice..."

He thumped his glass, as if angry.

"Come on, drink up."

"I feel a bit squiffy now."

"All right. We can't have you arriving home rolling in the lee scuppers."

"Why always lee scuppers? Running with blood. What's wrong with the windward scuppers?"

"They're uphill—must be. Everything rolls into the lee scuppers."

"Of course—how simple. Look, Clive, we ought to start. We've got to get back to the hotel and get the luggage.."

"No hurry."

"But I detest being late at trains. I always like to have time."

"Oh, hell," he said. "I wish I hadn't promised Old Monty. But he's such a real chap—I'd hate to let him down."

"I understand—of course you couldn't."

"If I hadn't promised, by God, I wouldn't go for anything, Prue. You know that. I'm not cutting away because —because I'm tired of it."

"I know that, darling. You've got to go out and have fun with men. You've only five more days and then..."

He sat looking at his hands. Then he lifted his eyes to her face. She turned away and looked from the window.

"Oh, Christ," he said.

He thumped the table and got up.

"I'll go telegraph Monty I'll be late."

She sat by the window, feeling the minutes tick away. She finished her drink, and sat, rocking her head slightly as if in answer to some induced rhythm. Then she heard him coming. She looked up at his face. He was grinning.

"Now, all fixed," he said. "Uncle fix everything. We've time for lunch."

"Well, what train will we take?"

"None. We're not going."

She shook her head, slowly.

"But—Monty?"

He waved his hand.

"Oh, that's all right. I sent him a telegram saying I was unavoidably detained—that's the correct phrase. But if he felt like it, he could run down here for a binge. You'll like Monty. Aren't you glad?"

She put her hand to her throat, in a halting gesture.

"You really want to stay?"

"What the hell do you think I did it for?"

She swallowed and smiled.

"You're an idiot, darling."

"That's right," he said. "I am, aren't I? But all the same we stay."

"But you've a wonderful mind, too."

"Of course I have. The executive type of mind. Solve things—pop—like that. The thousand-pound-a-year mind. I wanted to stay—bang, like that! The answer came. Stay. You wanted to stay, too, didn't you?"

"Of course I did."

"Then why the hell didn't you say so?"

"A woman can't be—be forward. I thought you might be fed up."

"Well, isn't it the same for a man? I thought you might be fed up."

"I'm not, darling."

"Give me a kiss, then."

"Right here?"

"Well, if a man can't kiss his own wife in a pub..."

He felt the awkwardness of his words.

"Well, as far as anyone else here is concerned, you're my wife," he said.

She held up her face. He rose and bent over the table. When he sat down again, she shook her head.

"You know," she said, "it's unbelievable."

"My kisses?"

"Oh, they're unbelievable, too. But I mean this town, this place, this window, this table, you, me, us being here. Five days ago—none of it existed. Ten days ago you didn't exist. Then nine days and fourteen hours and about thirty minutes ago a very stuffy male voice said: 'Shall we go to the concert; or would you rather walk?' And you were born."

"Was I stuffy?"

"Oh, very. I hated you."

"I'm sorry."

"Oh, no. It wasn't your fault. Only—it's hard to remember it's true. Everything's unbelievable."

"I get that feeling, too, sometimes. All is imagination! What was it the man said? Some day I shall revenge myself on my enemies—I shall kill myself, and thus end the world for all of them."

"Perhaps it's wartime that does it," she said. "There's so little—so little time... oh, let's have lunch."

"I'll get Mine Host," he said.

It was only afterwards, when they came down from the cliff top in the darkening evening, that they remembered the clerk in the hotel. They stood on the Esplanade and looked at the ornate stone front of the Channel Hotel with the acanthus-leaved panels, and the twin potted palms by the door.

"Oh, that poor little man," she said. "He'll have an attack of apoplexy."

"We could get our bags and move out—and go to another hotel."

"That's cowardice."

He stood, looking at the building.

"Up the rebels," he said, finally. "Here we go."

They came into the lobby. The assistant manager jumped into a sort of electrified activity, as if that would erase his tardiness of the morning. He nodded his head, and spoke.

"Your statement is all ready, Mr. Briggs!"

He saw them halt, stare at him, and then, as if by a single signal, turn in laughter and run to the stairs.

"Well," he breathed to himself. "Well!"

There was nothing else for him to say. The holiday world had been torn so completely from its age-long routine that he now lived as if in a dream. If the town could be so empty in such beautiful weather—well then, anything —really anything—could happen.

Nothing would ever be real any more.

CHAPTER XXI

"At a steak fry," Lachran had boasted, "you eat steak. You're in the cattle country now."

It had sounded absurd, childishly flamboyant. And yet it was happening. Prentiss Saintby looked over the electrically lit glen. Beef! Nothing but beef! People at the long tables eating it as if it were a regional rite. No potatoes, no vegetables. Just slabs of beef.

Lachran himself, in a white apron and chef's cap, was flipping it happily onto an outdoor grill.

That was the boastful side of the American nature, Prentiss thought. The side that was so hard for a Briton to understand. The Americans were constantly springing to exaggeration to remind themselves of what they were—while the Briton constantly turned to depreciation lest he should be guilty of reminding anyone of what he assumed everyone knew he was.

There was the cult of more and bigger here, always as a sort of reminder. A man put six telephones on his desk to remind himself that he was a busy executive; they built bigger and better skyscrapers to remind themselves that they were now a bigger and better nation; they ate nothing but beef to remind themselves that they were in one of the beef-wealthiest spots on earth. The rich constantly did absurd and crudely magnificent things to remind themselves that they really were no longer poor.

Yet back of it there seemed to be a fear. There was too much fear in America. No one took anything for granted. They were afraid it might not be true.

Even the cult of bigger and better was based on fear. All the advertisements in the land seemed based on some fear. If you don't use this dentrifice, you'll have black teeth, bad dispositions, floating waistlines, and you'll lose your job. If you don't buy insurance you'll be killed suddenly, leaving a pretty but helpless wife with four children and a mortgage company ready to take the home. If you don't use this, or eat that, or buy the other thing, you'll lose your social position, your health, your beauty, your life—you'll never be slim, or beautiful, or married, or popular.

That was the mass fear. The fear of the wealthy was—that the wealth wasn't true. Of course, back in the East where the wealthy families were older, they had more poise about it. But here, it seemed as if they must constantly remind themselves of their wealth by a flamboyant gesture. Hadn't learned how to take it for granted.

But taking for granted—there was a danger in that, too. You could see that in Britain. After all, one wanted to be fair. There was a sort of rude, crude, lusty honesty to this life—a sort of—of Elizabethan lustiness. That was it —Elizabethan.

Undoubtedly when the first great fortunes came rolling into England from the Spanish Main in Elizabeth's time, there had been the same silly, magnificent, flamboyant aspect to life—eating too much to show they had enough, drinking too much to show they could. A loud, wasteful generosity.

But had they feared as these men did?

Here, there was fear behind everything they said. Fear of the people, of their own Government. The violent hatred they voiced of "the goddam reds!" The utter depth of their antipathy to their own governmental regime. There was no political discussion. That was an important difference between England and America that he should remember. At home, he could walk into a pub and hear workmen putting up intelligent arguments for their political beliefs. Here there was only a chorus of empty phrasing. And there was no appeal through prides. Only through prejudices.

The way the wealthy spoke of Roosevelt, one would think that instead of being elected by popular and democratic majority vote, he had somehow stolen his office.

Prentiss left his thought abruptly. Lachran was advancing to him, a steak held on a long fork.

"Come on, eat up!"

"Thank you—I really couldn't. Not any more."

"You having a good time?"

"Oh, excellent."

"Now when you get back home, you can tell everyone you've been to a real American steak fry!"

Lachran was waving the fork happily. His face, under the great chef's cap, was purple with the exertions of his hospitality.

"When the King and Queen came over here," Lachran boomed, "I see where they gave 'em a hot dog roast! Hot dogs! Good God Almighty! Hot dogs! If they'd ha' come here, we'd ha' given them real man's food!"

A man clutched Lachran's shoulder.

"That was New Deal economy," he shrilled.

The people squealed in outrageous appreciation. Prentiss heard the high, strangulated laugh of a woman rising higher than the rest.

He backed away, but the man left Lachran's shoulder and clutched Prentiss's arm.

"You know, I don't think you should call Roosevelt a bastard," he said.

Prentiss drew himself up stiffly.

"I quite agree with you, sir," he said.

"No. Not unless you can't think of anything worse!"

The man bent over in laughter, and the ring of people screamed appreciatively.

Prentiss suddenly felt isolated and outrageously British. He was fearfully embarrassed. After all, it was their matter. He was an outsider and had no right to any opinion —or to express one.

Then, too, he had the deep British traditional respect for a man in office. After all, it was *the* President of the United States they were speaking of; the man holding the most august office in this country of more than one hundred million people. Yet they ...

Probably that was democracy—being free and equal. But it was something he'd never understand.

"Pardon me," he said, stiffly.

He squared his shoulders and pulled away from the group. Quickly he left the lighted glen. Then, in but a few yards, the world changed. Behind him the lights through the pines were but a glimmer. Here the world was in moon-touched dimness. One could even see the glittering white of the snow-capped peaks far away, hanging as if detached in the light-flooded air.

Only the howl and laughter in the glen behind him remained to challenge the austerity of the place. That woman's laugh, rising in high stridency, now sounded all the more vulgar. A profanation of something splendid— the sweep of this country with its cool-wine night air— more magnificent in some ways than the Scottish Highlands.

He turned by the lake, heading up the path to his cabin. It was then he saw a moon-halated splash of white down the dock. He paused.

"Hello, there," he said, inquiringly.

"Hi!"

It was Mary's voice. He walked along the planking slowly.

"Aren't you at the party?" he said.

"Yes, don't you see me there?"

Her voice was strangely petulant. He laughed a the emptiness of his own remark under analysis. He sat beside her.

"Don't you like it up there?" he asked.

She made a quick, explosive sound with her lips, and waved her hand as if brushing something away.

"We're not supposed to stick around," she said. "They get going on stories—and anyhow, we cramp Uncle Mickey's style when he gets wound up. He doesn't like us to hear."

"Oh, I see."

"Not that I haven't heard everything worth hearing," she said, quickly. "When we were kids, we used to creep up through the trees—me and Jim—my cousin. I've heard 'em all, anyhow. Pretty filthy most of it, if you ask me."

She kicked her legs disconsolately.

"You'd better be getting back," she said.

"Oh, not at all. I'd much rather stay here—if you don't mind."

She turned her head, abruptly.

"Do you really mean that?"

"I most certainly do."

She drew in a deep breath, as if suddenly happy. Then she straightened.

"I tell you what," she said, animatedly. "Let's me and you do something."

"Do something? But—er, what?"

"Oh—something. Look, we'll get a car and go to town. How's that?"

"Why—if it's all right."

"Of course it's all right. Come on."

She jumped up before he could move, and he followed her up the path to the garage.

"You stay here," she said, quietly. "I'll get a car."

He stood in the cold light, hearing the rumble of sliding doors. He saw the glow of light, and then, long after, the roar of an engine. The gravel spun beneath wheels and clattered tinily into the night. The headlights swept dazzlingly, and then she opened the door of a small truck.

"Hop in," she said.

Before he was in the seat, she slipped in the clutch, and the car jumped away. The door slammed itself in the leap. He held the catch of the door, staring out onto the road where the headlights fought against the wash of the moon. The car rocked slightly at the curves and the gravel slatted up under the mudguards. He glanced at Mary. The dash light underlit her handsome face. She drove with a sort of hard, nervous intensity.

"Steady there, girl," he said, almost involuntarily, as they rounded a curve.

"Don't worry," she said. "I know the roads."

He saw that she did not turn her head as she spoke.

"Aren't there speed limits?"

"We're still on our own roads—and nobody cares anyhow. Unless you have a smashup. I've been driving since I was six."

"Six!"

"Uh-huh! Me and Jim used to swipe the cars when we were young. Once we took the Mack truck. Uncle Mickey had a Mack up here for hauling and stuff. We came down here and got it stuck at the ford, and a flashflood came down. I wish you could see what it did to that truck. It took it three miles down the canyon, and buried it under a few tons of rock."

"But what did your uncle say?"

"Oh, he was hopping mad. Said we might have been killed, and if we ever got a car stuck in the ford again, he'd tan our hides. But right after that he got a bunch of contractors up and put the bridge in, so we don't ford the river any more. I used to like it. See, it's down here."

She swung the truck over the stone and concrete bridge, and then up the ledge road on the other side where a sheer face came down to the water. He clutched the door handle.

"Don't be scared," she said. "This is still our road, and there'll be nobody coming the other way."

The car raced along, climbing up the steep, narrow road. The chasm was splendidly rugged—like a setting for the *Walküre*, Prentiss thought. He turned his eyes back to the girl. And there was something splendid about her—a goddes of the machine—the dash light a temple lamp before her.

"There," she said.

The car was at the top.

"That wasn't bad for a light truck, was it? I wanted to get one of the cars, but they've taken all the keys out, so I had to take the pickup."

"Pickup?"

"Yes. This truck. It's what we call a pickup."

She swung the car from the road onto the open ground of the mesa, and headed back toward the canyon. Prentiss ground his teeth and pushed with his feet as if he would jam on a thousand invisible brakes. He reached for the door. At the last moment she put on the brake and the car halted at the rim of the gorge.

"Isn't that nice?" she said.

Prentiss swallowed.

"Yes," he said. "Really magnificent."

"I knew you'd like it. I like to sit here at night, and just look out!"

She threw off the lights, and immediately the tortured rock land below them came into moonlit relief. The sharp shadows cut the myriad flutings and outcroppings of the rock. It was hard to believe that the earth really contained places as impossibly wild and angular and immense as the scene before him.

"Wonderful," Prentiss said.

She lifted her arms lazily behind her head and stretched. Then she turned and looked at him.

"I like it here," she said.

As she spoke, at that moment, Prentiss again was swept by a flood of sexual awareness. Without turning his eyes he could see the girl completely — the golden-brown columns of her bare legs where the tiny dash light still shone on them; the almost Negro-black of her arms and face and throat in the moonlight.

One part of his mind was prompting him, urgently. It said: "Wake up. She has driven you here—for what?"

He turned as if on a challenge and looked at her. She turned her head, too, and looked at him frankly.

"You know," she said. "I like you!"

Even while he was surprised at his own temerity, he turned, and cradled her head. She kept her face upturned —waiting. He cupped her face and then kissed her full lips.

"You're beautiful," he said.

She smiled, slowly, as if buoyed by a satisfied and happy interior wisdom. She bowed her head and he sat upright again. Then she leaned forward to the ignition keys.

"Let's go to town," she said. "And we'll have a drink."

He pushed his hand over his brow. He was trying to read the meaning of what she had said.

"All right," he said.

He felt, somehow, like a swimmer who has just learned to swim, and who, feeling the first exciting tug of a river current, ins't sure whether he likes it or not.

She was backing the car. Then she raced over the open land, and onto the dirt track. The car sped, racing, down the long incline. He could smell, now, the scent of the dry flatlands—the rank odor of long-dried dust and sagebrush and baked air.

At first, as they went racing through the night, he felt strangely elated.

"She suggested it herself," a part of his mind said. "It won't be your fault, one way or another."

But as the sense of physical desire ebbed from him, this feeling was replaced. He began to feel trapped. He wished he had never come. Suppose she—she were—expert—in these matters? And he was not? So long ago, at the university, he hadn't been particularly expert that night. Things had been so terribly muddled. He had let himself be trapped.

"How—how far?" he shouted.

She smiled without turning her head.

"Forty miles. See the glow on the horizon? That's the town. I can do it in a half-hour."

He felt the absurdity of his position. The best thing to do was get out of it all. To-morrow—to-morrow he would see Lachran and demand a showdown and get the whole business over with.

He sat stiffly, fortifying this resolve, until the machine reached the town—first some shacks, then dark houses, then lonesome streets with nearly all the shop fronts dark. It was somehow ramshackle and yet had that mountain sense of cleanliness.

One lighted place glowed garishly in the night. He watched Mary nose the truck in toward the half-dozen cars by the curb and turn off the ignition.

"All right," she said, happily.

He followed her, wondering how often she had done this, how well she knew the route to take. He wondered just where she would lead him.

Then she turned by the dazzlingly lit window in the night street.

"Here it is," she said.

She opened the door. Prentiss following her in, stood in amazement.

Somehow he had pictured a den—a sort of Wild Western place where one sat at a pine table under the wooden balcony that led to the cubicles. And here...

Here was an antiseptic place alive with eye-smiting light, with white tile, with sanitary architecture, with noise. Even the magnified wail of a screechingly loud automatic music box was triumphantly defeated by that deafening noise of gabble. Youthful gabble. American youth again —too tall, too handsome, too well-fed. It was almost an abhorrent monotony of youthful handsomeness. Behind the counter similarly handsome young men and girls indistinguishable from the others except by their white caps and uniforms of starched snowiness, were lifting great beakers. It was an outrageous conglomeration of whiteness, noise, and that strange American vitality.

And he had thought...

Even before he could laugh, Mary was pulling him to two vacated stools at the counter. She manoeuvered him in ahead of a rush of youth from the other direction.

"Got 'em," she said, triumphantly. "My treat. Whitey! Whitey!"

A youth with his white forage cap set at an incredible angle on the back of his blond head looked over and grinned somehow austerely.

"Less noise from the ten-cent seats," he said.

He slid thick glasses along the tile counter, and then came over to them. His eyes swept Prentiss quickly.

"Hi, Mary," he said, affably. "What'll it be?"

"Jumbo malted frost," she said. "How about you, Mr. Saintby? A malted frost is awfully good."

"Oh, the same."

"Two, Whitey."

The youth swept away. With an incredible dexterity

he held glasses, flipped levers, ordered whirling machines to obey. It was a perfect, time-taught poetry of motion. The glasses seemed to flow from his hand along the counter and stop before them.

"Service," he said.

"Thanks," Mary told him.

He put his arms on the counter, and glanced again at Prentiss, quickly. Then he said:

"Your superman's in here."

"Oh, my gosh," she said. "Well, I can't help it."

She turned to Prentiss as Whitey moved away.

"Isn't this a snaky place?"

"Snaky?"

"Yes. Everything's snaky this year. Last year it was super."

"Oh, slang."

She nodded as she bent her head to the straws. Then she lifted it.

"Isn't this the best ten-cent drink?"

"Oh, decidedly."

Mary rocked her head to the drowned stridency of the music machine that not only played records, but sent out a sort of aurora borealis of strident lights from primary-colored panels of glass, where, in addition, awe-inspiring and endless bubbles of air rose through liquid-filled tubes.

"Artie Shaw," she said. "Do you like him?"

"I don't know him," he said, puzzled.

"Don't you get Artie Shaw in England? Do you like Ray Noble?"

"I don't know him, either."

"But Ray Noble—he's English!"

"Is he?"

"Of course. He's..."

She stopped abruptly.

"Uh-uh!" she said. "Here he comes."

She looked round quickly. Prentiss saw a wavy-haired young man edge gloomily beside her.

"Hi, Mary," he groaned, sadly.

"Hi, Joe College," she said, brightly. "This is Mr. Saintby—he's just over from England. Bill Southers!"

Prentiss felt that she said it with a curious possessiveness. The young man looked up, blankly.

"Hi," he said, tonelessly, and then moved away.

"Who's that poor young chap?" Prentiss said.

"Oh, him? He's just gloomy. Getting over a crush. Have another?"

"I'm afraid I couldn't."

"No, that's the trouble. They make such big ones. Check, Whitey!"

She edged from the stool as Prentiss took the slip of paper. He paid the cashier and they went back to the small truck with its square body and enclosed cab. She clicked on the switch, and backed away.

"Thanks—I was going to treat you," she said.

As they left the town, Prentiss felt suddenly happy. It had turned out very well, he told himself. It hadn't been what he expected—and thus he'd never had to put certain parts of him to—to a test. He was very relieved, on the whole, that it had turned out as it did.

He leaned back comfortably as the car went out over the flat, rising land. Mary flicked her eyes at him.

"That was an adequate drink, eh?"

"Yes," he said. "And very interesting."

"Interesting?"

"Yes. You know—seeing that part of America. I suppose that's America, too—very typical in many ways. One likes to see things."

"Oh. Don't you have ice cream dives in England?"

"Not quite like that. Where do all those young people come from?"

"University. There's a university here."

"O, I see."

Prentiss lay back. Suddenly he felt aged, alien. He sat quietly, and they did not speak again until they were at the bridge. Then she stopped the car.

"It was nice of you to go with me," she said. "It was swell."

She lifted her face calmly to be kissed.

Prentiss bent over and kissed her, meaning to do it casually. But as he did so, he felt again the wave of desire that was so foreign to his nature. He wished to press his hands against the fullness of her soft breasts. Even as he considered it, she straightened.

"Thanks," she said.

She started the car and they went up the winding road, into the pine grove. By the house she turned in the garage, quietly shut off the engine, and reached for the lights. Then Prentiss started. A voice cut in, rasping, hard:

"Where've *you* been?"

There was anger, challenge, in the voice. Prentiss felt himself go chill, like a schoolboy caught in grave sin. It had all been harmless—but how could Lachran know that? He saw Lachran's face by the open door.

"I just went riding with Mr. Saintby," Mary said.

As she spoke, Prentiss saw Lachran's face ease, and break into affability.

"Oh, *you* went with her!"

He laughed, quickly.

"Young lady," he said. "You were just going to get particular hell. I thought you'd gone off gallivanting alone."

He walked with them from the garage.

"You know, she has a habit of taking them goddam machines and racing all over the country. I don't give a damn, but if she has an accident out there all alone, hell's fire, she could lay out there all night without anyone finding her."

"Oh, I drive perfectly well," Mary said, angrily. "You imagine things."

"All right," Lachran said. "But all the same, you don't dare drive alone all over the countryside. Now I tell you again. I got a right to have some peace of mind. It's all right though, since you weren't alone."

He put his hand on Prentiss's shoulder as they neared the rustic bridge.

"Well, I'll be seeing you. I left something for you—sent it up to your cabin."

"Oh, thank you," Prentiss said. "Er—good night."

He walked unsteadily over the narrow bridge toward his cabin. He put his hand to his brow. It was slightly damp with perspiration.

Curious, he thought, that a man could be innocent, and yet feel so guilty. Or that a young woman could be so innocent and yet sound—otherwise.

He looked at the night world about him. The moon was low, now, and the place seemed darker.

A paradise. But a sort of foolish paradise. And all this had nothing to do with his mission. To-morrow—to-morrow he must get Lachran down to figures. There was absolutely no reason for the man to waste time any more.

He went into the cabin and clicked on the light. On his bed was a great, pearl-gray Western hat. On the leather band inside was stamped, in tiny gold letters:

"The owner of this hat is a friend of J. Michael Lachran."

He stood, staring at it.

CHAPTER XXII

WHEN Clive turned from the telephone she was still standing the same way: with the two fingers of her right hand pushing the hair under her hat.

It's the color of dead grass, he thought. That's it. The color of dead grass.

"Monty's blown right down here," he said. "I told him to come up."

"I heard," she said.

She took her hat off and went over to a chair and picked up Clive's dressing gown. She hung it in the cupboard. Then she went to the chair by the window and sat down.

"Now we can all eat together," Clive said. "You wait. He's a great old Monty, Monty is."

They both waited until the footsteps sounded, and then Clive threw open the door. Prue, sitting there, thought she had never seen him do anything so gladly.

"Glad to see you, Nipper. Bloody glad to see you!"

Then the man saw her, and he paused. His voice had been rasping—too overbearingly loud. His figure was bulky in the ballooning uniform of a private. He was squat—almost fat—and she thought his face coarse and brutalized. When he pulled off his cap at the sight of her she could see short-cut black hair standing on end. She knew that his thick neck went straight up to his skull at the back.

"This—this is Prudence, Monty!"

The man put on a smile of welcome, and his teeth shone, too perfect and white—like a dentist's advertisement.

But he did not move toward her. He looked back at Clive, and nudged him.

"So, this is why you wouldn't come up to London. Can't say I blame you a bit, my lad. Can't blame you a bit."

As he spoke the last he grinned at Prudence as if he expexted approval. She felt as if she were a horse being inspected. Everything about the man was coarse, vulgar, low-class. She turned to the window.

"Won't you sit down, Mr. Montague?"

She had waved her hand to the chair, but she saw he was sitting on her bed. She tightened her hands.

"You might as well call me Monty, Prudence," he said. "Everyone else does. Montague. The moniker doesn't fit the kisser, does it?"

He grinned at Clive as if it were a great joke. She sat quietly, forcibly opening her hands. She let them lie in her lap, and then, from some dim purpose, left an awkward silence between the three of them.

Clive stirred. He was thinking: You can never do it— never make a woman understand why you like and love and admire another man. They see only externals.

He turned angrily to Monty, and cupped his hand and brought it down on the other's knee.

"Well, Monty the Monte Carlo millionaire! By God, it was good of you to come down here," he said. "We'll have a beano! Wasn't it good of him to come down, Prue?"

He wanted her to say yes. Even though he understood her dislike, he wanted her to say yes, just for Monty's benefit.

"Did you have a good trip down, Mr. Montague?" she said.

"That I did!" He turned to Clive. "Couple o' Wiltshires on the train, and a commercial traveller. We got the civvy into poker, and we squeezed him every pot. I got near two quid."

Prudence turned away as she saw Clive shaking his head

admiringly, as if this were a fantastic achievement, but one to be expected of such a great man. She heard him say:

"It's good to see you, Monty. You get a room here?"

"Too posh for me, my lad. I'll kip at a lodging house somewhere."

"Well, we ought to get you set first. Then we'll have a real celebration. How's that, Prue?"

She turned her head.

"You two go," she said. "I'll meet you at Mine Host sevenish."

Clive felt angularity in purposes. He wanted to protest. But Monty cut in.

"Righto. Let's go, Nipper. We'll see you later, Prudence."

Unwillingly Clive got up.

"Well," he said to her. "Be—be careful."

"Of what?"

"Oh—blackout, and walking alone—and . . ."

"What's there to that?"

"You can't tell. Motorcars. Damned things racing along without lights and—well—anything."

She waved her hand.

"Good-by."

Unwillingly Clive turned. Monty was waiting at the door. They went out together, not speaking. On the street Monty said at last:

"That was smart of her."

"What?"

"Sending us out alone. Knew it'd give me a chance to ask you who she is, and why and where and what for and also."

"She didn't do it for that reason."

"You don't know much about women, then, Nipper. Where'd you get her?"

"Oh—I've known her a long time."

"You don't mean to say so?"

"Look here, Monty. She's a nice girl."

"Of course she is."

"Well, she is."

"I said she was, didn't I?"

"But the way you said it..."

"Oh, come off it, Nipper. I wasn't born yesterday, and I'm not a bloody Y.M.C.A. Jesus-singer. When a chap goes on leave with his girl—what's wrong?"

"She's a good girl, Monty. You just don't like her."

"I don't even know her, Nipper, so don't get upset. I don't know much about that kind."

"What kind?"

"Now don't get narky. I mean her kind—class. She's class, Nipper. Anybody can see that. She's high class. Educated. But that's all right. So are you. That's the kind of girl you ought to have—not no tart. You can see she's got class—and looks like a million pounds."

"She is beautiful, isn't she, Monty?"

"That she is. But then everybody's girl's beautiful. Don't you know that? There never was a woman too bloody ugly that somewhere there wasn't a man believed she was the bleeding picture no artist could paint. Same with a man. Never a poor bleeder so crummy-looking there wasn't a woman somewhere believed him every statue in the Tate Gallery rolled into one. Why—there's even been times when a woman has thought something of me."

Clive lifted his head. Now it was the same, he thought. Now things were the same.

"No," he said.

"And no sarcasm, my lad. I don't boast. I just use that as an example."

"It was your wealth, Monty. That's what attracted them."

"Wealth. I'll say one thing. I've always had more looks than money—and you can figure that one out."

254

"That leaves you bankrupt both ways."

"Not half, it doesn't."

They walked in step down the pavement. Now they were in a unison. Clive felt light-hearted.

"But she is beautiful, isn't she?"

"All right, if you want me to say it, she's the icing on the cake."

"You don't have to say it. I don't need corroboration."

"Then what did you ask me for?"

"I didn't ask you. I told you."

"And you've known her a long time, eh?"

"Yes—pretty long."

"Well, you deserve a good un."

"No, Monty. I don't deserve her."

"Oh, don't put 'em on a pedestal. There's just good uns and bad uns, that's all. If you draw a bad un then hell's a promised land where you'll get relief when you die. And if you get a good un, then you'll be willing to go to hell when you die because you'll have had all the heaven one man can ask while you were alive. But don't put 'em on a pedestal, and then some day you can't cry your bleeding eyes out because you think they've fallen off—because they never was there in the first place."

"The sage of Soho. Shall we have a drink first?"

"No, let's get a place to kip first. How was your hospital?"

"Oh, all right. How was yours?"

"Oh, cushy enough."

They went in silence, each comfortable in it.

"Bleeding dead hole," Monty said.

"It's crowded to the roofs in summer, ordinarily."

"Good job it ain't now."

"What for?"

"Jerry'll come knocking soon. Stands to reason, don't it? He's no bloody fool."

"I suppose so. I'm on leave now—let's forget it."

"Righto, if you're fed up. This seems to be the right area."

"What makes you think so?"

"Smells like it, Nipper. Lodging house streets smell the same all over—fried liver and onions in the cellar-kitchen and cat muck in the hall upstairs. Same smell everywhere. See—there's a sign."

Mine Host's was crowded that evening when Prudence came in. She knew that they did not see her coming. Through the layers of cigarette smoke she could see Clive's mouth moving as he spoke, animatedly, but his words were shut out by the hubbub back in the bar. Then she stood by the table, and Clive looked up.

His eyes are happy, she thought. He is stimulated and excited and happy. Men need men.

"Now we're all here," he said. "A drink! Whisky soda!"

"No, port please."

"Busy tonight. I'll go dig one up."

She turned to watch him go. Then she began pulling off her gloves, slowly. When she was finished, there was nothing else to do. She looked up at the man opposite her. He was letting his eyes travel over her, and his face held a half-smile.

"Well," she said. Her voice was cold.

Monty lit a cigarette, almost insolently. He left it in his mouth and the smoke trailed down his nostrils.

"I don't care," he said. "But you might make it nice for him. I know it's bloody hard for a woman to meet her chap's friends. She always wonder: 'What can he see in that chap?' You don't have to lay it on."

She folded her gloves neatly, and left him without answer.

"All right. You're class. I'm not. But he's class, too.

He's educated, too—but he don't stick it in your face. That's being a real gentleman. He's so real you don't think about it after you've been talking a couple of minutes. He's sky-high."

The force of his admiration left her disarmed.

"He—he thinks a lot of you, too," she said.

The man smiled. When he spoke again it was as if everything was settled.

"Oh, that's just because we're in the same push," he said. "You know—sticking together. When you eat and sleep with a chap for months, like in the army, well, you get chums. And he's all right. You're all right, too—for him."

"I don't know."

"Oh, yes. I'm not talking of what kind of woman I'd like. I'm talking about what'd be good for him. He's bright, and young—and he'll get along if he gets someone good. A lot of thinking goes on in that kid's napper. And he's got stuff—he could stick, that kid could."

She looked at the table.

"Was he—was Clive a good soldier in France?"

"Was he a good soldier!"

When he went no further she looked up. She noticed that his eyes seemed incongruously gray. He spoke evenly, holding her gaze.

"Was he a good soldier!" he repeated, slowly. "You know him, don't you? What do you think?"

He looked at her, almost distastefully, she thought. Then she saw him lift his gaze and smile. He spoke over her head.

"Got it, eh? Leave it to an old soldier to scrounge the rations quick."

She turned as Clive set the glasses down.

"I got a couple of rounds while I was at it," he said. "Never seen it so busy here."

He sat down, and smiled at Prue.

"Well?" he said. "Where were you when I came in?"

"France," Monty said.

She wanted to stop him from talking.

"We started to talk about France," he went on. "And that reminds me, Nipper. I hear you're up for a bloody medal."

Clive shook his head in a sort of angry disbelief.

"No," he said. "No!"

"God's truth. Saw the R.S.M. in Piccadilly and I asked the old sweat to have one on me—I knew him back when—so he unbends enough to shift three or four, and he says both you and me go up for ribbons for the do with Allen."

"No," Clive said, distastefully. "No—no!"

"All right, you bloody hero. You wait and see."

"What's it for? Prudence said. "What about Captain Allen?"

"The bloody hero pulled him out. Didn't he tell you?"

"Oh, no. Don't start building it all up, Monty. Forget it. Here, let's drink."

Monty ignored him.

"He was a bloody hero, Prue. I don't like bloody heroes," he grinned. "I'm an old soldier. Do you want to hear about it?"

"No, she doesn't."

"Oh, don't be so bloody modest, Nipper. I hate a modest bleeder worse nor I hate a hero. You did it—and now you got to put up with it."

"What did he do, Monty?"

"I got scared, that's what I did. Truly. I was so scared I had the trots. Now let's have a good time—we're on leave..."

"Everybody's scared, Nipper, at the time. Not right at the time. Either before or after. Anybody who says he wasn't frightened—he never was in it. The thing is, right at the time..."

"Monty likes war, Prue. He likes it so much he didn't

get enough out of the last one, so he had to get into this one. And he likes talking about..."

"I'd just as soon go to war as try to gyp a living out of the wholesale greengrocery business. And that's no lie."

"But what about Captain Allen?" Prue said.

"Didn't he tell you about Douai?"

"No."

"I did."

"He didn't, Monty. Don't listen to him. Just tell me."

"Oh, it was a bloody do for fair."

"You can have it," Clive said.

"It was Ess, Pee, and corruption all around."

"You can have it."

"See, modest, Prudence. That's what I don't like about him. See, we're in Douai. We've got to hold."

"We will hold this position to the last man. I've told her, Monty."

"That's right. To the last man, it was."

"And the last drop of blood."

"That's right, and..."

"The thin red line of heroes, Prue."

"Let Monty tell it, Clive. Now don't interrupt."

"He can have it."

"What then, Monty?"

Clive nursed his glass.

"Never introduce your girl to a pal," he said. "Or first thing you know you'll be on the outside of a triangle."

Prudence smiled at him. She knew he was glad because she and Monty seemed to be friendly to each other. He didn't wear modest as a pose, she knew. He didn't like talking about the war; but he was so happy to see that she and Monty were friends that this came first.

"Well, we're by a bit of a greenhouse," Monty went on, expansively. "A bomb'd hit near and sort of pushed it over on a wall—a bloody regular natural pillbox it was. Cover overhead, perfect field of fire through a hole in the wall. Snug as a bug in a rug we are, and no planes can see us. Camouflage—we look like a ruin, that's all."

"Shut up, Clive."

"Well, there we sits. And over he comes. And oh—we took them typewriters and knocked our initials all over him. He'd pushed us around ever since it started and when we took Douai that was the first real crack at him we'd had. Been waiting so long we was happy to see the bastard coming."

"He means it was a change from the monotony of running away, Prue."

"Nothing wrong with a retreat, my lad. And we made up for it. Oh—wiped 'em down—like playing a hose on 'em. Make you laugh and cry your bloody eyes out at the same time to see the way he come walking up. Cruel the way he walked into us.

"We melted him right away to nothing. Then another bunch came, and we plowed 'em under. Skittles, it was. Cruel! After that he starts bunches rushing to get us, but they wasn't sure where we was. Cat and mouse—and he was the mouse. We pinned his ears back all afternoon, and then all night. Just ticky-tacking. Then I remember I scrounged around and happened to find a bottle of whisky..."

"You happened to steal a bottle of whisky."

"Don't be rude, Nipper. It's the same thing in war. Any old soldier would..."

"Old soldiers never die."

"The simple fades away. Well, we certainly faded him away, all right."

"And then we faded away. Tell her how we faded away when he got rough."

"Well, you didn't expect he'd come marching up at the halt on the left form platoon for the whole bloody war, did you? You had to expect he'd bring up nasty stuff. But it was certainly good while it lasted. Like knocking dollies down at a shy. Then it was *his* turn, and he brought up a few mortars and a few tanks..."

"Don't forget that nice *flammenwerfer*. You wouldn't have her think just a few tanks could make the British army run."

"Oooh, that was a bloody thing, wasn't it! Well, you can't grudge him. It was his turn to play cat and mouse, and him the cat for a change. I still have to laugh, when I think of how he chased us round that bloody town—to hell and gone and back again."

"Take a laugh for me, too. You've got a good sense of humor. Look, if you don't want that drink, I'll take it."

"You leave it alone. Well, Prudence, then I comes round a corner and there's Nipper again, sitting right on top of a pile of bricks, cussing something fearful and taking a bloody Bren apart..."

"Putting it together, I was."

"Either way, you was on top of a pile of bricks. So we chucks his Bren and keeps mine and hunted around for a place where there wasn't Jerries. Lumme, there was Jerries everywhere. Every bloody cellar in town was filled up and standing room only. Clive runs up out of one, and I have to laugh. He's white as a bloody ghost, and he says: 'Oooh, there's about fifty Jerries down there. I almost walked into 'em.' So I says: 'Well, they can share part o' what I've got among 'em.' And I chucks down a bomb. After that we started to retire..."

"We ran like hell."

"All right. We decided on a strategical advance to the rear. That's what. We go down a street—and funny thing, you remember there, Clive. I had to laugh. There was a bloody top hat sitting right in the middle of the street. A top hat, mind you, Prudence. Imagine, in the middle of a bleeding war. A top hat, lying there right in the middle of the street. And I starts laughing, thinking how that got there. You remember that, Clive?"

"No. You're making it up."

"God's truth, I'm not. Just before we come to that street where them poor bleeders were lined up."

"I know. How about a drink? I don't see how you talk so much without a drink. Don't you get dry?"

"Lumme, that street was something, though. They'd plastered 'em pretty. First off I thought it was our outfit that was moving out and sat down to rest. That's just what it looked like—like a full company on a route march, flopped for a five minutes' rest. But they was all dead— every last bloody one. They must have been filing out, and they copped 'em from both ends of the street, and mowed the whole bloody lot down.

"Lumme, that street give me shivers now I think of it. All of us there—maybe a hundred of us in that street. And every bloody one dead except me and Clive. Sitting there like they'd fallen out for rest on a route march. Some sitting, like, and some just squatting against the wall and in doorways, and some lying down like they were tired, but easing the straps on their packs and resting peaceful.

"And us stepping over the bodies of our own chaps, and the street quiet, and only us alive. Like being in church, it was, if you know what I mean. Very respectful, of course. Funny, we didn't even run—you wouldn't think a Jerry would open up on you then, any more than he would in church.

"So we come up out of that street, and then down by a square, and we could hear him tap-tapping at us, and we'd spray around a bit with the Bren to keep him respectful. Then we begin to come on a few of our push that'd been dropped.

"I saw Young Harris, there, Clive. Dotted right through

the head, he was—bloody hole at the back you could put a dinner plate in. We sees more of our push, and we knew we'd gone out that way. Then we happens on Captain Allen—lying in the gutter—dotted him with a half dozen emma gee bullets right across his chest."

"Why don't you hold your trap?" Clive said.

She heard his voice ugly with coldness.

"Well, I'm telling her, not you," Monty said, pugnaciously.

"You're telling her! For Christ's sake, forget the war for ten minutes, will you? I don't mind, but Jesus Christ, you're going to be like these old soldiers who go on yapping about it all the rest of their lives. You'll kill more men with your mouth before you die than the whole bloody army did in France in the war—this one and the last one."

"Don't get nasty."

"I'm not getting nasty. I'm saying I'm bored."

"I'm not," Prudence said, quickly. "I'm not, go on."

The two men looked at her. They had forgotten about her. Her face was set, and her teeth were held together so that the lower ones showed.

Why is she like that? Clive thought. What can make a woman go into another person like that? In a sort of trance. Women are more terrible than men. God help the world if women ever start fighting wars. It'll be worse than anything men ever knew. God help the world then.

"Oh, Ess, Pee, and corruption," he said. "I'm going in the bar. You fight your war."

Prudence watched him go, her face not changing.

"Now. Go on and tell me," she said.

"You really want me to?"

"No. But you've got to tell me. I've got to hear it. What about Captain Allen?"

"Well, I just looked down, and I was saying: 'Lumme, here's Allen copped it, too.' And then he opens his eyes, and says: 'Clear out. Didn't you get the order to clear out?' Just as if he was balling us out. And I says: 'No, sir. We've been hiding in too many cellars—we didn't get no order.' 'Well,' he says, 'clear out. You should have cleared out last night.'

"Then he closes his eyes like he's very tired and impatient with us for keeping him awake. And Clive says: 'How about you, sir?' And he opens his eyes and says: 'To hell with me or anybody else who can't make it. If you can get out, go on out.' Then he closes his eyes again.

"And there we were. I sit down on the edge of the pavement, and there was Allen in the gutter, and Clive standing up, nursing the bloody Bren and about fifty bloody Jerries across the way somewhere taking rising shots at us, and bouncing them bullets all over the pavement. It was like standing up in the middle of the rifle range, hearing 'em smack and sing and go ricocheting.

"Well, we couldn't leave him there, and we couldn't stay there, so Clive passes me the Bren and gets him by the shoulder straps and hoists him up, and I get down in the gutter and start dotting a few where it'd do most good.

"I could hear Allen saying: 'No, leave me here. Please, you're only making it worse. Leave me here, please.' And Clive saying: 'Oh, you bastard. I'll be a sod if I will. Oh, you bastard!' Cussing the Captain with everything he could lay his tongue to.

"Now that's funny. But it takes lots of chaps like that. Chaps you know never said a bloody or a damn in their lives—cussing like that. And never remembering it afterwards. Especially young chaps in their first do. Some of 'em cry, and some starts to puke and go on puking and puking all the way trough a push—and some gets the runs, and I've seen 'em going over with their gun in one hand holding their trowsis up with the other. And sometimes some of 'em sings at the top of their lungs. And some just cusses solid through the whole thing. But it's funny, now I think of it—I never heard one of 'em pray through a push. No, most often it's cussing with everything they can think of, and they don't know it. Because if they did, you wouldn't think anybody would pop off into the next world with such language on their lips, now would you?"

"No. Then what? Captain Allen?"

"Oh, we got him out. It was a bloody do, though. The Jerries got their hair up—you'd think got enough of us without wanting just the three of us left. We'd been horsing round that town among 'em nearly all day. Now we was like a couple of burglars trying to get away with a sack o' silver through London in daylight. Everybody was after us—more and more. It was all right while the ammo held out. I'd spray 'em with the Bren, and then hop it quick after the Nipper. Then I'd flog and spray 'em again till he was round the next corner. Then I'd hop it after him, like that, you know. Then the ammo ran out, so I chucked the Bren and let 'em have it with bombs. Then when them was gone, I yells after the Nipper, and he lets me have what he's got. Then when them was gone, I'd yell for more. And that way we got through the bloody town. Clive'd pull him round a street, and go hunt for bombs, and I'd suck-hole and bomb 'em for a while till they started getting round us, and then we'd pull out. I'd yell: 'More bombs, Nipper.' And every time he'd say: 'This is the last one. Theyre isn't any more,' to make me not waste 'em. But he always got more..."

„There isn't any more," she repeated. "Yes—but where did he get them from?"

"Oh, pick 'em up, you know—from bomb bags that'd been dropped by somebody—or scrounging around among the dead chaps. Every time he'd kid on it was the last—so's I wouldn't waste 'em, see. But every time when I was out, I'd yell: 'More bombs, Nipper.' And like a good kid, he'd have 'em. He'd drag the captain up the street, and then he'd scrounge around and find some and say they was really the last..."

"There aren't any more. I can't find any more," she said.

"That's right. Then we're getting by a street with a row of trees each side, and we're playing peepo round the tree trunks, and he says: 'Really, this time, Monty. Really—there aren't any more. I can't find any more.' He sounded so bad that I knew he meant it. And there we was, stuck. So I says, 'Well, here's where they're one up on us.' 'Hell,' he says, 'So-and-so, and Ess and Pee and Effingwell this and that. Come on.'

"So we grabs Allen, him the shoulders and me the feet, and we run till I'm so bloody near dead I can't hold up. And Allen keeps waking like and saying: 'Please, put me down. Please! It's worse this way. Please.'

"I was so done in, I says: 'We can't do no more, Clive.' I was finished—you know how I mean—you don't care whether you sit there and just get killed—as long as you sit. You're so tired, you're through. And I didn't know what we'd do—I didn't care, neither. And then Clive looks round, and there's a bloody motorcar, sitting up the street—you'd see lots of 'em round, you know. Deserted. Refugees get as far as they could, and then run out of petrol or have some trouble. This had had a war walk over it. Windows smashed, and front tire hit and everything. So the Nipper says we'll drag him up there and see. So we drags him up. There was a couple of our chaps knocked off there—been firing round the car and then been knocked out—heavy gun from a tank, I should say. We stuffs Allen in, and the Nipper says: 'There's petrol, Monty.' 'What about ignition?' I says. Well, of course, there wasn't no key, but the Nipper says: 'I'll start this Essing Effing thing, I will.' Cussing top of his lungs, he was. And he takes a safety pin out of one of the dead chap's first aid dressing, and dives under the

266

steering wheel. Laugh, I nearly falls over. There's his legs sticking up in the air and a bloody war going on. They was popping us proper. So I flops down and gets one of the dead chap's rifles, and gets two of 'em before they start to get careful again.

"I hears the starter turn over, and the Nipper shouts to jump in. I jump in, and he'd shorted the ignition—regular trick it is, for nipping a car—you know, chaps steal a car once in a while—some chaps. There we sit, and the starter going whoo-whoo-whoo-whoo, and I can hear the battery getting weak, and still no start. But you could smell the petrol, with the carbureter being flooded.

"'No juice,' I says.

"So the Nipper hops out, and throws up the bonnet, and out I get again, and go back to me dear little hipe—you know, a rifle—in the gutter to keep 'em back. I'd fire a clip, and then take another off the dead chap—out of his pouches, and look around for more targets. And they was working up through the houses and making it nasty. I looks up once in a while to see how the Nipper's coming along. You know, that was funny. For the first time he's stopped cussing. He wasn't saying a thing. By God, I'll never forget that. He was just standing there, working on that car, as cool as if he was home in his own garage. I remember, as I looks up at him he pushes his helmet back with the back of his hand, and then wipes his nose with his wrist, and gets a smear o' grease up his face, and wrinkles his forehead.

"It wasn't like he was in a hurry. It wasn't like he didn't hear the bullets or are about 'em. It was just like he'd forgot about the whole bloody war and everything, and was just very interested in his job. Almost like he was saying: 'Now isn't this a very pretty and interesting piece of repair work!'

"Oh, I was proud of him, I'll tell you. Cool—cucumbers

is boiling compared to what he was. Then he slams down the bonnet, runs round the wreck, hops in, and wuff! Off she went. I get in, and he slaps her in gear, and off we go, flippety-floppety-flop, with the front wheel flat and the tire slapping on the valve.

"And—now this is the cream of the lot—we gets to the corner and right then the tire comes off as we turn. The tire goes straight ahead, we goes round the corner on the rim, and we come smack into a bunch of Jerries that's creeping round to cut us off. And right beside the curb there's a tank just stopped and a Jerry officer talking to the chap in the tank, telling him something.

"Round the corner we come, right into that. And what do you think the Nipper does? He sits up straight behind the wheel and I can see this Jerry officer looking straight at him and Clive looking straight at the officer. And Clive lifts one hand, half like he's saluting and half like he's waving. And the officer almost starts to salute and then looks as if he'd changed his mind. Then I couldn't see him no more. But surprised! Those Jerries were that surprised, they stood there, and didn't fire a bloody shot. Not one bloody shot! Can you believe it?

"And mind you, we got past some of 'em as close as I am to you, and I puts up my hand and cocks my snook at 'em, and I looks back, and there they are, cocking their snooks back at us—like a bunch of kids—all of us, wiggling our fingers at our noses.

"Now you tell that to anyone! You tell 'em that, and ask 'em to believe you. But so help me Christ, that's the way it was. And if the Nipper had ha' stopped, or tried to turn round, or tried to back away, I'll bet that tank'd ha' shot the living be'jesus out of us. Course, it didn't take more than a minute or so. But just the same, there it was —us driving right through about a hundred Heinies, and all cocking snooks at one another.

"Laugh! Afterwards I start to laugh till I can't sit up straight any more. What with the look on their faces, and the front rim o' that car sounding like a steam roller on concrete, I nearly died.

"And that's the way we come out of Douai. And up the road, we pick up a couple of Guards that's wounded, and then a couple of walking wounded hop on the running board until we hit a rear-guard emma gee post, and go through that. And then a real ambulance comes along, and everyone's swapped over. And we run about a mile more before the petrol gives out, so then we hoof it and finally run into some Green Howards, and then the Welsh Guards coming marching up from Arras, through the Jerries, and then we knew we'd held Douai long enough for the Arras chaps to get away.

"Well, we got in with a bunch of casuals—oh, Green Howards and West Kents and Durhams and Northumberland Fusileers. We was all mixed—except them Welsh Guards. Lumme, they come out of that scrap, going in step like they was on regimental parade. But they wouldn't have if we hadn't held Douai, or they'd ha' been cut off.

"Well, we got out all right, and they got the Captain to hospital and out of Dunkirk all right, and I hear he's coming good. He's a good one, Allen is. I knew him in the last war. I knew him well.

"He had plenty of the old stuff. When we left him I ask him how he is, and he doesn't say anything. After a while he says: 'Thank God we got a navy, Monty.' That was kidding, y'know. We used to say it in the other war. He didn't know how right he was, at that, the way it turned out."

He sat, staring at the table. Then he lifted his drink.

"Thank you for the story," she said.

"Ah, that's all right."

"No, thank you. I wanted to hear."

"I don't tell it so good."

"You do. There wasn't many came out—out of your regiment?"

"Oh, not as bad as you'd think, you know," he said. He said it cheerfully. "Quite a lot of us. Ones and twos and threes—like me and the Nipper. Surprise you how many got out."

"How many did?"

"Oh, couldn't say about numbers—'course, a rear-guard action—well, that's what a rear guard's for, you know. Can't everybody get out, now can they?"

"No. That's it. They can't."

She sat fingering her glass, and suddenly wishing that Clive would come back.

Clive stood in the bar at the counter, cupping his glass, not hearing the mixed talk sounds, looking at the white porcelain tops of the long levers on the beerpulls.

He was thinking: Killing and getting killed, it didn't count much. When you killed, you didn't mind it. If you were killed yourself, you couldn't mind it. It was only afterwards, thinking about it, away from it, that it was bad. When you were out of it, your not-fighting mind ruled you and you were able to look back at the motion-picture of yourself and neither understand it nor like it. But when you were in it, it wasn't really bad. It was only when you were out. Then you couldn't talk, unless you lied, because you couldn't believe or justify yourself. But when you were in it a different mind and force ruled you, and you did what you had to without hurt or concern, doing it quickly and coldly, removed from any peacetime moralities.

When you were in it you could take life as impartially and decisively as in peacetime you could take scissors and snip a rose—and think no more about it. Not just Jerries—enemies. Anyone—any life. Your own men.

The chap who came down along the wall, bending, running quickly, coming through the smoke of the burning houses, dodging round the tangle of fallen wires in the street. And Monty yelled: "Hey, chum! Where you going!" Then the man came over, running, his feet crunching in the shattered glass of the old greenhouse. He crouched down, holding his rifle as by force of habit, his lips beyond control. Then he said at last: "I'm getting out of here."

"Oh, get the wind down," Monty said. "Get it down, we're all right here as long as they're holding out over in the houses on the left. They can't get at us. Just move down the end of the wall there and take a pop at 'em once in a while."

"No," the man said. "No. I'm getting out of here."

"Oh, take hold of yourself, and get down the wall," Monty said.

"No. You can't order me around. You've no right!"

"No right, eh?" And Monty had crawled on his hands and knees. "No right? I have a right. I'm senior soldier here—and I tell you to get down the wall."

Then, jumping into motion like a suddenly released spring, the man had stood, facing Monty, his rifle thrown forward at the on-guard, the bayonet at the throat, the left knee bent in the semi-classic parade-ground style.

"I'm oing out, and I'll shoot any bugger who tries to stop me."

He had turned, quickly, pointing the bayonet first at Monty, then at Clive, then at Monty. Clearly the chap was insane, then. Insane as a man could be. Dangerously insane—pointing the bayonet first at one, then the other. Insane or a spy.

Whatever he was, the second time he had turned to

Monty, Clive had lifted his Lee-Enfield quickly, and shot him through the side of the head.

"Nice going," Monty said. "The poor barstid."

That was all. And then they had gone back to the low greenhouse wall. It was over. Forgotten.

Forgotten then; but now remembered, it had different dimensions. Dimensions so great, you didn't talk about it. You only thought about it:

How could I—I, this person, me, who owns these hands that I can lift before my face and see—I, the owner of these hands? How could I have done it like that—and never think about it any more at the time, nor say any word about it then? If then I could do it without remembering, why can I see it now with not forgetting?

Oh, hell. Forget it. He deserved it!

Deserved it? Who are you to say any man, any creature, should suddenly stop having being and knowing?

Perhaps he was a spy.

He wasn't! He was a tired, exhausted man.

He was dirty with panic.

All right. He had done what he could, and stood it as long as he could. Who knows how brave he had been until he couldn't stand it any more? Modern war fare bears on the nerves until...

O.K. then. O.K. I should have stopped and had him psychoanalyzed. We should have tested his reflexes...

He was a live human being.

He was rotten with fear.

And you—you weren't racked and hounded by fright?

I did what I had to. So did the others. They had guts. They stuck it out. He was no different than the rest. He should have stuck it out like everyone else—even the wounded, and the ones there was no hope for, they didn't go rotten with fear. Even the ones hit, who knew it was all over for them, they lay there and wrapped themselves in some fine, faraway dignity that removed them over and beyond you so that you, the living, were less than they, the dying, and they never spoke a word, and waited there to go out that way.

They did it! He wasn't even hit. The only one in hundreds like that. The others, they died properly.

Hell, died properly. What a neat phrase. How would you like to take an afternoon off and go die properly?

It doesn't matter about the phrase. There's a truth behind it I don't know how to say. They died properly—kids, youngsters. By God, by Jesus, by Christ and Mr. Chamberlain and the Cabinet, they died—and the way they did it will be a reproach forever to us who didn't.

Coming up through the garbage of the streets, coming up through a lonesomeness like Sunday in a business center, coming through the mist that was smoke of burning houses and the pall of pulverized brick dust and smashed mortar, you saw them among the rubble: the dead ones in the myriad unbelievable undignified postures that sudden death invents, and the badly hit and dying ones wrapped in some curious isolation that made them untouchable.

It was no use trying to touch them or help them. If you, torn by the shame and hatred of your own being alive and going out and leaving them, if you tried to help, it was no use.

You knew that, yet you went to them. You went to them for exactly the same reason that a wealthy man gives a beggar a half-crown—to quiet your own conscience.

If you couldn't walk on past the next one, and you stopped and said: "Can I do anything, chum?" the way they looked at you was reproach enough for having trespassed blunderingly into a place where your livingness gave you no right to be.

They said no, or they shook their heads no, and sometimes their faces were wrenched up in pain, or sometimes calm because the wound and their own dying had shocked them beyond pain, but the eyes were always the same. The eyes always looked at you pityingly, as if excusing you for the tremendous blunder you had made in talking such inconsequential silliness.

If you tried to rouse them from it, they resented it. They wanted to die properly. "No, no—leave me here, chum!" What made them do that? Captain Allen the same—even though he pulled through. So many said that—as if a narcotic had lulled them and they no longer wished to be free of it.

It was no use trying to help. The one with the ginger hair that he'd tried to get out before they got to Allen.

"No—no! Leave me here, chum!"

"Come on! Here, you'll be all right. Slip your arm round here. Monty, get his other arm there."

Three, four, five steps. Then:

"Chum, chum!"

"You're all right."

"No—chum! Will you—I've got to—undo my breeches."

"You haven't time!"

"I've got to! I've got to! Please!"

The ginger hair and the white-waxy skin that often goes with the redhead complexion, and the mixture of pain on the face, and embarrassment. A man, embarrassed even in death by natural functions.

Then they reached up under his tunic flaps and undid the leather belt with the collection of hat badges on it, and then found the buttons and undid the suspenders. His flanks were that blue-white color, amazingly light. They held his arms as he crouched, and strained, and nothing came. They pulled his breeches up and lifted him again. And again:

"No—again! I've got to! I want to go mates!"

Standing again, sweating, in the brick-shattered street,

and looking back, wondering in how many seconds the tanks or armored cars would come round the corner, and looking down again at the crouching boy.

Then dragging him along again, feeling him grow heavier and heavier between each stop when he crouched and strained and nothing happened. Dragging him until Monty said:

"Hey!"

Then you looked up and saw the ginger head thrown back to the sky, and the jaw, dropped on its hinge, hanging so wide open.

You let him down slowly, although dropping him now would have been no different, and you saw him there on the cobbles, and saw your own feet, and saw Monty's feet, and heard Monty saying:

"Shot in the gut! Makes 'em think they have to go!"

"Oh, was that it?"

"Yes. That's the way you can tell. Come on, let's get on with it."

That's all you said then. Like receiving a clinical report. And only now, afterwards, when your peacetime-mind came back, you saw it and tasted it and felt it and knew what you had done. You knew the enormity of it, and it had outrageous unreality. Not you—you couldn't have said it so! Nothing in it was true! Not really a man died— only a motion picture! Not in person!

All right, try to tell someone that was it. That was war: standing by a boy who crouched, trying to relieve his riddled guts and do it with humility for having brought his necessity out of privacy and placed it before them!

Tell that for your war story! Tell her that, Monty, when you're going good! Tell anybody that at your next afternoon tea, and watch how patiently and humbly they'll listen!

Tell them about the other one—the one leaning by the

car that you got away in. When you went over and said: "Can you get this car running," thinking that the two of them had wanted to start it. Only one was down in the gutter in the impossible posture that meant he was dead, and the other, leaning against the car, half-sitting on the mudguard, half-leaning, his hands crossed over his belly, opened his eyes and you knew that it was another of them, somehow satisfied now death had come, only waiting for it to come quickly and leave behind a world in which he might cry out or scream.

Only he didn't look wounded. The one in the gutter— yes. The leg half torn away above the knee, and the already-blackening pool that was dusted over with gray from the settling grime. But the other, the stillstanding one; seeing him clutching his belly, you reached out a hand.

"No, chum! No! Leave me be!"

But there was no mark on him. He couldn't be badly wounded. You lifted his weak hands to see, and started to unbutton his tunic, and then it all fell out, sliding and wet, cascading onto your boots as the man, too, slid sideways and down, his head thrown back against the spokes of the wheel.

Then—there you stood in the entrails of a living man, and lifted your feet back politely from under them, and listened to the snoring, shuddering groan that should have stopped but that went on and on...

Monty saying:

"Put the poor bleeder out of his misery, Nipper. Here!"

You stepped back, carefully, gravely, and Monty turned from picking up the rifle and placed it quickly against the turned neck, under the ear, and pressed the trigger, holding the rifle one-handedly.

The next minute it had no meaning and no reality and you were trying to get Captain Allen in the car and then, knowing there was petrol, saying: "Short the ignition under the lock." And then, under the hood, checking back from the dead plugs—the distributor, the mag—the—mag—what in the name of God kind of carpenter calling himself a mechanic last taped over this half-made joint to fall apart and... "Now we've got it, Monty."

That was real—all that part. But not the other. Only until now. Why was it real now?

Because I remember it and know it and can say even out loud:

That is true and it happened—and if it were not true and did not happen to you, you could not know it.

I could invent it.

You could not. No one can. You can invent a bandage on the brow set esthetically at the right heroic angle, or an arm in a sling, or oh, let me like a soldier fall upon some open plain this breast expanding for the ball to blot out every stain, or Florence Nightingale in high-heeled shoes, or mid the war's great curse stands the red cross nurse she's the rose of no man's land, or Lady Sylvia Putz has completed her course as a nurse without anyone becoming aware of her identity until she had concluded it.

You can invent an arm off, and a leg off, and the edges all tucked in neatly, and the sleeve that is empty, and he fell in Flanders Field and skylarks and poppies row on row—except that it was the crosses row on row. You can make up a war memorial and an unknown soldier, even.

You can make those up.

But you can't make the other things up.

No one could be that good. Nobody could be as daringly inventive about war as war can be itself. Therefore it is true—and you did it—and the hands you had are those hands now before you holding the glass—and because they are there, then all the rest is there, too. Only if you can invent your hands away, can you invent the other away?

It is true.

Well, what of it? It's been going on for centuries—thousands of years. I didn't make the war. I didn't make myself, nor my brain nor my memory nor my nerves. Maybe you have to be like that while it's happening. You have to be, or you couldn't go through it. And if you're that way when it's happening, then it's no use being another way when it's over.

Hell. Sit up, pull yourself together, and don't think about it. Take a swift one. Drink it up and live, love, and laugh like anyone else. Who are you to be unlike anyone else, you lousy egotist? Are you any better than the Duke of Wellington, and Nelson... oh, kiss me Hardy! Kiss me Hardy, kiss me long. It's all the same in the long run, and you made no difference. The dead ones would be all the same dead—and if they hadn't died there, then old age, or occupational disease, or gallstones, or hardening of the arteries would have got them.

Drink up. And now—order another round and see how Monty the Monte Carlo millionaire is getting on. Never introduce your donna to a pal.

I don't mean that. Monty wouldn't try anything.

The hell he wouldn't. Any man will if conditions are right.

But Prue wouldn't.

Any woman would if conditions are right.

Not Prue. You can tell. They're that way, the ones like her. You can trust them a thousand miles away, or you can't trust them while you run out to the latrine. And she's the kind you can trust. You know—no man was ever really fooled. You know the many women you can't trust, and you know the few you can.

How do you know?

How do you? You can't say how you know—but you know it all the same.

What a fine philosopher you are. A two-whisky philosopher!

He held up his forefinger to the barmaid.

"Three whisky sodas," he said.

"Three?"

"Not all for me. The others."

She grinned. When the drinks were ready he walked slowly and too concentratedly to the table. He saw Prue look over Monty's head and smile, and then Monty saw the smile and turned and grinned.

"Y've been long enough, Nipper. I've been talking her to death."

What was the use of taking it one way or another? Take it as it came.

He edged into his seat beside Prue.

"Well, did you make it good and heroic, Monty?" he said.

"He made it funny, Clive," Prue said.

His brain began going quickly again.

Funny. Oh, my God! Saying it's funny, but using the phrase to cover up admiration. The way she looked up when she said that. That's the last straw—being looked at like that—eyes bright—a sort of excitement in them. Funny! She doesn't know about the boy who couldn't go, or the one disembowelled owner my feet. Women are crueler than men—crueler in their ignorance. Let them see war—civilians—women. The French women know.

"Yes, it was very funny," he said.

She caught the curl to the edge of the words.

"I mean, coming out—he was telling me about the car you fixed and coming out, laughing fit to die, and thumbing your noses."

"Unfit to die, you mean."

"Remember, Nipper?"

"No."

"There, you see. I said I had a better memory nor him, Prudence."

"I never denied it. You're full of memories. You're the official reciter."

"Who is?"

"You are. Tell her some more stories. Go on spilling your mouth."

"I don't spill my mouth, my lad."

"You do. You're the official reciter. You're just full of military *contes*."

"Now is that any way to talk before a lady?"

Monty was laughing, but Prudence saw that under it he was getting angry.

"I'm merely using a tea-party phrase of the upper classes, Monty," Clive said. "You wouldn't understand it. Give us a military *conte*."

"I'll give you a *conte* over the napper in a minute. You're drunk."

"Give her the *conte* about the way you talked over the telephone to the Divisional General."

"That was in the last war."

"That wasn't the way I heard it. It was this war. I'll tell her. It's my turn to be *raconteur*—see, that's same root, Monty?"

"It was last war."

"He's the one that's drunk, Prue. It was this war. He found a phone and hooked in on a wire with a safety pin, and a voice said—a very pretty voice: 'Who is this?'

" 'This is the commander of the advance guard echelon,' Monty says. 'Let me speak to the Major General.'

"And by God, if he doesn't get the Major General and kidded the life out of him. 'This is Private Effingwell Clancey of the Covent Garden Clanceys,' he says. 'The Jerries are throwing things at us. Can't you do something about it?' 'Look here,' the General says, 'this is no time for practical jokes. We're busy up here.'

"'Busy?' says Monty. 'What the hell you think we're doing down here? Punting on a lake? Why, you dugout king, why don't you come down here and bloody well reprimand me?'"

"You're drunk, Nipper."

"I am not drunk. Just because I tell one on you..."

"That wasn't the way it happened. It wasn't like that. It was the last war and..."

"Ah, you see? You see the way truth gets twisted when too many people get talking. By this time even you don't know what really happened."

"You're drunk."

"I'm not—and if I am, who's got anything to say about it?"

"You talk like that to me, Nipper, and I'll smack your behind."

"And how many besides on the detail?"

"No more—just me. Any day!"

Prudence lifted her hand to her mouth as she saw Monty rise up, his paws on the table. Clive stood, too, his finger tips spread, touching the table lightly.

"Please," she said. "Now, please..."

As she spoke Monty lifted his hands, palms in, and weaved his head in a quick, flowing motion. As Clive lifted his own arms, the squat man reached out in a motion almost too quick to see, and, flat-handedly, smacked Clive on the buttocks, and then was away again before Clive could move.

Prue could hear it—like the dull sound of a paper bag popping. Monty was beginning to smile.

"Now," he said. "Now then."

Clive straightened slowly and suddenly shook his head

as if in pleased and puzzled admiration. He rubbed his buttock with a childish motion.

"By God, you're the only man can get away with that, Monty. You know why, Prue? That's because he's Monty from Monte Carlo, the sweetheart of P.B.I., the Old Man of the Infantry, the bloody perennial of the Foresight Fusiliers. Come on, sing us the 'Foresight Fusiliers,' Monty."

"Now, now, Nipper. That ain't proper—not afore ladies."

Clive watched Monty sit. Then he sank to the seat, turning to Prudence.

"You see, he doesn't know it."

"Well, if it isn't proper to sing, don't embarrass him."

"Embarrass who? Him? Old rhinoceros hide? Ha, if he can't sing it, he doesn't know it. Do you or don't you know it?"

"All right, I don't know it, Nipper. Now, does that suit you?"

"Yes. But you know 'Old Soldiers.' "

"Ah, that's proper."

"That's Monty's song, Prue. That's our song. Come on, Monty. Give her 'Old Soldiers,' and make it loud. Wait, we'll finish this round first."

Clive finished his drink as they watched.

"Now, come on, Monty. 'Old Soldiers.' Ready?"

He beat time with his hand, and they sang. Prudence looked from one to the other, hearing the words, the grating voices:

>   Old soldiers never die,
>   Never die, never die.
>   Old soldiers never die
>   They simply fade away.

When they were done they looked at her and saw her face crinkled in an expression of pain.

"Now what's wrong?" Clive said, happily.

"My heavens!"

"It's a good song. Monty learned that in the last war. It's our favorite."

"The song's all right—you're not kidding?"

"Kidding? Why, what about?"

She knew they were not.

"Why, you're both absolutely tone-deaf," she said. "Now I know why you and Monty are friends. You're the only two people in the world that could be as tone-deaf as each other. You know—two of you together is—why, it's as if two sets of quintuplets were born in the same town."

"Listen, thousands of people like to hear us sing that."

"What thousands?"

"Why, we never had a concert without us singing that by request. Popular request. Acclaim. It wouldn't have been a concert if we didn't sing it. The Colonel said me and Monty singing 'Old Soldiers' was always the hit of the show. We always did it to thunderous applause. Isn't that so, Monty?"

"Right, Nipper."

"I'll bet they'd applaud it," Prudence said. She felt happy for them. "You don't really know you're tone-deaf, do you?"

"What's that, Nipper?"

"Like being color-blind in the ears."

"That makes it all simple."

"You don't know you're tone-deaf—do you, Monty?"

"Sounds all right to me—once we get started together we're all right."

"It's marvelous," she said. "Do you know that you both changed key twice—and each time you jumped a whole fifth?"

"What's that mean, Nipper? Make that simple, too."

"A fifth. It's United States slang for a quart of whisky. She says we need another fifth. How about it?"

As he rose, he felt her hand on his sleeve.

"No, Clive! Don't drink any more."

Clive looked down and brought her into focus.

That's always the way, he thought. The reforming urge. At first they were all right, and took drink for drink with you. And then, before you knew it, they were saying: "No, please. Don't take any more." You could hear it all over. "Oh, come on home, Alf. You know you've had enough!"

He kept his head steady.

"I don't want to be made into something I'm not," he said, unsteadily.

"No," she said, putting out her hand. "Sit here and sing me another song."

"No. 'Old Soldiers' is the only one we do good."

"Well, I'll sing you one."

He looked at her, his head unsteady. Then he sat, suddenly.

"All right. You sing us one. That's fair, isn't it, Monty?"

She bit her lip, feeling suddenly embarrassed. She thought of songs—songs. Then she lifted her head, and started. She felt her voice nervous and small amid the hubbub.

> Believe me if all those endearing young charms
> Which I gaze on so fondly today...

Though she sang quietly—or perhaps because she sang quietly and unlike the usual alcoholic roaring of a public house—people at the near-by tables turned and listened. The place grew quieter, and she wished the roar and babble would start again to cover her confusion.

Suddenly, in that moment, she felt her head whirl with unreality. What was she doing here—she, with two common private soldiers who now called her by her first name, sitting in the common room of a workingman's public house? Among these common people who stared at her?

She fought back her own snobbishness. The people

were so friendly, she said to her mind. There was a warm, close friendliness—an acceptance of her—an unashamed group feeling that one never had in the West End. She looked at Clive. His eyes, unmoving, were fixed alcoholically on her face.

Did love—did love mean that? All of it? Beeriness and going with a man down into the places of his life?

Oh, hell, she thought. It means everything. The best and worst—the rough and the smooth. And the difference between this man and the others she had known was that he wasn't proud of his best and wasn't ashamed of his worst, and thus brought to them both a covering of humanity.

No pose. No everything-good-on-the-surface and the bad things hidden. No putting a best foot forward. No company manners. There was a deceit in social nicety that he didn't have and these people didn't have—and scorned to have.

She looked at him, singing, still self-consciously:

> As the sunflower turns to her God when he sets
> The same face which she turned when he rose.

Then she felt warmly excited and happy in a foolish way, for the people were clapping their hands.

Monty was saying: "Here, I'll take a bow for you!" And he was standing, bowing like a variety artist to the people who laughed and picked up their drinks again.

But Clive was looking at her, and he reached out his hand almost as a blind man might, and barely touched the tips of his fingers to her hair.

There was the moment, with Monty standing, and Clive's hand reaching out; with the hubbub of noise and smell of tobacco smoke and ale.

She wanted to cry: This is it! Stand still, time! Stand still here and let me breathe. Don't hurry me along. Please time, stand still! This is it!

CHAPTER XXIII

CLIVE lay back in the sand, hard-packed between the rocks. The cliffs, going up overhead, were much bigger, it seemed, than when one was on top. Now they had an awesome quality—like going into a cathedral when you were young and your senses tasted everything, and feeling the immensity of stone.

Up overhead the seagulls screamed, turning and angling their wings as they hovered near the cliff face.

He closed his eyes. The hot, queasy, morning-after feeling in his stomach robbed him of any desire but to lie there and not move. The light hurt his eyes and made the violet flashes of pain go through his temples. He lay, listening to the strumming of the wind against the great chalkstone face, listening to the swirl and crash of the sea, the scream of the gulls, the sound of Monty and Prue talking, as they sat, back against the rock face.

"... it was a great and brave thing."

That was Prue's voice—talking about the war again. Oh, why not? History in the making. Anyhow, she liked Monty now—you only saw what was real in Monty when you got over the first shock of his exterior, his uncouthness, his unschooled manner.

"... do what you have to do. It ain't being brave nor a hero. You know you've got to do it and you do. If you knew you didn't have to, you wouldn't."

"You'd obey an order, though, wouldn't you? I mean, if you were told to do something, even if it were foolish, you'd do it, wouldn't you—as the Germans are supposed to?"

"Someone had blundered," Clive said. It hurt his head to speak. Perhaps they hadn't heard him.

"It depends. If there was sense to the order."

"Suppose you didn't think it was sensible?"

"Oh, then. It depends on how many officers there was round watching me. Some officers is all right, though. They'll help you swing the lead. Like once we put on a raid, and didn't. Soldiered on the job. You don't just go out and get killed."

"What raid?"

"Oh, this was in the last war—that was how I got friends with Captain Allen. Only he was Second Lieutenant then. I had to laugh."

Clive could hear Monty chuckling, hear Prue's voice, caught by the wind.

"Tell me about it."

Like a child. Tell me a story. Wanting to have stories to confirm and strengthen her own conformity with the popular patriotic surge.

"Well, it was on the sector above Ypres. First off it started with measuring the lake there. Man had to crawl out every two hours and stick a wire-post down beside a rock to see how deep the water was."

"What for?"

"Knock me blind if I know. Probably they were afraid Jerry might be getting ready to flood us—you know, turn it into our trenches—we had pumps going all the time in that sector.

"We had to measure it six times a night or so. Jerry had to measure it, too. Nice and friendly. He knew we had to. We knew he had to. Nobody hurting anybody else.

"We'd hear him crawling out and pretend we didn't. He'd hear us crawling out, and pretend he didn't. It got so we'd give Jerry the signal when we was back—the old tiddley-winks on the Lewis. Chap we had—name o' Bogie Miller—had a trigger finger that was a knockout. He could play tunes on a Lewis. So when our man got back, he'd play the tune. You know: shave-and-a-haircut—bay-rum. And same with Jerry. When their man was back, they'd do the same. Shave-and-a-haircut—bay-rum!

Everybody knew. Even the blokes on the brigade emma gees—heavy ones, firing over our heads—they knew about it and would keep quiet. Then when everybody was back, you could send up Very lights and sweep the old typewriters up and down if anybody came around, and you knew nobody was out there to get hurt and everybody was satisfied.

"Well, everything's fine until the Major goes down on two weeks' leave, and his second in command—Captain Goss his name was—takes over. Iron-monger collector, he was—you know, had the M.C. and bar, and dying to get a D.S.O. So this is his chance. Moral superiority. We own no man's land right up to his wire. Patrols out all the time. That was his line.

"So patrols go out, wandering all over, one of 'em gets lost and starts coming in the wrong post, and the kid on the emma gee gets the wind up, and pours it all over two men and a lieutenant—kills the officer. Bloody near cut him in two.

"Well, Captain Bloody Goss has to report casualties. He's all red hot. Got to have revenge. More patrols out. Blood for blood. Second night, he's out with a patrol and happens to catch the poor Jerry that's measuring the lake, and they grab him, but he yells, so they shoot him and get back.

"Well, we'd just give Jerry the shave-and-a-haircut to tell him our man was back, and then we knock off his man. The only way he can see it, it's a dirty trick. So he starts patrolling.

"That's one thing about this moral superiority up to the other fellow's wire. The other side is liable to get exactly the same idea. Then there's no more peace in life. Patrol, counter-patrol, bombing party, raid in force, counter-raid. Finally Jerry puts on a box-barrage party, comes in and captures three and knocks off four. The C.S.M. copped it. Nice old bleeder, he was. Put in years, and donkey's years, in India, and was up for his pension and retirement in three more weeks.

"Goss is going bloody raving. Well, just then Allen comes back. He'd copped one and had been down the line at hospital. So Goss picks him for duty—since he'd had such a nice long rest.

"You know how it is: Party will leave post number three at zero minus whatsizname, establish moral superiority, if possible bringing back prisoner for identification, harass all enemy patrols and return at zero plus a banana through post nine.

"Well we're all blacked up and over we go. We get in an old crater, and then Allen sits down and says he's going forward to reconnoitre.

"He says: 'I'll take Old Monty.'"

Clive lifted his voice.

"Did they call you Old Monty even in those days?"

"Well, I was younger then, of course, but I was a little older than some of the kids."

"A little older! You must be older than God now. How old are you—no kidding?"

"Let him go on, Clive. What about the raid?"

"Oh. Well, Allen says: 'Where are you, Monty?' 'Here,' I says. 'Damme,' he says. 'I didn't know you in your nigger minstrel outfit. But even that don't improve your appearance. Come on.'

"So we crawls—and crawls and crawls till we're finally in another shell hole.

"Then he says: 'Montague, what would you say if I'd told you we'd been right through the enemy wire?'

"'If you says so, it's true, sir,' I says. 'And when I know something is true nothing could change it. Not even a court-martial before ten generals and a bloody pile of drums high as Nelson monument.'

"'Thanks,' he said. 'But it isn't a very exciting raid.'

"'Well,' I says, 'they pulled a minnie back today and I don't think many people know of it. It could have moved tonight, if we bombed the position pretty heavy—over by the old ruin. Maybe we killed a couple of Heinies doing it.'

"'You're too artistic,' he says. 'If we killed any Heinies why didn't we get a mark of identification?'

"'I know where there's a dead Jerry with shoulder straps,' I says.

So we fix up a perfect story. And off we crawls. I had to laugh, 'cause Allen grabs my foot, and whispers: 'My God, no wonder you were sure you could find him in the dark. Is that him?' 'It ain't no rose garden we're smelling,' I says.

"So off I goes and saws a shoulder strap off this Jerry. When I get back, Allen's holding his handkerchief very dainty in front of his mouth.

"'I don't know what regiment, he is,' I says. Then he starts laughing. 'I know,' he says. 'He must belong to that famous Limburger regiment we've heard so much about.'

"After that Allen takes out his Webley and lets fly up in the air, and I chuck a dozen bombs. Right away the Jerry line starts writing signatures all over, and it sounds like a hell of a battle for five minutes. When it's all over, we crawl back and pick up the patrol.

"Next day Allen says to me: 'You remember the mule going up by the Menin Gate?' 'Indeed I do,' I says. 'It's a clear memory.' 'By God,' he says. 'I thought that was the ripest thing I ever smelled until last night. It was a mere violet. Private Montague, last night you performed as heroic a deed as any man in this war.' 'It was nothing, sir,' I says. 'When I was a nipper we used to live right opposite a tannery.' 'You're still a hero,' he says, 'and I'm going to see you get the M.M. first chance I have.' And by God, he did, and that's the way I got my M.M.—all for cutting a shoulder strap off of a corpse.

"And we took it back and everybody was satisfied. Allen told Goss all about how we had bombed a minnie out of its post, and Goss was satisfied, and a week or so later the Major comes back off leave, and we're satisfied. Everybody's satisfied. That's the way it is."

Monty threw up his hands, as if to say that was the end of the story. Prue shook her head, slowly, her forehead creased.

"Was there much of that?" she asked.

"All the time," Monty said. "Any man who was ever at the front did something like that. They all did it. It's an old story."

Clive lay, feeling the throbbing in his head—a delicate pounding that played syncopations in between the crash of the surf.

"You bet it's an old story," he said. "Too good to be true."

"The sleeper wakens," Monty chanted. "The sleeper wakens! All the same, it's a fact."

"A fact is a lie and a half," Clive said.

"I tell you, it's true."

"Go on! It's full of holes."

"What holes?"

"I'd answer that properly if Prue wasn't here, too."

Clive lay and laughed, and then felt his own laughter streaking pain through his head.

"Now what's wrong with the story, Nipper?"

291

Clive rolled onto his stomach. He looked at Prue, sitting with her back against the rock, her hands clasped aboud her knees, her skirt tucked tightly between her legs. He smiled, suddenly loving her for her neatness. Some women slopped their bodies and clothes around...

He turned to Monty.

"All right. How do you explain about the detail? They weren't in on it."

"Well, they'd heard bombing and shooting, and he told 'em we'd been on a raid, but he said he was going to report they were all in on it. If anybody come to you and said he wasn't going to mention that you weren't in on a dirty detail, you'd say O.K., wouldn't you?"

"Yes. I suppose I would, in the final analysis."

"There you are, then."

"No, it still doesn't smell good. How about the shoulder strap. If he'd been there long enough to stink, it'd be from some outfit that'd left long ago."

"Ah, we didn't care. But that turned out best of all afterwards. Goss sends in a big report about how in the last ten days he has so established our moral superiority that the Saxon regiment has been withdrawn, and Jerry's brought up a fresh Wurtemberger regiment to face us."

"Oh, come on," Clive said. "Intelligence would know where that Wurtemberger regiment really was."

"True, my lad. But what are they going to do? Ask questions in Parliament? No, they'd laugh and say it was one on Goss. Intelligence knew what was happening. Everybody knows what's really happening in a war except bloody boy scouts like Goss. When the Major come back, Goss was transferred to some school or other—to get him out of the way.

"Real soldiers never wanted his kind around—but you take men like Goss—you can't keep 'em down. I see him again once—back of Amiens in the '18 push. We're going along, full pack. A big motorcar comes along behind us, tooting us all off into the ditch and covering us with mud and corruption. And there was Goss—a major, and wearing a brass hat and red tabs, and looking executive as General Haig.

"Ah, he was a bloody ribbon collector, that Goss. Some's like that. You can't keep them down."

Clive looked again at Prue. She was staring into infinity. She brought her eyes into focus, and smiled at him.

"Hello," he said, quickly.

"Hello."

"You like stories?"

She smiled, half-ruefully.

"I don't know. It all sounds so strange—so incredible. It's not at all like the stories you read in the papers."

"Of course it ain't," Monty said. "But it's true though. Nipper here says I'm a bloody liar. But I know what happened. I won't argue."

Clive sat up.

"Not, I don't call you a liar, Monty. Oh, undoubtedly you embroider the edges and hemstitch the story up. But, in essentials, the story is probably correct. I suppose it's been so in every war."

"I'll bet," Monty said.

"Of course," Clive said. "Popular imagination and the soldier. Why, I'll bet when Julius Caesar landed somewhere near here—I bet he did plenty of fixing up to send back to the constituents in Rome—making things sound as they ought to have been instead of as they were.

"And who then, or now, is to question Caesar's version?

"Why, I'll bet that nine-tenths of history as we know it never happened that way at all. And it will go on that way as long as we have lowly human beings fighting the wars, and generals writing the reports.

"If a general loses, does he admit his lacks? Not one

bit. If he loses, he says he foresaw it, only the politicians wouldn't give him more tanks or rifle-brigade men, or more maps, or better toffee for the troops, or whatever it was—and if his troops happen to win, he says that's exactly the way he planned it."

Prudence shook her head.

"No," she said. "There must be something to generalship and strategy. Napoleon—Marlborough—their great campaigns."

"Ah, but Nipper's right. I don't know much about 'em, but first I want to know who said what happened in the campaigns. *They* did, didn't they, and the rest of the chaps had to take their word for it."

"But they won the campaigns!"

"I don't know," Monty said. "I picked up a book about the last war once. About scraps I'd been in myself. Why, it would make you laugh to read it. It was all too cut and dried. Not like it happened at all."

"But a private soldier can't know the larger issues?"

"In the sum he knows the largest issue of all," Clive said. "Whether he comes out with his life or not.

"And that's what soldiers know and historians don't. The first duty of a general is to keep his reputation alive, and the first duty of a soldier is to keep himself alive."

"What happens when the two run counter?"

"What do you think? Soldiers lives are far more common than general's reputations. Soldiers, like ammunition, are expendable and re-supplies may be indented for."

"Darling. What a face you make!"

"Why shouldn't I make a face?"

"But every soldier can't feel like that. If he did..."

"No more war."

"No, it ain't that," Monty said. "Way I look at it is this. You don't have to say anybody who went through Douai and Dunkirk wasn't all right. There's plenty of chaps willing to die for Old England and so on; but good soldiers or old soldiers won't go chucking away their lives unless they see some sense to it.

"There never has been a time when there wasn't men in England, ready to go out and die if there was some sense to it that they could see."

"If you can see any sense to getting killed at all," Clive said.

"Well, way I look at it, Nipper, a chap admits he's ready to die the day he 'lists. But the trouble with green soldiers they don't know enough to be able to tell whether there's sense to it or not.

"If you had all green soldiers, they'd go risking their lives for nothing, and the first thing you know you'd have a dead army. But, the first thing an old soldier knows is.."

"To keep his rifle clean and his bowels open," Clive said.

"No, now..."

"To obey the orders of superior officers at all times."

"That's eyewash."

"To walk my beat in a smart and soldier-like manner.."

"Come off it. His first duty is to stay alive, as you said, so's he can go on being a soldier."

"Sooner let it be said: 'There goes a live coward' than 'here lies a dead hero,' eh?"

"Dead heroes don't fire no guns. While a live coward can chuck a bomb tomorrow."

"If he was a coward yesterday, why should he fight today?" Prue asked.

"Ah, now y're asking something," Monty said. "Nobody knows what makes a chap run one day and fight another. I've seen 'em do both—and I've done both myself. Mostly, a chap fights because of one of two things. He's got to fight or be killed—or he can see some sense to what he's doing. If it's like at Douai or Dunkirk, well that makes sense. If it's like Goss's raid and don't make sense, he'll just do enough so's he can't get shot by a firing squad for disobeying orders, and not do enough to get shot by Jerry."

Prue stared from one to the other.

"You mean to say, then, that wars are fought with millions of individuals deciding whether they will or won't fulfill orders—each man deciding whether it makes sense to him?"

"That's exactly true," Clive said. "And its what generals never understand. Individual men reason it out, and when it gets to the point that individual men can see no more sense to the way their lives are being used—then the war's over. You didn't win the World War because any general solved it. It was just the Jerries couldn't see any more sense to the way they were being killed so they went home."

"That's true," Monty said. "If you've got to be killed you want some sense to it."

"But, when is it sense?" Prue asked.

"Well, Douai was, and Dunkirk," Monty said. "They made sense. So the chaps stayed and got killed. Now the papers says they're heroes. That's pig-wash for the people to read. It wasn't being heroes. It was just common sense that a rear guard would have to pick a place to hold so's the others could get out.

"So when they said: 'Take Douai back and hold it,' and 'Hold the Canal de Bergues,' nobody was being a bloody hero, and getting killed didn't come into it.

"You didn't say to yourself: 'I don't want to get killed.' You just said: 'Well, it makes sense somebody's got to stay behind and cop it, and it's just our bloody luck to get the detail, that's all.' Oh, and maybe you said too that it showed the command must think you're a bloody good outfit to get what they call the honor of staying. When you're a soldier you've only got two things to believe in—to take pride in yourself for being a clean soldier, and to think your regiment can knock the ears off of any other that ever lined up on parade. Oh, maybe you get the wind up a bit, but then you laugh and say: ,Well, any bloody band o' jam-wallahs can pull out and keep on going; but you've got to have a regiment of real troops to stay behind and stick it. That's what I figure is the big thing the British nation's got, if you come right down to it. We can stick it. We can stand up and stick it better than any other bloody nation on the earth.

"Anyhow, we knew we had to stick it at Douai and Dunkirk, and chaps would do it because it made sense, and if it hadn't made sense we wouldn't have done it.

"Likewise, at Dunkirk the navy could see the army had to be got out, so that made sense to them, and they come in and got us out, and a nasty job it was for 'em. But nobody groused.

"I tell you, if you could have seen the way they were pulling them wounded up on the boats and laying 'em on deck in rows, and not one of 'em saying a word, only just lying there and waiting and holding on to themselves so they wouldn't say anything, and chaps like the Nipper, up to their necks in water all day and then letting other chaps have their places and going back to take another day on the beach with them Stukas—well, nobody can grouse. Remember, Clive, that Colonel brought that outfit out— every man he had left carrying two rifles so's Jerry couldn't cop 'em?"

"Yes," Clive said.

"Well, that was all sense," Monty said. "Arithmetic! Lose 50,000 to get 250,000 out. You had to. If the 50,000 didn't hold, the whole bloody push would get smacked.

"Funny, one time I got thinking that if you were dead you were just as dead if 50,000 went with you as if 250 000 went. But there's cockeyed thinking there somewhere, and

297

I knew it. Most of the time I'd say: 'Well, if you cop it, you cop it, and Ma was right and I never should have enlisted in the first place. But you've been lots of places and seen lots of things, and there isn't much to do you haven't done, and so what the hell! Do you want to live forever!' So I says: 'Yes!' So I says back: 'Well, you ain't going to anyhow, so if you go now you might as well take as many Jerries along with you as you can and then it's a fair swap.'

"And we did take a few, too. That first wave that come over—did we spray 'em clean! Remember, Clive, that first bloody push, coming over singing?"

"Yes, I remember."

"The way them bastards were singing, it sounded like. Remember?"

"Yes."

Clive got up slowly, feeling the breeze come cool on his aching head.

"I'll take a walk," he said.

He went to the water's edge and leaned against a rock, gnarled and studded with limpets and smelling harsh of the slow rot of sea life. He watched the edge of the wave trickle up through the runnels of sand, almost to the rock— almost.

He thought: When a wave reaches this rock, you are dead. As surely as that, as surely as time itself, it shall come. Dead, like the others dancing over the gun sight.

When the first wave came, lines of them, it was not real. Perhaps they were singing. You only remembered now that there was, far away, a noise—timy, torn gusts of sound. Had that been singing? You were too busy with so many things in yourself to know clearly then. You were saying: "At last, you bastards! At last! You've made us run, and march, and dig, and march and run—and now, it's our turn. At last!"

When you looked over the sights at first they blurred, and then you saw the target—just figures like ants, bobbing and dancing on the gun sight. Slowly you realized the targets weren't dancing—they were still and it was your gun shaking.

That was when Monty said: "About eight hundred yards! Let 'em come to two hundred. Don't tip em off yet."

You looked up at him and smiled and licked your lips, feeling them cracked and hot and dry. Your throat was dry and your heart was thumping up high in your chest and you struggled to keep from puking.

You waited and tried to swallow, and your gullet seemed to scratch your dry throat and at last you could hold it back no longer, and you turned your head and puked—and puked. And there was nothing to puke. You hadn't eaten for so long. Only bitter water in the retching, and you spat and flung the stringy slime from your mouth and wiped the smear of tears from your eyes and thought:

"Now he knows it. Now Monty knows how stricken with terror I am."

But when you blinked and looked at him and made the muscles of your face smile to show you were all right, he said: "That's O.K. Lots of 'em do it either before or after."

So you got your eyes clear and looked over the sights and found your body shaking with a stagefright that sent the gun jumping all over the landscape.

Then you gripped yourself and concentrated and ordered your lungs to breathe slowly to stop the gasping for breath, and the sights became still, and you lay, balancing the crawling ants on the top of the foresight—until a gun opened on the left almost making you fall from sudden fright at its sound.

Then Monty said: "Ah, why didn't they let him come in closer? Why didn't they let him come?"

Then you knew it was no use waiting, and you steadied

the gun and squeezed, and the clatter of your own machine gun deafened you and you fought to keep the butt to your shoulder so that the jumping would stop, and you blinked and saw the men dropping.

At first you couldn't believe you had harmed them. It was inconceivable that such a small action on your part had played any part in the tearing of flesh or bone, or in the finality and utterness of death to some human. You wouldn't believe it. You even hoped it wasn't so. They weren't dead. They were just hiding. They'd heard your bullets, and they'd just flopped.

So you waited, the gun still at the point, waiting until they got up again, and you'd spray them again. But they never got up, and you waited and waited, but they never got up. And you looked for something else, but there was nothing else. You looked at Monty, and he said:

"Round one! Round two coming up!"

After that it was not the same. The next time they came you thought impersonally. You thought of the range, and of what a good place this was, with plenty of protection and a fine field of fire. After that you did it over and over and over like a timeless dream that only changed its monotony when the Stukas found you, and dived and dived, and the flash blinded you, and your head felt like a gourd being squeezed and let go, quickly, time after time.

That was the second day. Time moved so curiously. Yes, the second day. Curious, the voice over the housetops, calling: "Are ye all right still down there, A Company?" and you'd shouted back: "O.K.!"

Then Monty had pulled his good one. He pretended the Stuka had knocked them out and they lay quietly. When the Jerries came crawling, half-bent, they'd not fired. They watched them come on, with more and more confidence, coming nearer and nearer, until the gun on the left had begun sweeping them, trying to cover the extra field of fire.

It had been like a moving picture, watching the German officer crouching, hiding from the gun on the left, but in full view of your field of fire, waving his men round to the flank. You'd lain quiet and watched him as he waved and shouted. You'd watched them sweat and bring up their machine gun and start getting it in place. And just when it was about ready to fire, Monty had nudged you: "Now let 'em have it!"

Then your guns chattered, and above their cracking stutter you heard them on the left, shouting: "Good old A. Company!" They'd thought you'd been knocked out.

That was a dirty trick—lying doggo and letting the Jerries believe they were safe. At two hundred yards—you couldn't miss. But after that you knew men didn't hide because of your bullets. For you'd seen them go down—over the top of the sight you saw the officer jump up, and then spin round as if an irresistible hand had plucked him by the shoulder. And he got up again and started to crawl, and then suddenly sagged flat. After that he never moved again, and every time you looked out, there he always was—just as you had stopped him while he was trying to crawl away. Never any different.

Then the heavy stuff started coming, and you saw chunks of houses erupt with a roar. But you didn't feel really bad until you heard the awful roar of a *flammenwerfer*, and the gun on the left went dead. Monty went crawling by the greenhouse wall and into the cellar to see what had happened. Then for no reason, it seemed, the tanks came in behind, and you turned round and fired from the shoulder, the gun's recoil swinging you in a wild pivot. You heard the flame thrower roaring and knew you were firing silly bullets at a thing of armor plate and steel. You heard the shriek of its cannon—being fired point-blank at fifty yards and you knew it was all over. The front had broken somewhere else and you were cut off. You shouted for Monty, feeling terribly alone, but he never came. So you ran, crouching, going with an agony of speed, and dove into the cellar. After that it was like cops and robbers on a city-wide scale. You tried to find your way out through the town. But Jerry had the town. You hid from the tanks and climbed through windows and went out back doors—hiding from the tanks and firing at the enemy infantry that had seeped in from the broken flank, and that went running and hiding through the empty streets. You abased yourself and skulled, and came out for a vicious minute of freedom and revenge when you saw a chance.

You ran, and hid, and fired and ran, until you were so tired, and in that tiredness so empty of fear of even death itself, that you dropped on the pile of bricks and ludicrously, hopelessly, began trying to make the gun work again.

That was when, from nowhere, Monty came up, large as life—his chunky, solid figure coming steadily up the street, carrying the Bren, his hand lifted in signal—just as cheerful as ever. And somehow, seeing him, you became alive again, and had fear again, and thus believed in life again. So you got up and said: "Hi, Monty." Ah, a great chap, Monty! A great chap!

The water almost reached the rock. Clive reached out and dug a runnel with his heel. The next wave camp up the runnel and lapped at the rock.

That was the end.

He went back to the cliff face.

"We ought to go," he said. "The tide'll cut us off soon."

Monty nodded and went on talking:

"I suppose when the chaps on one side come to the conclusion that it ain't no sense any more to what they're getting killed for, then the war's fini, napoo!"

"But," Prue said, "the Germans may consider it right

to risk being killed for something that we wouldn't consider worth it."

"I'm sorry. I don't follow you. If there's two rights, I can't be worried about their right. It's what we think is right that's important to me, and to hell with their ideas."

"Spoken heartily, Monty," Clive said. "Let's go. You've got to the point where you admit finally it's all prejudice. It takes a brave man to say it, Monty. To hell with their ideas, and up with our own. That's the simplest and most truthful analysis."

Prudence looked up and smiled at Clive. He held out his hand, and she swung up taking his arm. They went along under the cliff face until at a headland the waters lapped up to the cliff. When each wave ebbed back there was a momentary path over the puddled sand between the chalky rocks.

Clive ran through. Then he turned, and as the next wave ebbed, he watched Prudence. Laughing and jumping, she came through the puddled water, her skirts held to her knees, and, above the roll of her stockings the white of the well-made legs showing. The slanting sun was striking full on her, and as she ran, she laughed as a woman will.

And like the bursting of sudden and new sunlight, he found himself knowing that it was important to remember all this.

Remember it all, a fierce, hidden part of his mind shouted. Remember it! The time, the place. Remember it as you see it, all frozen to bring back at any time. It will always last, this crystallized moment. Everything will last for you in this second. You will remember the sound shut in by the cliff, the sound of her laughing, and the sound of the sea, and the smell of the water, and the sun coming flatly at her as she jumps over the pool, and Monty back there, standing, and waiting his turn to run through. This you will never forget.

And as he thought it, she came and he opened his arms to her and she ran to them. He lifted her from her feet and swung her round and shouted:

"Jesus Christ!"

Then he looked down at her and they knew what they both felt and thought. But she looked up at him and said:

"Hello!"

He bent his head to her face.

"I wish to hell Monty wasn't here," he said.

She lay unmoving in his clasp.

"Behave yourself," she said.

"Then we'd go home and go to bed!"

She looked at him, her eyes laughing.

"I'll tell Monty. What a thing to say about your friend!"

"Go on and tell him. You daren't!"

"I've too much decency and modesty."

"That's right," he said. "You have. I'm glad you have."

He put her down, gently, and then linked his arm with hers.

"Wait for Monty," she reminded him.

"Let him find his own girl," he said.

But she made him wait, and then she linked arms with Monty too.

That way the three went back to the town, and to Mine Host's, and listened to the B.B.C.

A lot more German planes had been shot down, and everyone was very confident about Churchill and what he had said to Parliament.